make me yours

A FORBIDDEN ROMANCE

FORBIDDEN BILLIONAIRES
BOOK 2

LILI VALENTE

make me yours

A Forbidden Romance

By Lili Valente

Created with Vellum

about the book

Rule Number One: Never lose your virginity to the man who ruined your family.

It's a rule I never meant to break, but the night our paths collide, I have no idea who Weaver is.

He's just a drop-dead gorgeous man with no qualms about sleeping with a virgin. By the time I realize he's also the man who destroyed my father, I've spent the hottest night of my life on his yacht.

I'm ashamed of what I've done.
I'm even more ashamed that I want to do it again...

I don't care about our age gap or that he'll be leaving town in a few weeks. This war between our families isn't mine to fight, and my father hasn't been there for me in a long time.

But Weaver is. He's there for me when I need him most, proving he doesn't have ice water flowing through his veins.

I'm falling for this forbidden man hard and fast...and then he gives me proof that my father was right all along.

Can our love survive Weaver's dark side?

Or will he ruin me the way he ruined the people I once loved?

For my Ream homegirls. Love you all. Thank you for being the best readers ever!

prologue

HIS FIST IN MY HAIR, his lips on my neck, his rough voice whispering—"You're mine. This is where you belong. With me. Always."—is the stuff of my most erotic daydreams.

In the past week, my ice-cold billionaire has made all those dreams come true.

He's also set off a bomb in the middle of my life.

Nothing will ever be the same, even if I walk out of this room right now and never set eyes on him again. I can't go back, and I have no idea how to move forward.

It's terrifying, and a part of me wishes I'd never met Weaver Tripp.

The other part clings to his shoulders as he drags his teeth over my nipple and begs him never to stop, never to let me go.

"Never," he promises, ripping my pants down my legs with one hand as he continues to torture my electrified skin with his mouth.

It's torture, what he does to me, the way he makes me burn.

The sweetest torture I've ever known…

"That's my girl," he says, groaning as he slides his hand down the front of my panties. "So wet for me. I love feeling you soaked and ready for me to fuck you, baby. I love it so fucking much."

I whimper, lifting my hips to welcome the invasion of his thick fingers driving inside me. He hasn't even touched my clit yet, but I'm already so close it feels like I'm being swept up in a tornado, carried higher and higher into a churning funnel cloud of desire.

And like with an actual tornado, there's a serious chance I won't survive giving myself to this man again.

He's a danger to my family and possibly the most gifted liar I've ever met.

"I love you, Sully," he says, shoving his own pants and boxer briefs down far enough to bare his erection. I feel his cock feverish against my thigh and fresh heat rushes between my legs. "I'm always going to love you."

Except that.

That isn't a lie.

That's the truth, I can hear it in his voice, feel it in the way his hand trembles as it smooths down the back of my thigh.

Before I can respond, he shoves my knee up toward my ribs and then he's inside me, making me gasp as he fills me—deep and fast. I moan at the hint of pain that swiftly transforms to pleasure as he rides me hard, staking his claim in a way he never has before.

This man has spanked me and restrained me and whispered filthy, forbidden things into my ear, but he's never taken me like this.

Like he can't get close enough...

Like he's terrified that this will be the last time...

"Mine, you're mine," he rasps as he captures my uninjured wrist, pinning it to the hard floor above my head. "You're mine, and I'm yours. Can't you feel it? This is right. *This* is what we should be fighting for."

I arch my back, straining against his hold, knowing he won't let me escape. He'll bruise me first, because he knows this is how I like it. Using every bit of my strength to fight him as he fucks me turns me on like nothing I had the guts to imagine before Weaver.

He's changed me, ruined me, liberated me.

He's an anchor dragging me down to the bottom of the sea and the port in the storm I've been aching for my entire life.

He's my devil and my savior and when he releases my wrist long enough to slap the side of my ass hard enough to send a shock wave through my nervous system, I come like the shameless creature I am.

I come screaming his name and crying out for mercy, but I should know better.

Mercy is in short supply these days.

And Weaver isn't a man known for sparing anyone —his enemies, his friends, or anything in between.

one

One week earlier...

Gertrude "Sully" Sullivan

*A woman on the verge of
making some very risky
decisions...*

THIS IS STUPID.

I shouldn't be here, and I certainly shouldn't have sent that text...

I don't love Mark Tripp.

I don't even *like* Mark that much.

Yes, making out with him was fun, but our "situation" ended when the September chill set in. Getting handsy behind the dock house or in some secluded beach cove after work wasn't nearly as much fun when the temperature was barely above freezing. And we didn't have anywhere to go to hook up indoors without being found out.

Mark lives with his two cousins—both Tripps who loathe the Sullivan clan for "stirring up trouble" at dock meetings for the past fifty years. If he'd brought me to his place, he would have been labeled the black sheep of the family.

As for the Sullivan clan?

My grandfather hates Rodger Tripp, Mark's father and the Tripp patriarch, with the passion of a thousand giant lobster claws, snapping closed all at once.

For as long as I can remember, I've heard tales of the greedy, selfish Tripps, the family that created an illegal fishing empire in our town by bending the rules and paying off crooked politicians. According to Gramps, the Tripps are trying to squeeze out and destroy anyone who doesn't share their last name.

The Tripps won't be happy until every boat in our harbor has their ugly logo painted on the hull. The Tripps lie and cheat and steal. The Tripps don't sort their recycling and never return their shopping carts to the corral and are probably descended from Satan worshippers.

"There's a reason they don't brag about their roots like the rest of those Mayflower assholes," Gramps is fond of saying when he's had a few too many at the pub. "They came running up here from Salem right before the witch scare. No noose or burning for them. Oh no, not for the Tripps. They knew when to pull up stakes and run. That's the problem with witch hunts. Real witches get tipped off by the Dark Lord and get out of town, and you end up burning innocent people."

And while I'm eighty percent sure he doesn't *really* believe in witches or that his nemesis, Rodger Tripp, has a direct line to the devil himself, Gramps would have a cardiac event if I brought a Tripp boy home.

My grandfather has been like a father to me since my own dad proved uninterested in the task, and he's usually the ultimate "cool" parent. In elementary school, Gramps let me have as many friends over for my Saturday night sleepovers as I wanted and ordered pizza for the entire crew. He worked extra hours to help pay for my braces and my first car and never imposed a curfew. And when I announced my intention to move into the old apartment above his garage after high school, he helped me replace the carpet and install a kitchenette.

Not once, in the six years since I "moved out" has he ever said a word about me bringing boys back to my apartment.

Gramps and I don't talk about romance, but he never stopped having lady friends over, even when I was little and sleeping right across the hall from his bedroom. And he's made it clear with his occasional winks across the bar when I'm flirting with a cute tourist that he thinks girls should be allowed to have as much fun as the boys.

As long as that girl isn't a Sullivan with her eye on a Tripp.

If Gramps knew I'd let Mark Tripp put his hand up my shirt at Whale Song Beach, he would be so disappointed. If he knew I sent Mark a cleavage shot earlier tonight, when I was lonely and wishing I didn't live in a one-lobster town with men I've known since we were children and zero chance of finding a long-term boyfriend, he would toss my phone into the sea.

And maybe me along with it...

I have to get to Mark's cell phone before he shows that picture to anyone else. Gossip spreads like wildfire in Sea Breeze. Our tiny Maine town is hopping during the tourist season, with music and art festivals, bonfires on the beach, and outdoor movies at the community center. But in October, there's nothing to do except drink beer, pile on extra layers before you head out on the boat each morning, and talk.

And Mark likes to talk.

He swore he didn't want anyone to find out about our little secret, either, but he's the one who kept staring at me across the hall at the Moose Club's annual lobster feast in August. He's the one who let his hand brush mine at the farmers' market, when we both reached for the same loaf of sourdough bread. And he's the one who told Maya Swallows, one of my best friends, that he thought I looked "beautiful" when I was taking pictures on the dock one afternoon after work.

"He said you looked like a movie star," Maya had

relayed that evening during book club at our friend Elaina's café. "Isn't that sweet?"

"No, it's stupid," I'd said.

Because it was.

If anyone in our families had been close enough to hear, we'd both be in deep shit, and all for nothing.

Mark doesn't love me, either. Mark likes the way I look—despite my permanently chapped lips from being on a boat all day, I have the blue eyes and long blond hair he tends to go for—but he likes the way a lot of girls look. He likes inviting other girls to sleep over on his dad's yacht, too. But not me. I was never special enough to score an invite to stay the night on The Merry Way. Not even when it was basically the only place in town where we would have had a chance of being alone without our families catching on.

The Merry Way has a private slip at the edge of the cove, shielded from easy view by the ice cream shack, with access to the beach trail on the other side. I could have parked at the trailhead, hiked over the dunes to ravage Mark on his dad's yacht, and been back at my truck before sunrise, with no one the wiser. I'm used to getting up at the ass crack of dawn to be out on the water and so is Mark. If we'd wanted to take things to the next level, it would have been the perfect solution.

But Mark never issued the invitation, and I never hinted that he should. We both knew what we had wasn't worth the potential fallout.

If only I'd remembered that before I had two hot toddies with Elaina and walked home feeling hot all over and way too alone. If only I'd never snapped that shot while I was stripping down for a shower. If only Mark had responded to one of my five texts begging him to delete the picture once I sobered up.

If only I had magical, time travel powers and could turn back the clock far enough to tell Elaina not to mix me that second drink.

"It's okay. You came to your senses in time. You can do this. How hard can it be? He's probably already asleep," I mutter, creeping farther down the dock and peering around the edge of the shuttered ice cream shack.

It still smells vaguely of waffle cones, even two months after it closed for the season, and my stomach rumbles at the scent of sugary, toasted dough. I press a hand to my midsection, promising my tummy a bowl of ramen when we get home, if it will just keep it quiet for a few more minutes.

Rodger Tripp's boat is a yacht, but it's a small yacht. There are only so many places Mark—and his phone—can be. And he must be sleeping pretty hard if he isn't answering his texts.

Like most of our generation, Mark's cell might as well be permanently attached to his hand. He always answers texts in a minute or two, even when he's out on his boat or with another girl. The only time he goes quiet is when he's unconscious, and even then, only when he's had a few too many.

It's Friday night and all the boats in town will remain docked tomorrow in deference to the hurricane sweeping through New England. The storm will pass by a good distance from the coast, but the water will be choppy as hell tomorrow and not worth fishing. Which means every lobster man and woman in town was at the pub tonight or tossing back a few with friends around a backyard bonfire.

I passed three gatherings on my half-mile walk from home and can hear music coming from farther down the shore, where the folks in the heart of town are likely in full, block party mode.

For a moment, as I peek around the side of the shack, I hope that Mark is out at one of those parties. Maybe he dropped his phone on the yacht earlier in the day and forgot about it, and that's why my "track your friends" app led me here. Maybe I'll be able to sneak in and grab his cell without risking discovery, after all.

But when my gaze lands on The Merry Way, there's a light on inside. It's just a faint light, but it's a sign of life that wouldn't be there if no one were on board. Say what you will about the Tripps, but they don't believe in wasting money or electricity.

I hear Gramp's voice in my head, insisting that's another sign that they're a bunch of greedy bastards, but I ignore it.

I have to stay focused on the task at hand.

Pulling my black hoodie up over my hair and ducking my head, I hurry quietly around the ice cream shack and over to the narrow stretch of dock connecting The Merry Way's private slip to the rest of the complex. The clouds are on their way, but for now the moon is high and bright, emitting enough light to make my blond hair glow like a beacon.

But that's why I put on dark clothes before I left the

house. Now I blend into the shadows as I creep up the gangplank and step onto the deck, my boots making an unexpectedly loud *thunk* as they make contact with the polished wood.

I freeze, my stomach dropping and my heart lurching into my throat. I hold my breath, my ears straining for the sound of movement from below, but there's nothing, just the whistle of the wind through the tattered wind sock on the ice cream shack and the lapping of the waves against the hull. After a beat, I feel safe enough to follow the faint glow of the deck's solar lights around to the entrance to the living quarters.

I swallow and will my racing pulse to slow.

Mark is a strong guy, but he's not a gun fanatic like some of the men in town. If he catches me, worst-case scenario, he jumps me before he realizes who I am. I'm not going to get shot for trespassing or stabbed with a rusty fishhook, for goodness' sake.

The thought reminds me of Sea Breeze's most persistent local legend, about the sea captain with the hook where his right hand should be, who hunts teenagers at the local make-out spots.

Many towns have versions of this particular legend, of course, but what makes Sea Breeze's special, is that our sea captain, in his big yellow slicker streaked with blood, always leaves a piece of his coat behind when he claims a victim.

Teens have been finding pieces of that blood-soaked slicker around town for generations. It doesn't matter that no one's been murdered around here since the early 1900s, news that a scrap of coat has been found always gives me the creeps. Elaina thinks it's hysterical. She hates scary books and movies, but for some reason, real-life evidence that someone wants teens to be too terrified to make out in their cars around these parts, gives her the giggles.

At this point, I doubt I'm ever going to giggle again.

By the time I reach the base of the stairs leading down into the yacht's main living area, my heart is punching holes in my chest, and my throat is so dry it makes a strange sound as I swallow.

So, I stop trying to swallow.

No sounds. No noise.

Just a silent journey to the bedroom where I will retrieve Mark's phone from where it hopefully sits on the bedside table, delete my five text messages and the incriminating photo, and then make an equally swift and silent retreat.

For a moment, all appears to be going according to plan.

I make it through the graciously appointed living room, down the narrow hallway, with the bathroom and smaller bedroom on either side, and back to the master, where Mark lies sleeping beneath the covers.

I can just make him out in the gloom.

The room is dark, lit only by the faint glow of the moonlight penetrating the curtains on the left side of the space. The curtains appear to be a lighter color, but they're thick, rich people curtains, with a dense weave that keeps light out and sound in. I bet Mark could be banging his girl of the moment in this bed and no one on deck would hear a thing.

As I step inside, my footsteps silent on the lush carpet, I have the sensation of being swallowed. Everything feels muffled, like I'm in the belly of one of the whales that arrive here in the spring to gorge on plankton and fish.

Later, I'll blame the sound-dampening properties of the space for the fact that I don't hear Mark moving until it's too late.

As for the fact that I don't realize the man in the bed *isn't* Mark until I'm pinned under his powerful body?

Well, I'm not sure what to blame for that except the darkness and bad fucking luck.

two

Weaver Tripp

A man who just captured an intruder.
A very beautiful, intriguing intruder...

WAKING up to a man trying to kill me in my sleep in New York, would have been shocking, but not completely out of the realm of possibility. New York is a big, bad city, after all, not a sleepy hamlet like Sea Breeze.

Sea Breeze is one of the safest small towns in the country, a fact proudly proclaimed on its website, and one of the reasons I went out of my way to avoid coming back here, once I finally got out.

I couldn't stomach the hypocrisy or the disconnect between the propaganda and reality.

This town wasn't safe for me or my mother, not by a long shot, and hearing everyone from the mayor to the principal talk about how lucky we all were to live in such a sheltered haven, made my blood boil. I couldn't get out of here fast enough. The second my diploma was in hand, I was on a plane to New York City, bound for a high-profile internship before starting business school at Columbia.

But that was fine. No one was sad to see me go.

Rodger, my much older brother and Dad's favorite, was champing at the bit to take over the family business. By the time I graduated with my MBA and a job waiting for me at one of the biggest banks in the world, Rodger had the seafood empire well in hand.

He also had several dirty politicians in his pocket, men and women who, in exchange for large campaign donations, were happy to overlook the fact that the Tripps were violating Maine law. According to the state fishing code, professional lobster harvesting must be done by small, independently-owned operations.

Our operation is independently owned, but there's nothing small about it, and nothing legal about the way my father and brother organized the business. For two generations now, they've forced members of our own family to pay a percentage of their profits to them in exchange for "help" with boat maintenance. Once my brother took over, he added another fee for shitty group health insurance that leaves everyone paying for most services out of pocket.

If I were a better man, I would have stepped in and called my brother on what he was doing. I would have protected the younger, more vulnerable members of the family. I would have been the hero our mother believed me to be before she died just six months after my abusive father, proving there's no justice or mercy in the world.

But I'm not a hero.

And I'm not a good man, a fact I prove by remaining on top of my intruder once I realize he is actually a *she*, and that she's probably one of Mark's chaotic group of friends.

Or one of the many girls he's fucking...

She looks like his type.

As I roll her onto the mattress beneath me, her long, wavy blond hair spills across the sheets. The moonlight reveals plush lips parted in an "O" of surprise, cheekbones a princess would kill for, and big eyes I'm guessing are blue, though I can't make out their color in the darkness.

Mark's conquests are always blondes with blue eyes, girls who look like they could use a sandwich and an intervention with whatever they use to dissolve the filler dermatologists pack into women's lips these days.

But this woman's lips aren't artificially plumped, they're too soft-looking for that, and she isn't his usual waif. When she shifts beneath me, trying to wiggle free, I can feel the strength in her long frame. She's in amazing shape, but not strong enough to buck me off when I grasp her wrists and pin her to the mattress.

I'm not like the other Wall Street lifers at my investment firm. I don't rely on my power or money to make me attractive to the opposite sex. I wake up every morning and hit the gym at five a.m., exorcising my demons and honing my body into a loaded weapon in the process.

I'm obviously not going to hurt this woman with my superior strength—I'm not my father—but I'm not above pressing an advantage.

"Who are you?" I demand.

"P-please, I'm sorry," she says, her breath coming in swift, shallow pants. "I thought you were Mark."

The words disappoint me for some reason. I guess a part of me was hoping this girl was different in other ways, too, that maybe she was intelligent enough to realize my nephew is a self-centered idiot, unworthy of her time and attention.

But that doesn't seem to be the case.

Unless, of course, she's lying...

She looks like she's lying, her eyes darting around the room before returning to mine. "Please." She gulps. "Just let me go? I'll leave and never come back. I promise."

"Do you always sneak in to join Mark in bed dressed all in black?"

She gulps again, and her voice is wobbly when she says, "I like black. There's nothing illegal about black."

"But there *is* something illegal about trespassing." Higher education gave me tools I've used to make myself rich, but at the end of the day, my gut calls the shots.

Right now, my gut is screaming that this woman has something to hide.

Something big.

"What do you say?" I nod toward the bedside table, where my phone sits next to the darkened lamp. "Should I call Mark? Ask him if you have permission to board The Merry Way?"

She chews her bottom lip for a moment. "Please..."

I arch a brow, not saying a word or moving a muscle.

She sighs, searching my face for weakness she isn't going to find.

When she apparently realizes neither of us is going anywhere until she gives me an answer, she whispers, "Please...don't call Mark. I don't have permission to board, but I can explain why I'm here. I'm not trying to hurt anyone or take anything, I promise."

"Then explain." I ignore her pointed glance up to her wrists, still pinned in place by my much larger hands. I'm not letting this woman up until I get some straight answers.

After a beat, she sighs again. "I texted Mark a picture earlier tonight, after I'd had a few drinks with a friend. It was a...suggestive picture."

"A sext," I supply, wondering how old this girl thinks I am. I may be a decade or more her senior, but I've received my share of racy texts. I have a few on my phone right now, in fact. An ass shot from Raya, my hook-up in the city, and an artistic nude from Angeline, my fuck buddy in Paris.

But it isn't Raya or Angeline I'm thinking about as

my captive shifts beneath me again, making me even more aware of her strong thighs and the full breasts beneath her hoodie.

"Right, a sext," she says, and I swear I can see her blush even in the dim moonlight. "As soon as I sobered up, I was mortified and texted him again, begging him to delete the photo, but he didn't answer. Then, I realized his number was still traceable on my 'track my friends' app. I saw he was spending the night here. On the boat. I thought if I could just sneak in and delete the texts myself, while Mark was sleeping..."

I hold her gaze, trying to decide if I believe her.

Her tongue slips across her lips, making them look even more plush and kissable. If she weren't one of my nephew's lovers, I would definitely consider it. Her shyness over sending a sext is cute, and her body is built for the kind of athletic fucking I haven't enjoyed in a while.

Raya and Angeline are both model thin and too delicate to do more than wrap their arms around me and hold on for the ride.

But this woman could keep up with me, I'm sure of it, and the more I study her plush lips, the more I want to see them open in an "O" of pleasure while she comes on my cock.

"So...can I get up?" she asks after a beat, her voice a sexy rasp in the darkness. "I can find Mark's phone, delete my embarrassment, and be out of your hair before you can say 'I'm a big, scary man who likes to bully people half his size.'"

Her words send ice water rushing through my veins.

I don't mind being called big or scary, but I'm no bully. I'm not my father and she's not some innocent waif I pounced on while she was lost in the woods.

"You're trespassing," I say, my voice a low, ominous rumble. "In Maine, that gives me every right to defend myself. With force." I curl my fingers tighter around her wrists, until I can feel her pulse racing beneath her skin. "That's something you should have thought about before you walked into someone's bedroom in the middle of the night without an invitation."

"How do I know *you're* not trespassing? This is Mark's dad's boat," she says, proving she's as brave as she is uninformed. "And you're not Mark's dad. Not unless you had a hair transplant and grew six inches."

"No, I'm not Rodger," I say, my jaw tight. "Rodger's dead. Now, like it or not, everything that was his, is mine."

Her jaw drops. "He's dead? What? When?"

"Yesterday. Late afternoon."

She blinks and shakes her head. "But no one said anything down on the docks. Not a word. And no offense, but that would be big news around here."

"Because people hated Rodger?"

She has the decency to blush again, but she doesn't hedge. "Yeah. We did. He was an asshole."

My lips twist in a hard smile. "Guess you won't be speaking at the funeral Sunday morning."

"Guess not," she says, her eyes narrowing on my

face. "What about you? You don't seem too broken up about the news."

"Are you always this blunt?" I ask, returning her glare.

"Are you always this determined to stay on top of women who don't want you on top of them?"

I smile again, a more lethal grin this time. I may not know how to make a relationship last more than a few months or have any idea what love feels like, but I know when a woman wants me. And this girl isn't backing up her words with nearly enough struggle for me to believe she wants to be anywhere but where she is right now.

Dropping my lips closer to hers, I whisper, "Didn't your parents teach you not to lie?"

"I'm not lying," she says, even as her back arches slightly, causing her breasts to press against my chest. "I don't even know your name."

"Is that all it would take?" I smooth one hand down her forearm, over her elbow, to curl around her bicep, impressed again by the muscled flesh beneath my fingers. "A name?"

"I don't want to sleep with you."

"Are you sure about that?" I slide my palm lower, over the hollow beneath her arm until I'm cupping the side of her breast.

I tell myself that I don't want to fuck a girl who's already fucked a relative, but in a town the size of Sea Breeze, a girl like that might be hard to find. I'm stuck here for at least the next few weeks, until I can get my family's affairs in order. I don't want to spend those weeks alone. The past haunts me in this town, but the ghosts are quieter when there's a warm, eager woman in my bed.

And this girl is eager, whether she wants to admit it or not. When I skim my thumb lightly over the swell of her breast, teasing closer to her nipple, a soft, hungry sound escapes from the back of her throat.

Her voice is breathy as she says, "I've never had a one-night stand."

"Who said anything about one night? I want you in this bed, coming on my cock every night until I leave town in a few weeks."

"You don't even know me," she says, her chest rising and falling faster. I drag the zipper down on her hoodie, revealing a tight, shiny black tank top that holds her full breasts close together, creating a creamy valley I'm dying to explore with my tongue.

"I know you're beautiful, brave, and seem relatively intelligent despite having fucked Mark." I curl my fingers into the fabric at the top of her shirt. "What else do I need to know?"

"I didn't fuck Mark," she says, her lips parting as I tug on the satin, guiding it beneath her breast. She gulps, her throat working as I mold my hand to her soft, hot skin. But she doesn't look away. She holds my gaze as she says, "I've actually never fucked anyone."

I hesitate, genuinely surprised.

Surprised, but not put off...

I've been with my share of virgins. They tend to get more attached, making the end of the relationship messier than usual, but most of my liaisons end badly, sooner or later. When it comes to women, I don't think too far into the future. I enjoy the heat and connection for what is—pleasure, pure and simple.

There's only one thing I'm concerned about at this point.

Well, maybe two...

I move my hand from her breast, bracing it on the mattress beside her ribs.

"How old are you, Cat Burglar?" I ask, studying her face again. She doesn't look like a teenager, but Mark's a douchebag, just like his father. Rodger was still fucking high school girls when he was married with a baby on the way, and I fear the apple didn't fall far from the tree.

I don't mind an age gap, but I want a *woman* in my bed, not a child.

"I'm twenty-four," she says, her chin hitching higher. "And I'm not a prude or a hopeless romantic, if that's what you're thinking. I'm just not into being the subject of small-town gossip and almost everyone I work with is a man. I know how they talk. Lobstermen are worse than desperate housewives, and I don't want a bunch of horny, chatty dudes speculating about my sex life."

I grunt, surprised again. "You're a lobsterwoman?" I've known a few in my life, but it's still an over-whelming male profession.

And none of the ladies I saw coming off the boats as a kid looked anything like this woman. She's a Viking shield maiden, strong and beautiful and living proof that women can doing anything men can do, while remembering to wear sunscreen so their skin doesn't dry into a windburned husk by their mid-twenties.

"Harvester is the gender-neutral term," she shoots back. "And yeah, I am. Sixth generation. I have half a dozen ancestors out there at the bottom of the ocean and another couple dozen in the cemetery on the hill. Fishing is in my blood. I couldn't leave this town if I tried."

"And you don't want to try," I say, reading her correctly if the pride firming her features is anything to judge by.

"No, I don't," she says. Her tongue slips out to dampen her lips as she adds in a less certain voice, "But I don't want to be a twenty-five-year-old virgin, either, and my birthday is in November, so..."

"Happy early birthday," I murmur, my gaze flicking down to her tight nipple, my fingers aching to capture it between my fingers. But I need one more question answered first... "What's your name?"

"Gertrude," she says, in a tone that dares me to comment on the old-fashioned name.

I smile, liking her more with every passing minute. She'll be the perfect distraction while I'm here, a way to blow off steam when the stress of dealing with my dysfunctional family gets to be too much.

"Well, Gertrude—"

"Call me Sully," she says. "All my guy friends do."

Guy friends...

I'm not sure if I'm going to be one of *those*, but, "I'm happy to give you a sexual education you won't forget,

27

Sully," I say. "But I'm going to need something from you in exchange."

Her brows shoot up. "Wow. You think a lot of yourself, don't you?"

I don't dignify the question with a response. I *do* think a lot of myself and so will she, once I'm done making her come hard enough to banish her little sexting problem from her mind.

Aloud, I say, "I'm a private person, too, and the people of Sea Breeze haven't earned the right to know anything about my life. If we decide to fuck, we keep it a secret. If our paths cross in town, you don't say hello. You don't so much as look my way. You don't call me or text me or disturb me when I'm dealing with business during work hours. And when I tell you I want you, you come down here just like this, quickly and quietly, dressed all in black so no one sees you, and you leave before the first fisherman arrives on the docks in the morning."

Her jaw drops as she shakes her head. "Bastard."

"Indeed," I agree.

"And proud of it. Awesome." She huffs. "Well, you can fuck right off, Mr. Whatever Your Name Is. I don't need your bullshit or your 'education' or your ego the size of—"

I cut her off with a kiss, crushing my lips to hers.

At first her mouth is hard and unyielding beneath mine, but when I cup her breast, dragging my thumb across her tight pink nipple, her lips part on a gasp of pleasure. A moment later, my tongue is sparring with hers, stroking and teasing, demanding her submission as I jerk her top lower, baring both her breasts.

"I need your promise, Cat Burglar," I say, plucking both of her nipples now as I knee her thighs apart. "We pretend we don't know each other and you come when I call, or no orgasms for you tonight."

"I have a condition, too," she says against my mouth, her fingers clawing into the bare skin on my back. "You never tell anyone about this. Ever. I don't want it getting out that I'm a Tripp fucker. I may not know your name, but you have to be a Tripp, and your family is the worst."

I kiss her harder and smile, my teeth pressing against hers through our lips. "Agreed. You have my word, Sully. Now lift your arms. I need your clothes off. Now."

To my surprise, she obeys without another word, returning her arms to their place on the mattress above her head. I grip the bottom of her hoodie and tank top, ripping them both off at the same time, revealing a body that would launch a thousand ships. Her breasts are large, but firm and high on her chest, with pale nipples only a shade darker than her skin. Her stomach is taut and flat, with muscles visible on either side of her torso.

She's fucking perfect, and I can't wait to see the rest of her.

I grip the top of her sweatpants and cotton panties, dragging them down slowly, inch by inch, revealing more firm flesh, sexy hip bones, and finally, a thatch of dark blond hair. It isn't neatly trimmed or tamed in any way. She's a natural girl, just like her Viking fore-bearers must have been, and even though I haven't been with a woman who doesn't shave since I was a teenager, I find her untamed beauty completely sexy.

Suddenly, I can't wait another second to taste her. I need her pussy on my mouth, her taste on my tongue. I need this bold girl helpless and writhing beneath me, proving I still have some control over my destiny.

Sea Breeze has pulled me back into its web for now, but it can't keep me here. I'll bury my brother, clean up his mess, pass the hideous mansion on the hill on to whatever relative wants to live in that house of horrors, and get back to my real life.

But in the meantime, I'll distract myself by giving this girl a first fuck she'll never forget.

chapter 3

I'M NOT EXACTLY sure how it happened, but suddenly I'm naked in front of a man for the first time in my entire life.

Naked with a *stranger*, no less.

I know this man must be a Tripp—probably one of the older cousins who was sent away to business school, while Mark stayed here to learn the operation from the docks up—but I don't even know his first name.

I'm about to lose my virginity to an anonymous asshole who thinks he can treat me like his own personal small-town prostitute.

Well, he has another think coming on that. No way in hell will I be trotting my ass down to his yacht every night to service his cock and sneaking out like a shameful secret the next morning. Yes, I would have been willing to sneak around with Mark, but Mark is a friend—sort of—not a pompous, arrogant shithead who thinks he's—

"Oh my God," I moan, my hands flying to tangle in the pompous shithead's hair as he buries his face between my legs, his tongue swirling against my clit with a firm assurance that sends electric shocks of pleasure pulsing across my skin.

He kisses me *there*, in that place no man has ever kissed me, and I instinctively know no other man will ever measure up to this jerk's mouth. His lips, his tongue, his teeth...he employs every tool at his disposal with the kind of skill I'm guessing only comes with hours and hours of devoted practice.

His tongue pushes inside me and I die a little. Then his tongue is on my clit and his fingers are inside me and things are happening that have only ever happened while I'm alone in my room with my vibrator between my legs and a steamy romance in my headphones.

I come.

And not just come, I come *hard*.

I come writhing and bucking into his lips and squirming shamelessly closer to his magical mouth. I come with an intensity that leaves my head spinning and my breath rushing so fast I can barely bleat in protest as he abruptly flips me onto my stomach and swats my ass.

Once I've managed to pull in a breath, I jerk my attention over my shoulder, in time to see him swat me again, hard enough to make my flesh sting.

"What was that for?" I demand, outraged and pissed off and...so fucking turned on I can barely stand it.

"For trespassing," he says, swatting me again even as his other hand moves between my legs from behind. He strokes his fingers through my swollen, sensitive flesh, making me tremble. "And this is for having the most delicious pussy I've ever tasted." The next two slaps are softer.

Or maybe I'm just getting used to the sting.

Getting used to it and liking it way more than I ever imagined I would...

But still, I've read enough kinky romance to know you're supposed to ask for permission to introduce pain into pleasure. "That's the last time you spank me without permission," I say. "Next time, you ask."

His lips curve into a wicked smile as he continues to finger me. "Yes, ma'am."

My brows shoot up and my thighs ease farther apart, making more room for his talented hand. "It's that easy?"

"It's that easy." He smooths his free palm over the flushed skin on my backside. "I won't spank you at all, if you don't like it, but...I think you do." His fingers push deeper into where I'm dripping for him, making me moan. "Tell me you like it when I spank you, Sully."

"I..." I trail off, biting my bottom lip as he proves just how good he is at making me forget how to speak. "I don't understand why you spanked me for tasting good."

A beat later, he's hovering over me, his hands on either side of my shoulders and his heat warming my entire body as he whispers in my ear, "I didn't say good. I said delicious, so delicious I'm not going to be able to stop thinking about it for a very long time. Your sweet little pussy is going to haunt me, Sully."

"Good," I murmur, feeling wicked and wonderful as he wraps his arm around my waist, flipping me onto my back with an ease that makes me feel delicate for the first time in my life. Then, his big palm is between my shoulders, sliding me higher on the mattress with one hand, and I feel every drop of feminism leech from my body.

At five eight, I've always been taller than a lot of men. As a former rugby player, who's only gotten in better shape since high school, I'm also stronger than a good number of them. I've never felt small or dainty with a guy I've dated, but I've never imagined I'd enjoy feeling that way, either.

I like knowing I can handle myself in a scuffle with just about anyone and that, worst-case scenario, I could drag my date out of a burning building as easily as he could do the same.

I never thought I'd melt for a man who could move me around with one hand, or with thighs even stronger than my own.

But as my stranger guides my legs apart and settles between them, the feel of his hard, muscled body makes me tremble.

"Nervous?" he asks, mistaking the reason for my shiver.

I shake my head, marveling at the power in him as I skim my fingertips over his chest and up around his firm shoulders. "No." I lift my hips, relishing the way he sucks in a breath as my bare pussy rubs against his erection through his boxer briefs.

He's big there, too, but I'm not worried. I'm too turned on to be worried. I just want him, every inch —now.

"I just want you," I say, rubbing against him again, moaning as he captures my nipple between his fingers. "I'm dying to know what it feels like."

"And you're sure you won't regret having your first time be with a stranger?" he asks, a gentler note in his voice than I've heard before.

It's my first hint that Mr. Pompous isn't all bad, which is nice, I guess, but it doesn't really matter. No matter what he wants, this is only going to be a one-night thing. I can't risk anything more.

I have one night to figure out what all the sex fuss is about and I've never been this turned on. I couldn't stop now if I tried, not even if he were the worst man in the world.

"No regrets," I say, squirming beneath him as he lowers his head, sucking my nipple into his mouth. I cradle his head, my breath coming faster. "But please, fuck me. I need more than fingers. I need it so bad."

Those must have been the magic words because he reaches for the bedside table, grabbing a wallet I didn't notice there before. A beat later, he's out of his boxer briefs, kneeling between my legs as he rolls a condom down his long, thick length.

His cock is gorgeous. For a moment, I'm sad that I didn't get the chance to touch it before he was covered in latex, to feel his burning hot skin against my fingers, or to lick the salt from the tip of him with my tongue. I've never received oral before tonight, but I've given it a few times, and I'm not too shabby at it. At least my high school boyfriend, Keith, never had any complaints.

But before I can dwell too much on my lost opportunity, my stranger is fitting his thick, hard length to where I'm already so sensitive and wet. He goes slow, gliding into me centimeter by centimeter, holding my gaze as he moves. When I wince a few inches in, he pauses, whispering, "Let me know when the pain is better, and I'll keep going."

"Don't stop," I say, digging my nails into his shoulders. "It doesn't hurt, it just feels..."

"Feels...?" he prompts as he sinks deeper, deeper, until he's fully inside and I'm fighting to pull in a breath.

He's big enough to fill every inch of me, pressing against my inner walls, but aside from a slight bruised feeling, there's no pain. There's only pressure and sensation and the curious need to move, to feel *him* move, to create a kind of friction I've never felt before but instinctively crave.

"Full," I supply, though that isn't the exact word.

I *do* feel full, but I also feel electrified, aware of every centimeter of my skin in a way I never have been before. The feel of his hand squeezing my hip as he pulls back and sinks inside me again sends electricity shooting through me from head to toe.

When he bends to lick my nipple again, I nearly have an out-of-body experience.

"Oh God," I breathe, clawing at the back of his neck as he continues to suck my breast into the warm heat of his mouth and rocks into me with slow, shallow thrusts that make the tension building between my hips spiral higher.

"Your nipples are so sensitive," he says, transferring his attention to my other breast as he lifts my hips into the air, adjusting the angle of penetration until he grinds against my clit at the end of every shift of his hips. "One night I'm going to make you come like this, just from touching you, sucking you, biting you."

"Oh God," I mumble again, panting now as the wave of pleasure bearing down on me threatens to break. "Oh God. Oh God."

"Not God, beautiful," he murmurs as he moves faster, deeper. "Weaver. Call me Weaver when you come on my cock. Fuck, yes, come for me. Come for me like a good girl."

His words penetrate the lust haze but it's too late, I'm already coming so hard it feels like I'm being turned inside out. I'm spiraling and pulsing and throbbing with bliss. I'm clinging to him as he comes, soaking up every word he murmurs about how perfect I feel on his cock, even as my brain is having a meltdown of unparalleled proportions.

Because this man?

This stranger?

He isn't an older cousin. He's Weaver Tripp—Weaver *fucking* Tripp, the man who destroyed my parents' marriage and sent my father on his final downward spiral, the one from which he's never recovered.

Weaver is a bad, bad man and I'm even worse for sleeping with him.

But before I can shove him off me and make a run for it—or beg him to fuck me again because I am a weak, spineless waste of a human who's pretty sure she just became an instant sex addict—a voice from above deck calls Weaver's name.

We're not alone, and I might be about to get caught naked with the one man I never should have so much as said "hello" to as we passed on the street.

chapter 4
WEAVER

CURSING Sea Breeze and my abundance of intrusive relatives, I swing out of bed, murmuring a soft warning for Sully to, "Stay put and stay quiet."

I pull on my pajama pants and charge out of the bedroom, shutting the door behind me. By the time I reach the living area, a shadow is creeping down the stairs from the deck, calling my name.

Judging by the hair sticking up in spikes around the shadow's head, it's Mark, my worthless nephew.

The kid who thought he could handle a woman like Sully...

A surge of irrational, unexpected anger washes through me as Mark squeaks, "Weaver? Is that—"

"Back upstairs," I say in a low growl. "You haven't been invited into the living quarters."

He stops mid-step, his chin jerking back into his neck in surprise. "What? This is the family yacht. We come aboard whenever we—"

"Not anymore," I say.

43

"But we—" His words end in a startled grunt as I spin him in a circle and shove him none-too-gently back the way he came.

"It's after midnight," I say once we're on deck and Mark is blinking in shock in the moonlight. "This is where I'm staying while I'm in town. It's my temporary home and guests aren't welcome in my home without an invitation."

"Okay," Mark says, though he's clearly not pleased. "Sorry, I just... I can't find my phone. I've looked everywhere, but it's not at my place or at the bar or in Simon's backyard. I think I must have left it here earlier, when I gave you the keys."

Grateful that Mark didn't set foot inside the living quarters this afternoon, I start toward the seating area at the front of the ship. "This could have waited until the morning. A lost phone isn't an emergency."

"I don't have a landline," he says, his tone lifting toward a whine. "And Mom throws a fit if she can't get in touch with me."

The mention of Laura, Rodger's wife, makes my jaw clench. By all modern conventions, my brother's assets should have gone to his spouse, but that's not the Tripp way. My father made it clear before he passed that he expected Rodger to secure the safe continuation of our family empire.

That meant ensuring a Tripp was in control, not a spouse.

As Rodger's eldest and only child, Mark was next in line, but the executor of the trust, Darren, is a friend of mine from boarding school. Our phone call last night left no doubt that I'm still in line to inherit my brother's assets and control of the company.

Sounds like Rodger didn't leave much to his twenty-four-year-old son.

Though, so far, I can't say I blame him. It was obvious from the moment my plane touched down this morning that Mark is more concerned about what he stands to gain from his father's death than what he's lost. There didn't seem to be much love between the two of them—another reason I feel comfortable kicking Mark off the boat without ceremony. If he were a normal, grieving son, I would have more compassion.

I'm an asshole, but I'm not a monster, not unless someone has proven they deserve it. And so far, Mark's proving to be the latest selfish, money-hungry bastard in a long line of the same.

He's going to lose his fucking mind when he learns how little he stands to inherit. He already knows some of the details, but the full picture is even more bleak... for him, anyway.

The full conditions of the trust won't be revealed until the official reading of the will, but Darren has already begun the transition of my brother's assets into my name, including the deed to the mansion and the yacht, Rodger's fleet of lobster boats, and a vacation home in the Outer Banks in South Carolina.

I want a McMansion in a community likely to be swept off the map by the next hurricane like I want to be standing in the cold ocean air with my nephew instead of down in bed with my sexy cat burglar.

But we don't always get what we want, at least not without a fight.

Speaking of a fight...

"I hope your mother knows I have no intention of removing her from the family home," I say, flicking on the lights near the outdoor living area. "No matter who Rodger left Brookhaven to on paper, she's welcome to live there as long as she likes."

"She'll appreciate that," Mark says, with a nod. Anger flares in his gaze as he adds, "She would have appreciated my dad not being a fucking asshole, more, though. We all would have."

I motion toward the sage cushions covering the couch and chairs. "Feel free to look around for your phone."

"Why do you think he did it?" Mark asks, making no move to start searching for his lost cell. "Why did he leave so much to you? Do you think he just forgot to modify the trust or something? I mean, no offense, you're obviously a great businessman, but you don't live here and you never wanted to be part of the family business. I've been busting my ass every day on a lobster boat, proving I could work my way up from the bottom, just like Dad did with Grandpa. I've put in the hard work. I deserve to be in charge now that he's gone."

I hold back a sigh. His father isn't even in his grave and he's turning on him.

But that's the Tripp family for you—mercenary to the end. It's one of the many reasons I don't intend to have children.

46

"It's late, Mark," I say. "I suggest you find your phone and go home. Get some rest, and we can discuss this after we know the full conditions of the trust."

His features tighten, his brow furrowing above his pale blue eyes. They're my father's eyes, but not nearly as clever or cold. "I think we should talk about it before then, Weaver. I have a right to know what you're going to do. It's my future on the line. Mine and my family's."

"Your family is my family," I remind him. "And despite what you may think, I have the best interests of that family front of mind."

"I'm not a child," he says, his tone pitching toward a whine again, making my jaw clench. "I can handle this. I can fill my father's shoes. I know I can. I can be the new CEO of Tripp Seafood. I deserve to be."

There's that word again, "deserve."

People are so eager to declare what they "deserve," when none of us deserve anything but the chance to walk the earth in peace, without another person interfering in our lives. But of course, very few people are granted even *that* opportunity.

In parts of the world, men Mark's age are trafficked into human slavery to harvest cocoa. In others, they're forced to comb trash heaps for scraps and live in squalor in the shadow of luxury skyscrapers. In still others, they grow up fighting rival gangs for resources or sacrificing their lives to pointless wars in the name of a God they were never given the chance *not* to believe in.

Mark is a pampered, privileged man-child, who has already been given far more than he "deserves."

Maybe that's why, when I spot the rectangular shadow of a cell phone under the lounge chair to my right, I don't stoop to pick it up. Or maybe it's just that I'm eager to get back to the woman in my bed.

The woman whose provocative picture is waiting in Mark's unread messages...

Of all the things Mark doesn't deserve, he certainly doesn't deserve to see Sully undressed. Not now or ever again.

I motion toward the gangplank. "Meet me at the café on Main Street at eight a.m. tomorrow. I can give you fifteen minutes. We'll discuss my preliminary plans for the company then."

"Fifteen..." He trails off, clearly rethinking his outrage when his eyes lock with mine. He swallows, shrinking beneath the full weight of my "don't fuck with me" glare."

I don't often utilize this expression with family members—it's reserved for business rivals and people standing too close on the subway—but I have a feeling it won't be the last time I'll need it while I'm in Sea Breeze. The Tripps aren't a normal family that knows how to behave in a power vacuum. My relatives are more like poorly behaved children, who become even crankier than usual in the wake of a disrupted routine.

Mark clears his throat and casts his gaze down to the planks beneath our feet. "Okay, great. Sure. Thanks." He moves toward the seating area, but I stop him with a hand on his arm.

"I'll look for the phone in the morning. It will be easier in the sunlight." I nod toward the gangplank again. "You should go. It's been a long day and tomorrow will be even longer."

Tomorrow, we'll be packed into a tiny funeral home together with my brother's body, forced to pretend we're a loving clan for an hour or two before the claws come back out. I'm dreading it even more than the Sunday morning burial parade through town to the family plot, where Rodger will be laid to rest next to our father and mother.

Mark tenses beneath my touch, but after a moment, he sighs and his shoulders slump. "All right. See you in the morning." His lips twitch slightly at the corners. "If you're there before me, don't order the dark roast. It's like airplane fuel. Elaina always makes it too strong."

I happen to enjoy my coffee strong enough to launch a plane, but I nod. "See you then."

I wait until he's on the dock, circling around the empty ice cream shack before I bend and collect the phone, tucking it into the pocket of my pajama pants. For a moment, I debate tossing it into the ocean, but that won't take care of the image Sully's concerned about. It would still be there, waiting for Mark in the cloud when he secures another device.

Hopefully, his password will be something easy to guess. If not, I'll just have to make unlocking his phone for me mandatory before we speak in the morning. He might think that's strange, but I don't give a fuck what my nephew thinks. He's going to make my life difficult no matter what I do, might as well get something I want from him before that happens.

Down below, I'm disappointed to see Sully dressed and pacing in front of the small kitchen island on the right of the living area. When I descend the final stair, she spins to face me, her eyes wide.

"He's gone," I tell her, casting a pointed glance toward the bedroom. "But you were supposed to stay put."

"I couldn't," she says. "Once I heard Mark's voice, I was too nervous. Was he here looking for his phone?"

I nod. "He was, but he left without it. I told him I'd look for it in the morning, when the light was better." I pull the cell from my pocket, pleased to see her expression lift in response. "You have approximately seven hours to crack the password."

"Yes! Thank you so much." She rushes forward, collecting it from me with shaking hands. "I won't need that long. It's one, two, three, four, five. I made fun of him for it when we were taking pictures of a lobster he caught a few months ago." She taps at the phone, her shoulders sagging with relief at what she sees on the screen. "He hasn't read it." She taps a bit more, then exhales, setting the phone on the island with a soft *thunk*. "Done. Thank God."

"Again, the name's Weaver," I say, resting a hand against the island. I'd prefer to put my hands on *her*, but there's something different about her energy.

The look in her eyes is guarded, too, as she emits a tight laugh. "Right. I caught that. Nice to meet you, I guess?"

I arch a brow in response and she edges to the right, dragging a hand through her magnificent hair.

"I mean, it was obviously nice to meet you. Or... orgasmic, at least." She winces and skitters a few steps closer to the stairs. "But I have to get home. I've been up for almost twenty-four hours. I should have been asleep a long time ago."

I reach out, looping my fingers loosely around her wrist, surprised when she flinches in response. I release her immediately and lift my hand in surrender.

"If you've changed your mind about seeing me again, that's fine," I assure her. "I only want you in my bed if that's where you want to be."

"Thanks," she says with a little shake of her head. "I just...I have to go. Good night, Weaver. And good luck with everything. Knowing the Tripps, you're going to need it."

She flees without a backward glance, before I can say a word.

But what would I have said if she'd given me more time? I'm not the kind to beg a woman to stay, no matter how much I enjoyed her company. I know better than to give my power away like that. Vulnerability, in my experience, only leads to disappointment. The few women I've let into my heart have all proven unworthy of my trust.

Or I've proven unworthy of theirs...

If Sully hadn't decided to run, I would have given her more pleasure, there's no doubt about that, but in the long run, one or both of us would have regretted our connection. She isn't the kind of woman who's easy to quit, and I'm not the kind of man who has anything to give a small-town girl looking for love.

After closing and locking the door leading down to the living quarters—I've had enough uninvited guests for one night—I slip back beneath the covers, but sleep is a long time coming. My cat burglar's sweet and sexy smell lingers on my sheets, sending memories of the way she moved beneath me pulsing through my head. Her passion was innocent but powerful, intense. I can't remember the last time I wanted to stay up all night with a woman, getting lost in her body.

I'm forty years old. As much as I enjoy sex, I thought I'd left my "fuck all night" days behind me.

But this girl, this woman, did something to me, something that keeps me awake nearly an hour before I finally take my dick in hand and jerk off to memories of her slick heat milking me as she came.

chapter 5

GERTIE

ON A NORMAL DAY OFF, I'd be in bed until at least nine, ten if I managed to ignore the birds squawking in the tree outside my bedroom window.

But today is not a normal day, and I'm up and dressed by seven, pounding down the stairs from my apartment above the garage. I swing into the kitchen of the main house to grab the raincoat I left in the closet when Gramps and I made chowder a few days ago, careful to circle around the creaky floorboards so I won't wake him on my way out.

"Where are you off to in such a hurry?" he asks from the living room, making me jump half a foot into the air and press a hand to my chest.

"Shit, you scared me," I say, spinning to face him.

He sits in his usual spot by the woodstove, a steaming mug in hand. If I'd been in my right mind, I would have smelled the coffee and known he was up, but I'm not in my right mind.

I haven't been in my right mind since I realized I had sex with the worst man in the world.

All Tripps are bad, but Weaver Tripp?

He's the worst.

He basically destroyed my father.

And he...*may* have had sex with my mother.

Ugh. The thought makes me want to gag. I press a hand to my stomach, willing it to settle until I can make it out the door. Gramps knows I never get sick. I only vomit when I'm really, *really* upset. Like when my cat died when I was four or when Elaina broke her wrist on the playground when we were seven, and I was the one who had to help her to the nurse with a bone poking through her skin.

Or like when I was eight, after my mom left and my dad ended up in the hospital...

My stomach was off for months after that nightmare of a morning. I woke up to silence in the house and neither of my parents' cars in the drive. My dad occasionally stayed out all night and came dragging in late the next morning, but Mom was always there. I could count on her to have food on the table and forms signed for school, even if she wasn't cuddly or "fun" like my father or Gramps. Even at a young age, I instinctively realized my mom didn't relish being a mother, but she was solid, dependable.

Until the day she wasn't...

I was alone and terrified for hours until Gramps showed up with the news that Dad was in the hospital. He was as surprised to learn that Mom was gone as I was, but his surprise didn't last as long as mine.

Gramps has been a lobsterman since he was seventeen and a gossip probably even longer than that. He knew the ugly story months before I did, but I eventually put together the pieces from scraps of things overhead whispered around school and down by the docks.

Apparently, my father went drinking that night, as usual, only to run into my mom at a bar in the next town over. It sounds like the start of a 1970s song about drinking piña coladas and getting lost in the rain, but it didn't end with my parents realizing there was still a spark between them.

Because my mother wasn't alone. She was with Weaver Tripp, a man about a decade her junior, and they weren't sharing a drink as friends. Apparently, that was clear from the moment Dad walked in.

My dad is usually a happy drunk, but that night he showed his violent side. He punched Weaver, Weaver beat the absolute shit out of him, and Mom dipped with her date, leaving Dad bleeding on the ground outside the bar. Dad, who'd already had several drinks at a different pub, pulled himself off the ground and got into his car to chase after them, but ended up running off the road instead.

He broke both legs and sustained a head injury serious enough to keep him in the hospital for weeks.

The therapist I talked to as a kid, after I moved in with Gramps and it became clear that I wasn't snapping back from the family tragedy as quickly as he'd hoped, said it was possible the head injury was the reason my dad was so different after the accident than he'd been before. It wasn't that he didn't love me anymore, but that he simply wasn't capable of taking care of me or communicating the way he had before he cracked his head open like an egg.

I wanted to believe her.

I really did.

But in my gut, I knew it was Mom leaving that closed my father's heart to everything and everyone, including his own daughter. He loved her *so* much. Even when I was a toddler, I remember being a little jealous of the way he looked at my beautiful mama, like she was an angel come to earth, better than all the rest of the people in the world put together, too perfect to be real.

She wasn't perfect, of course. She was just *really* pretty, and men are dumb when it comes to beautiful women. I understood that sometime around thirteen or fourteen, and it made me have even less respect for my broken father.

You don't stop being there for your child because you're not with her mom anymore.

You should love and take care of your babies no matter what.

Gramps gets that. Gramps has never let me down or stopped loving me, even when I ruined his truck by putting diesel fuel in it instead of regular gas or when we had a knock-down-drag-out fight about me staying to help him on the boat instead of going to college. He wanted me to get out of Sea Breeze and "make something of myself."

I told him the only thing I wanted to "make" of myself was to make myself useful to the people I love.

Gramps needed me on the boat. His arthritis was getting too bad to haul traps in all day on his own, and I had good friends in Sea Breeze, friends as close to me as sisters. They weren't going to college, either. Elaina was opening a cat café with an inheritance from her grandmother, and Maya was going to work for her parents in their rental property business. My family was here. No matter how much I loved taking pictures or how proud I was of landing a scholarship to art school, that made the decision not to go to college an easy one.

Eventually, Gramps came around to seeing my point of view and we're even closer than we were when I was a kid. He's not just my grandpa or surrogate parent, in many ways, he's my best friend. He just *gets* me, in a way not many people ever have.

Until this morning, I would have said nothing could come between us or damage the bond we've forged over the past sixteen years. But that was before I slept with a Tripp, the same Tripp who wrecked my family and ruined his son.

The thought makes my stomach roil again.

"Everything all right?" Gramps asks, frowning over the rim of his cup. "I haven't seen you that green since I made liver for dinner last winter. You didn't drink too much last night, did you?"

I shrug on my coat, averting my gaze. I don't want him to see the guilt I'm sure is plain in my eyes. "Maybe a little. Elaina was making the hot toddies and she's a heavy pour."

He grunts, his sharp blue eyes still fixed on my face.

I can feel his attention prickling across my skin, even though I keep my gaze lowered as I tuck my keys and wallet into my pockets. "You know better, Gert," he says. "Don't let anyone pour for you, not even a friend."

Gramps and I both enjoy a pint at the pub after work as much as the next harvester, but we're careful to drink in moderation. Neither one of us wants to be like my father. We leave the pub by no later than six most nights and have a three-beer maximum, even on Saturdays.

But better he thinks I drank too much whiskey than had kinky sex with our family's sworn enemy.

"You're right," I say, nodding as I rake a hand through my hair. "I'll be sure to mix my own drink next time. See you later. I'm going to run over to Elaina's for breakfast and cat therapy."

He grunts again, but seems mollified. "Be sure to use the lint roller in the carport before you come back inside."

"I know, I know. See you later," I say as I back through the door and pound down the stairs into the cool morning air.

Gramps' alleged "cat allergies" are the reason I don't have a cat of my own to love and spoil. Funny how his "allergies" didn't act up when I snuck a cat-hair-covered pillow into his bedroom a few weeks ago. Gramps slept just fine that night, and when we headed out to the boat in the morning, there wasn't a red eye or stuffy old man nose in sight.

I'm ninety percent sure he's been lying to me about his allergies since I was a kid who begged him ceaselessly for a cat. But considering what I did last night, I'm in no position to throw stones.

Fuck. Just thinking about it sends shame flooding into my stomach, making it so tight and heavy, it feels like it's dragging behind me as I hustle down the sidewalk toward downtown. I pass the fisherman's memorial on the way, a circular arrangement of stone plaques with a giant, wrought-iron wave in the middle. These plaques list the names of all the men lost to the sea from 1795 all the way to modern times.

When I was little, Gramps would take me there every Memorial Day and read the names of all the Sullivans who went to a watery grave. He knew which Sullivans were "our" Sullivans and which were from the other Sullivan family in town, the one that left Sea Breeze in the 1930s, looking for a better life out west. From 1930 on, all the lost Sullivans are ours. There are only two—my great-uncle and a second cousin who drowned when I was just a baby, but still...

I feel the weight of my legacy every time I pass the memorial. My ancestors gave everything for our family, sometimes even their lives. They're the reason Gramps has enough money to pay for Dad's bills and mortgage payment, even though my father hasn't held down a job in years. They're the reason we have enough left over to keep our gorgeous old Victorian in the family, instead of being forced to sell like so many of our friends who used to own waterfront homes.

I'm sure all the dead Sullivans are rolling over in their graves right now, ashamed to be related to such a Tripp-sexing, trash heap of a human being.

I walk faster, speeding past the memorial and the entrance to the docks, careful to not so much as glance toward the ice cream shack or the yacht behind it.

Past the hardware store, the fish market, the souvenir shops and the upscale resale shop, I push into Elaina's café, my shoulders sagging with relief when I see that she's alone at the counter and no one occupies the tables near the front.

Crossing the softly gleaming hardwood floor, I brace my hands on the counter and ask in a harsh whisper, "Do you think ghosts can see who we fuck?"

She cocks her head with a soft "thinking" sound, sending her sleek brown ponytail shifting to one side. "I don't know. I mean, I hope not. My grandmother would be horrified that I'm such a slut, but..." She trails off with a wicked grin. "Does this mean you finally nailed your lobster Romeo, my sweet Juliet?"

I roll my eyes. Elaina has been calling Mark and me "Romeo and Juliet" ever since she found out we were hooking up. The bad blood between the Sullivans and the Tripps is public knowledge and Elaina loves drama.

But this isn't a Shakespeare play, this is my real life, and I desperately need some sane, solid advice. "No. I did something much worse."

Elaina's eyes glitter with excitement as she claps her hands softly together, bouncing on her toes. "Oh, yay! I'm so excited. You have to tell me everything! Throw on an apron and get back here. We can gossip between customers."

"I'm serious, Elaina," I say, frowning at my still delighted best friend. "I did a bad thing. For real. A very bad thing, and I can't take it back, and if anyone in my family finds out, they're going to hate me forever. *I* might hate me forever. I haven't decided yet."

Her smile fades and a worry line forms between her warm brown eyes. "Okay, okay, I hear you. We're in crisis containment mode, not gossip mode. Got it. Just put on an apron and come sit next to your bestie, baby squirrel. We'll figure this out. We always do."

She's right. We *do* figure things out. We've been problem-solving together since before we could read.

Back in kindergarten, Elaina would give me half her cookie at lunch, supplying the sugar fix my mother denied me, and I would boost my much shorter friend up on the monkey bars during recess so she could dangle from her knees beside me. We've been making up for what the other one lacks for going on two decades.

If anyone can help me figure out how to contain this latest crisis, it's her.

"And get yourself a scone or something," she calls after me as I head into the cat-heavy section of the café, where lazy felines bask in the morning sun streaming through the big windows or lounge on couches and tattered wingback chairs. "You look hungry."

I'm pretty sure I look sick, not hungry, but she's right. It's hard to think straight on an empty stomach, and I didn't eat much for dinner last night, either. I punch the access code into the door leading back to the kitchen and slip into the spotless food prep area with a sigh. I don't remember baking with my mom as a kid, though Gramps said we made Christmas cookies together when I was really small, but I have enough warm memories of this kitchen to last a lifetime.

Elaina, Maya, and me—and sometimes our long-distance bestie, Sydney, from New York, who's here in the summers—have spent hours in here sipping wine in the evenings, helping Elaina bake for vendors at the local farmers' markets or for the country store down the street. We've helped make cakes for local friends' weddings and baby showers, soda bread for Saint Patrick's Day, and chocolate truffle candies...just because.

Because we like truffles and we relish a treat and because all four of us have been out with enough losers to know we shouldn't wait for a guy to give us chocolate.

We shouldn't wait for a guy to give us love or support, either.

I've always been proud that I have such strong emotional ties with my friends. I knew that my support for them and their support for me was what made it possible for me to be so picky about dating. I didn't need a man for anything, so I was free to wait until I met someone who was everything I wanted in a partner.

And sure, I have urges that weren't satisfied by a hug from a friend, but I also have a vibrator and a fabulous collection of kinky short stories on my phone. Until now, that's always been enough.

But after last night...

As I toast an English muffin and fetch my favorite

strawberry cream cheese from the fridge, I do my best not to think about all the things Weaver did to me...or how much I want him to do them again.

I can't step foot on his boat again, let alone anywhere near his bed. Having sex with him when I didn't know who he was is forgivable. Going back for more when I know damned well that he had a romantic relationship, no matter how brief, with *my mother* would be the rancid act of a depraved sex fiend.

And I am not depraved.

Or a sex fiend.

But as I finish my breakfast and fetch a mug for coffee from the collection hanging on the wall above the sink, I'm keenly aware of the ache between my legs. Part of it is being sore from having sex for the first time, but part of it is from wishing I were still in Weaver's bed, with his talented hands warm on my skin, making me feel things I had no idea my body was capable of feeling.

A vibrator just can't compare. It doesn't even come close.

Or maybe I just need better toys...

That's something Elaina will be able to help me with. She's unabashedly sex positive and a big proponent of meeting her own needs when she's in between partners. Bare minimum, I'm going to leave the café this morning with a list of top-notch vibrators and dildos, if not the absolution I'm pretty sure only a priest could give me at this point.

(And I'm not about to tell Father Thomas one word

about this. Not even if it means another century in purgatory after I die.)

After adding a touch of cream to my coffee, I push through the heavy blue velvet curtain separating the front of the café from the back to find Elaina busy with a customer.

A very familiar customer...

With a soft squeak of surprise, I drop into a squatting position, hoping the counter will conceal me from view.

But I should have known better. My luck is solidly in the shitter right now, a fact proven when a deep voice murmurs, "Good morning, Sully," from the other side of the cash register.

"Yep, good morning," I mumble, my face hot enough to sear a scallop. "Just...looking for lids. You said the lids were down here, right, Elaina?"

"Um, yes," Elaina says, rolling with me like the bestie she is. "And stirring sticks, too. You should find a box of both down there. On the shelf beside the little fridge. We need to get both of those restocked before the morning rush."

There's nothing but cleaning supplies down on this shelf, but I make a show of looking for lids and sticks until I sense Weaver moving away.

Before I can stand, Elaina nudges my hip with her foot and hisses, "What is going on? How are you and that gorgeous sexpot of a man on a nickname basis without me knowing about it, woman? You need to spill it, Gertie, and spill it quick. Before I expire from curiosity."

I stand, shaking my head as my heart does its best to punch through my ribs. "I can't," I whisper. "I have to get out of here. I can't see him again. Ever."

Her grin falls so fast I swear I hear it hit the floor. "Did he hurt you? If so, I'm going to kill him. I'll poison his bacon and cheese sandwich. Just say the word."

I shake my head harder, backing toward the curtain. "No. Nothing like that. It's...complicated. I can't talk about it here."

"Okay, meet me back here at three, okay?" she says. "I'll close a little early and we can shut the curtains and talk in private."

I nod. "Okay. Thank you. Love you."

"Love you, too, honey," she says, concern still writ large on her face. "Take care of yourself today, okay?"

I mutter something in response and fumble my way through the curtain. A few moments later, I'm pushing out the back door into the alley behind the café , not certain how to take care of myself in the wake of something like this.

I just know I need to put some distance between Weaver Tripp and myself.

I break into a jog, cruising into the narrow alley between Elaina's café and the souvenir shop next door so fast, that by the time I see the broad chest looming in front of me, it's too late to stop.

I ram into a cable-knit sweater, nose-first, and suddenly find myself in the arms of the last man I want to see right now.

Well, the second to the last, but who has time for semantics?

"Woah, there." Mark laughs, his arms tightening around me. "You're in a hurry. What are you doing back here?"

"I *am* in a hurry," I insist, ignoring his question. I try to pull away, but he holds me close, his thick fingers digging into the small of my back, making my skin crawl. Sometime in the past twelve hours, Mark's touch went from interesting to repulsive. "I have to get back to the house. Gramps needs me."

"Oh, come on, Gramps can get by on his own for one morning." His lips turn down hard. "I need you, Gee. My dad's dead. Heart attack out of nowhere on Thursday. It's been fucking crazy."

"I heard last night," I say, torn between the urge to comfort him and the urge to demand he get his hands off me. Now. "I'm sorry, Mark. That's really awful." He and his dad weren't really close—I'm pretty sure he hated Rodger most of the time, just like the rest of the harvesters in town—but losing a parent is still intense. "I can talk later, if you want to call, but I really—"

He tugs me closer. "I can't find my cell, and I don't want to talk on the phone, anyway. I need you, Gee. None of the girls I've been seeing lately get me like you do. When I'm with you, I can relax and forget about everything, and I really need to forget right now."

I dodge his lips as he bends to kiss me, pushing harder on his chest, but he's strong, and he isn't pulling any punches this morning. "Stop it, Mark. I'm serious. I have to go."

"Just five minutes," he says. "Just jerk me off, and

I'll return the favor later." He releases me with one hand, reaching between us to work open his belt.

I take advantage of his divided focus to twist free. When he reaches for me again, I act on instinct, bringing my knee up between his legs before shoving him again—hard. He falls backward, tripping over his own feet before colliding with an empty trash can and tumbling to the concrete.

Only when he's down, cursing a blue streak, do I notice the silhouette moving slowly down the alley.

Fuck.

It's Weaver Tripp.

And he looks ready to do some violence of his own.

chapter 6

WEAVER

I'VE ALWAYS HAD A TEMPER.

As a young man, it ruled me. I never started a fight, but if another man raised his fists to me, you'd better believe I finished it. I'd go from cool, calm, and collected to brutal berserker in six seconds or less.

It was easy. That rage, that violence, was always there, simmering beneath the surface. I couldn't get away with beating the shit out of my father, the true focus of my loathing and contempt, but bullies at school and drunken assholes at local bars were fair game.

Then, one night at Columbia, the summer after I graduated from grad school, when I was hanging out with old friends, I nearly beat a man to death.

He was a lacrosse player, a big guy, who'd thought it would be funny to stick his fat fingers under my friend Kayla's skirt without permission. He stayed on his feet a lot longer than most. By time I finally got him flat on his back, one of my eyes was swollen shut, my lip was torn, and my rage had become a wild animal, shaking me in its jaws.

The other guy—Blake—almost didn't make it. The trauma to his face and skull was too much. My father had to buy the university some high-tech chemistry equipment and pay off Blake's parents to make it go away.

I hated needing his help nearly as much as I hated the fact that I'd so completely lost control.

Just like dear old Dad.

That day, I swore I'd never let my rage rule me again. I went to therapy, worked on controlling my anger, and haven't raised my fists to anyone since. I haven't wanted to. The memory of how close I came to becoming one of the monsters has made it relatively easy to keep that violent part of me in check.

But right now, the urge to slam my nephew against the side of the brick building behind him and bury my fist in his stomach is so strong that I force myself to stay at the end of the alley for a long beat after Sully sends him to the ground. Only when it's clear that she's okay, and Mark isn't getting up anytime soon, do I take a breath and start slowly down the dimly lit passage.

She gulps when she sees me, looking like she might bolt.

Instead, she stands her ground, lifting her chin like the Viking warrior she is. If I were going to battle in ancient times, I'd pick Sully over Mark in a hot second. She might be smaller, but she makes up for her size with a courage Mark will never possess, not if he lives a hundred years.

"You're okay," I say, a statement, not a question.

"I'm fine," she says. "And I'm leaving."

"Please, don't," I say softly as Mark groans on the ground a few feet away. "I'd like to buy you breakfast. My way of apologizing for my nephew's poor behavior."

"We're dating, Weaver," Mark grunts from the ground, wincing as he braces a hand on the bricks and shifts slowly onto his knees. "I wasn't attacking her, for fuck's sake."

"I believe that's up for debate," I say, my cool voice belying the lava running through my veins. Even Rodger would have been ashamed this morning. My big brother was a greedy bastard who regularly cheated on his wife, but even *he* didn't make a move without consent.

"We're not dating and you were being an asshole, Mark," Sully says, backing away. I follow her, leaving Mark on the ground behind us. "I'll let it go because I know you're upset about your dad, but if you ever grab me like that again, you won't be walking away with something as minor as a pair of bruised balls."

"I didn't grab you. I don't know what you're talking about," Mark whines, a thin attempt at gaslighting that isn't fooling anyone.

"Are you sure you won't stay?" I ask in a voice for Sully's ears only.

"What happened to wanting me to sneak onto your boat in the dead of night?" she shoots back in a hushed voice. "So no one knows who you're spending time with?"

I lift a shoulder. "Things change." I don't tell her that I couldn't stop thinking about her last night or that her face was the first thing through my head when I woke up this morning.

The only thing worse than developing a fascination with this girl would be if she realized she's already under my skin.

"They do," she agrees, her eyes haunted. "I know who you are now, and I can't see you again. Not ever. Goodbye, Weaver."

Before I can acknowledge how good my name sounds on her lips, she's gone, vanishing around the corner, her swift footsteps fading away in the opposite direction. And suddenly, something about the way she moves, about the way her sandy blond hair catches the sun and her full hips sway, reminds me of a woman I haven't thought about in a long time.

"Who was that?" I ask Mark, returning to his side as he rises to his feet.

"Gertrude. Sully to her guy friends," he says, still doubled over, his forehead furrowed in pain. "Seems like you knew that. You said her name."

"What's her last name?" I demand, careful not to get too close to my nephew.

The urge to punch him is still stronger than I would like.

"Sullivan," he says, pouting. "Sully is short for Sullivan. She's John Sullivan's granddaughter."

My blood cools as rapidly as it began to burn, and

the few sips of coffee I consumed before I heard the café owner tell Mark he could catch Gertie on her way out the back roil in my stomach.

John Sullivan's granddaughter. Which means she's Leon Sullivan's daughter.

And *Tracy* Sullivan's daughter...

I should have guessed. Or at least suspected. Yes, it was dark in my bedroom last night, and Gertrude has a warm, earthy quality that's the polar opposite of Tracy's aloof energy. But she has her mother's hair, her mother's hips, her mother's big blue eyes...

And she told me to call her Sully for God's sake, clearly short for Sullivan.

Fuck. No wonder she never wants to see me again.

"I mean, you're not one of us anymore. You have no idea what goes on around here," Mark babbles. From his tone, I'm guessing he's been speaking for a while, but I've tuned him out.

And I intend to continue tuning him out.

Mark exhausted the last of my patience with him when Sully said "no," and he chose not to listen.

Pulling his phone from the pocket of my jacket, I toss it at him, unaffected by his, "What the fuck, Weaver?' as he scrambles to catch it before it hits the ground.

"Get your own breakfast," I say. "I'll see you at the funeral home. If you behave yourself, I won't tell your mother what I saw this morning."

"You didn't see anything!" he shout-whines. "Sully and I are fucking, Weaver. She was a cold fish this morning, but—"

His words end in a gulp of fear as I brace my forearm against his throat, pinning him to the wall. It takes what's left of my control to keep my voice low and even as I say, "You aren't fucking her, and you will never fuck her. You won't so much as share the same sidewalk with Gertrude Sullivan again. If you see her coming, you cross the street. If she's at the pub, you don't go inside. Do you understand?"

He swallows, his eyes wide. "Wh-what's wrong with you?"

"Do you understand?" I repeat.

Sweat breaking out on his upper lip despite the chill in the October air, he gulps again. "Yeah, sure, whatever. Fine. It's over, I'll leave her alone. It was just casual anyway, Weaver. It wasn't like we were in love or something. I know better than to marry a local girl. Dad taught me things, you know. He taught me to respect our family legacy."

He isn't good enough to lick a local girl's shoe, let alone marry one. Our family isn't royalty in Sea Breeze, we're grifters, predators who have used our influence to hoard wealth for ourselves while leaving less and less for everyone else.

But Mark will never understand that. Just as I'm sure he'll never understand why I won't be giving him control of the family business.

I turn without a word, striding back toward Main Street and my rental car.

"What about coffee?" Mark calls after me. "We were going to talk."

I keep walking.

"You can't do this, Weaver. You can't cut me out without at least having a conversation. Not because of this."

But I can, Mark. I just did.

"We'll talk later," he calls, his voice breaking. "Tonight maybe. I'll buy you a drink after the visitation."

I turn the corner, leaving my nephew behind me in the alley.

As soon as I'm in my rented Subaru, I head out of town, into the surrounding marsh, bound for the trail I walked a hundred times as a restless teenager, counting the days until I could leave this town. Here I am again, back to my old coping mechanisms—women I shouldn't touch and miles of marshland under my feet—a mere twenty-four hours after arriving in Sea Breeze.

So much for getting older and wiser...

chapter 7

GERTIE

I SPOT Elaina on the trail below me, huffing and puffing in red overalls with her dark brown hair pulled up in pigtails, but don't head down to give her a pep talk the way I usually would.

The stress of the day has left me feeling oddly depleted.

I can usually go and go, but today my get-up-and-go already got up and went.

So, I sit perched on the rock wall surrounding the lookout, staring out at the blue ocean under a cloudless autumn sky, while I wait for her to make it up the last fifty steps. Days like this are numbered. Soon, the skies will be gunmetal gray and the ocean faded to match.

Winters are always rough around here, but for some reason I'm dreading this one more than usual.

"Asthma," Elaina wheezes as she mounts the final step. She braces her hands on her knees, bending double as she sucks wind. "I have asthma. You can get that in your twenties, right?"

"Or maybe you just need to do some cardiovascular exercise on a regular basis," I say for possibly the hundredth time.

Elaina and I both played rugby in high school, but since graduation, Elaina has focused mostly on petting cats and baking cakes. Meanwhile, I spend my days hauling lobster traps onto our boat and my evenings jogging or lifting weights at the rec center. Being strong isn't just important for longevity in my job, it's a bit of an obsession.

I've watched my father go downhill physically with disturbing speed, the strong dad from my childhood transforming into a stooped man with a paunch who winces as he hobbles down the street. His body is a prison, trapping him in a life he hates but can't escape.

I don't ever want to live like that. I'd throw myself off the boat first.

"No. Asthma," Elaina continues to pant. "I clearly have asthma. And when I get a diagnosis, you're going to feel so bad for bullying me and making me hike instead of meeting me in my nice warm café."

"You look warm enough to me," I tease, laughing when she sticks her tongue out at me from the middle of her flushed face.

"The cats are mad, too," she says, hands on her hips as she sways toward me, gradually pulling in deeper breaths. "They were looking forward to a visit from Aunt Gert-Gert."

"I couldn't risk another run-in with the Tripps," I say. "Not until I figure out what I'm going to do."

She blinks, her expression sobering as she sits beside me on the rock wall, swinging her legs over to dangle beside mine. "I'm so sorry, Gertie. I shouldn't have told Mark you were leaving out the back. I thought he was looking for you to apologize for whatever happened between you two. I had no idea he'd do...whatever he did." She leans in, her brow furrowed. "What did he do, by the way? When he came in for coffee, all he said was 'your friend is crazy and kicked me in the nuts.' And that he wanted three scones to go."

I huff beneath my breath, annoyed, but not surprised. "He's such an asshole. I can't believe I made out with him for months. He's so gross."

"He's not gross," Elaina says. "Not physically anyway. He's cute. But if he did something bad enough to get kicked in the nuts, I'll never sell him a scone again." She bites her lip. "I did give him three today because I baked way too many and needed to unload some, but never again. Just say the word and he's banned for life."

It's tempting, but after a beat, I shake my head. "No, it's fine. He wasn't himself this morning. His dad just died. I'll give him a pass this time."

"A pass for what?" she presses again.

I briefly explain, leaving out the part about Weaver swooping in to glare daggers in Mark's face.

When I'm finished, Elaina's dark eyes are narrowed in anger. "Fuck that guy," she spits, like one of the cats after they get hit with the spray bottle for fighting. "No more scones for him. No coffee, either. Not even a mug of herbal tea without an ounce of caffeine in it. No one lays hands on my bestie and gets away with it."

"He didn't get away with it," I remind her. "I kicked him in the balls and he said he wouldn't mess with me again. It's fine."

He didn't exactly say that, but I feel confident that Mark got the message, and I don't want to start a town feud between his people and mine. Or *more* of a feud, anyway. My people are of higher quality, but Mark has numbers on his side. The other Tripps and Tripp minions might like me better, but he's the one with power and influence in Sea Breeze.

And that power might be growing very soon...

He isn't the oldest or most experienced fisherman in the Tripp crew, but he's Rodger's son. I can't imagine his dad passing the torch to anyone else. Weaver may have gotten the yacht, but Mark will get control of the fleet and everything else.

"But that's not what I need to talk to you about," I add, still not sure if Elaina is the best person to trust with this information, but I don't have anyone else.

Maya is a sweetheart, but she hates drama and has even less experience with men than I do. And she's out of town with her mom, doing some remodeling shopping for their vacation rentals, and won't be back for a week. Sydney would be a great source for advice—she has experience with older men—but she's in the middle of moving to Burlington, Vermont, and shifting the entire course of her life.

She's...a little busy.

Besides, Elaina can keep a secret, as long as she understands from the jump that I'm serious about this staying just between us. "I need you to pinkie swear you won't say a thing about this to anyone else, okay? Not a word. Not even to Sydney or Maya. I want to keep this quiet."

"Okay." Elaina nods seriously, searching my face. "You can trust me, Gertie. I hope you know that. I love gossip, but I love you more. Your secrets are always safe with me."

"I know." I squeeze her leg through her overalls, so grateful for her. I never would have made it through my mom leaving or my dad falling apart without Elaina.

She's always been there for me. Even when we were kids.

"So, who were you with last night?" she asks. "If it wasn't Mark? I didn't realize you were interested in anyone else."

I sigh, threading my fingers together into a fist, dreading this part. "I wasn't. I'm not."

Liar, the inner voice hisses, *you totally wanted to take Weaver up on his breakfast offer and stare into his sexy silver eyes over scones and a fruit plate.*

I clear my throat, screwing my courage to the sticking point before I blurt out the entire story—from the stupid text I sent Mark to tracking his phone to the Tripp yacht to ending up in bed with his sexy beast of an uncle.

By the time I'm done, Elaina's jaw is practically dragging the ground.

I tap the bottom of her chin, laughing despite the stress of the day. "You're going to swallow a bug."

She exhales another wheezing sound before swallowing with an audible gulp. "Oh my God, Gertie."

"I know," I say.

"Oh my God."

I nod. "Yep."

"God."

I widen my eyes her way. "Yes. I know. It's crazy. But you haven't heard the worst part yet."

Her lashes flutter as she clearly makes an effort to work through her shock. "Worst part? So far, it sounds pretty fucking amazing, Gert. Like, a little scary that you went out there alone, but so hot. And that man is unbelievably gorgeous." She blushes and hunches her shoulders closer to her ears. "I *might* have flirted with him a little after you left. But I obviously had no idea you two were a thing, and I will never flirt with him again."

"We're not a thing."

She arches a brow. "No? Sounds like you're a thing. He stood up for you against his own nephew and asked you to breakfast."

"But last night he acted like he wanted to keep banging me in secret," I remind her.

She waves a breezy hand. "That was last night, before he realized how obsessed he is with you."

I roll my eyes. "He isn't obsessed." My stomach sours as I force myself to get to the big reveal. "He's probably grossed out. Or he will be soon. As soon as he realizes who I am."

She frowns. "What do you mean?"

"We didn't exchange full names last night. I guessed he was one of the older Tripp relatives, but he looks way younger than he is. I had no clue he was Weaver Tripp, and he doesn't know I'm a Sullivan."

Elaina's features tighten. "I'm still not following. I mean, I know there's tension between your families, but I personally don't think that's a deal-breaker. Especially now that Rodger Tripp is out of the picture. It might be time to put all the bad blood in the past. Not all the Tripps are dicks, you know?"

I sigh. "Yeah, I know, it's not about that." Acid rises in my throat. "I thought you knew. About Weaver. About who he is and...what he did. But it makes sense that you don't. We were just kids. You weren't a gossip hound at eight."

Her frown deepens. "Sure, I was. I was just gossiping about third-grader shit like who had the coolest scented pencils and Maryanne Nicholson's boy-girl party in her garage and why I wasn't invited." She brushes my hair over my shoulder, her hand lingering gently on my back. "What did this guy do, Gertie? I've never seen you this pale. You're scaring me a little. Please don't have a heart attack up here, okay? I'm not in good enough shape to carry you down the hill."

My lips twist, but I can't force a smile. I can barely push out, "The night my dad caught my mom out at that bar with another man. The night of his accident..."

I suck in another breath that doesn't feel like it delivers oxygen to my brain. "That guy was Weaver Tripp."

Elaina's jaw drops again and her hand moves to hover over her open mouth. "Holy..."

I nod and swallow past the golf ball lodged in my throat. "Yeah."

"Shit," Elaina finally murmurs. "So were they..."

I shrug, every muscle in my body feeling too tight. "I don't know. But I mean, probably. Right? She was in her early thirties, and he was like...twenty-something or whatever. I doubt he would have been interested in an older woman with a kid for any other reason."

"Oh, wow," Elaina says, looking sick to her stomach.

"Do you think I'm gross?"

Her brows snap together. "Of course not! Oh my God, no, it's just the situation is kind of..."

"Gross," I supply.

She winces. "Well, yes. A little." She hurries to add, "But that isn't your fault. Or his! You guys had no idea. And that *was* a long time ago. You were eight so like... sixteen years? That's a good chunk of time."

"It doesn't matter. Having sex with someone my mother also had sex with is never okay. Never." I drop my head into my hands, muttering beneath my breath, "And I'll never be able to forget him. No matter how hard I try."

Elaina makes a sympathetic sound. "It was that good? I mean, I'm not surprised. He looked like he'd be good. Some people just have that air about them. That

'I know what to do with my body when I'm naked' kind of energy, you know?"

"It's not just that," I say, keeping my elbows braced on my knees and my head in my hands as I confess the secret I've kept from my best friend, "It was my first time."

She's quiet for a moment. "First time with a full-grown man?"

"No."

"First time on a boat?"

I lift my head, glancing her way, my cheeks hot with shame. "No, my first time ever. With anyone, anywhere."

The furrow between her brows deepens. "What? That can't be right. I know you and Keith never got around to it since he was scared of STDs or whatever, even though you were both virgins." She rolls her eyes. "Such a weird guy. But what about Felix at rugby camp, junior year?"

"We only made it to third base."

Her chin rocks back. "What? No, you guys snuck into the equipment room after hours. You even borrowed a condom from my stash. Remember?"

"I remember, but...I lied."

"What?" she squeaks. "Why?"

"My best friend had fully embraced her sexuality and was having an amazing time getting naked with boys, and I was still a virgin, who'd only kissed three people. I was embarrassed. I felt like I was falling behind on the whole growing up thing."

Her gaze softens on mine. "Sexuality is so personal,

Gertie. There was no need to feel rushed or embarrassed. I wouldn't have judged you for taking things at your own pace."

"I know that now," I say. "But at seventeen, I didn't. So, I lied and I'm sorry."

"You don't have to be sorry. I get it." Her head tilts thoughtfully to one side as she studies my face. "Are you sure you felt ready last night? Did Weaver steamroll you because he's older and wasn't thinking about his lady friend possibly being inexperienced?"

I huff. "Um, no. He didn't pressure me. I've been ready for more than making out for a long time. It's just this town. You know how it is. I work with half the guys my age and the other half are assholes or relatives." I lift a shoulder before adding in a softer voice, "And I told him. Before we... I told him I was a virgin."

Her eyes widen. "Oh. Wow. Well, that's good. Great, actually. Communication is key to a good relationship."

"It's not a relationship. It was a one-night stand."

She arches a brow. "Mr. Sexy's guest appearance in your life this morning would say otherwise. And anyway, it doesn't matter. Communication is still key, even if a relationship only lasts twenty-four hours." She leans into me, nudging my shoulder with her smaller, sharper one. "But I think you should consider seeing him again while he's in town. Men who are great in bed are hard to find. And I'm sure you didn't learn all the fun things he has to teach you in one night."

I roll my eyes. "I'm not an idiot, Elaina. Sex isn't

that hard. I've watched porn. I knew what went where way before last night."

"Sex is about so much more than that," she says calmly. "And you know it. And that's why you're scared."

"I'm not scared," I say with a tight laugh. "I'm disgusted. He slept with *my mother* before he slept with me. It's so gross, I want to vomit every time I think about it."

"Like I said, that was a long time ago," she says without missing a beat. "And the human body replaces all its cells every seven years. So, he's literally a different person than he was when he was with your mom. At a cellular level."

I shoot an "are you fucking kidding me?" look her way.

She shrugs. "It's true. And he might not have slept with your mom. That's purely speculation at this point. We need more data before you can make an informed decision."

I shake my head with a laugh. "You're crazy."

"I'm not, I'm logical."

"And how am I supposed to find out what happened with my mom?" I ask. "Call her up at that number she hasn't given me? Track her down in New York with her new husband?"

Elaina's nose wrinkles. "Ew, of course, not. Fuck her, she's the worst. And we couldn't trust anything she said anyway. Mothers who abandon their children can't be trusted." She bobs a shoulder. "But maybe Weaver can be. It would at least be interesting to get his perspective on everything that went down back in the day."

I snort. "Yeah, right. I'm not asking him about any of that."

"Why not? You've already been naked with him. Might as well bare a little of your soul, too. We can figure out a way to phrase things so they're as chill as possible." Her hand settles on my forearm, giving it a squeeze. "And this might be a blessing in disguise, Gertie. We were so young, and all the grown-ups did their best to sweep the scandal under the rug and pretend it didn't happen. Wouldn't it be nice to know what really went down? I mean, it was a major event for you. It changed your whole life."

I'm quiet for a moment, thinking about the girl I was before Weaver Tripp got caught making out with my mother and how radically everything fell apart afterward. I suppose I should be angry with Weaver, but...I'm not. After all, he hadn't made anyone any promises.

My mom and dad are the ones who swore to love each other for better or for worse. They're the ones who made the decision to bring a child into the world together. Weaver was just a kid home from college, and probably younger than I am now. His frontal lobe wasn't even fully developed and there's a chance he didn't know my mom was married. I doubt she wore her wedding ring out to the bars when she was looking for a good time.

"It would at least be interesting to hear his side of the story," Elaina prods after a moment.

I bite my lip, anxiety making my skin crawl.

"What's the worst that could happen?" she asks. "He says he doesn't want to talk about it? So what? Then you just thank him for the orgasms and walk away." She frowns before squeezing my arm again. "You did get orgasms, right? At least one?"

I nod numbly. "Two. And they were way better than my rabbit. Or my fancy Christmas vibrator."

Elaina sighs, her hand slipping from my arm. "Lucky girl. My lady parts are so lonely. I think I felt a tumbleweed blow through my vagina last night. No adult human should be expected to go without sex for this long."

My lips curve. "What's it been? Two months?"

"Three," she says, doubling down when I laugh. "That's a long time! And there's no end to the dry spell in sight. I've already banged all the decently cute and clever men around here, and I don't have time to drive into the city. I have a café to run. Scones don't make themselves, and I can't stay out until midnight and get up to bake at five a.m. I'm horny, but I'm also human. I need more than five hours of sleep to function."

"I'm sure you'll find another victim soon," I assure her.

Her lips purse. "They're not victims. They're failed experiments. It's not my fault none of the boys around here can handle a successful woman with a high sex drive. And I tell them I'm not looking for anything serious until I'm at least thirty. It's not my fault they choose not to believe me. When people tell you who they are, you really should listen."

Her words give me pause...

Weaver told me who he was last night. He made it perfectly clear that he was a man out for pleasure and nothing more. He was *very* honest with me about that. So, maybe he'd be honest with me about the past, too...

I guess there's only one way to find out.

Pulling in a deep breath, I let it out in a rush. "Okay. I'll do it. I'll ask him." Elaina claps her hands and starts to squeal, but I stop her with a hand in the air. "But not right now. I'm sure he's busy. He has the visitation tonight and the funeral tomorrow morning. If he hasn't run back to wherever he came from by tomorrow afternoon, then I'll make a trip out to the yacht."

Elaina nods. "That sounds smart. He'll definitely be in the mood to fuck all night by then. Funerals are inspirational that way. I always leave wanting to prove that I'm still alive and making the most of my one, precious life."

I frown. "Really? I just leave feeling sad."

"That's because you've only been to the funerals of people you truly loved. I don't think Weaver loved his brother, do you?"

I shake my head, feeling a little sad for him. But it's not his fault. The Tripp family has more than its fair share of bad eggs, and Rodger was the worst of the batch. "I doubt he even liked him," I say. "No one else did. Not even Mark. He was scared of him and maybe wanted to be like him a little bit, when it came to the money and power, but he didn't like his dad."

We have that in common, I add silently to myself.

92

I *love* my dad—I can't seem to help it, no matter how much he's hurt me or let me down—but I don't like him very much.

Which reminds me...

"I have to head back to town," I say, my bones feeling heavier now that I've remembered the task ahead. I can't believe I forgot today was the third Saturday of the month, but then...I've been a little busy. "I have to run groceries by my dad's place and grab his trash to add to ours before Gramps makes the dump run tomorrow."

Elaina puts her arm around my shoulders. "You're a good daughter. And a good friend. Don't feel bad about lying about Felix, okay? Seriously, I get it. I lied about my first time, too. It wasn't actually good. Not at all, really. It hurt, and I ended up with a bruised ovary."

"Wow," I say. "How does that happen?"

"Teddy had a giant schlong and no idea what to do with it. Two virgins hopping into bed together was a bad idea. You made a much smarter choice."

I don't know about that, but there's no going back now.

There's only forward and what I'm guessing is going to be a very uncomfortable conversation with the only man who's ever seen me naked.

chapter 8

WEAVER

THE VISITATION at the funeral home is packed. There's barely enough room to stand sipping a drink without bumping against one of the other people here to mourn the late Rodger Tripp.

Though "mourn" is far too strong a word.

Rodger wasn't a kind or good man. He was a bully. Most of his family members weren't sad to see him go, let alone the rest of the town. These people are here because they're afraid *not* to be—the Tripps can make your life difficult if we feel you've disrespected our clan.

And I'm sure the free food and drink were a decent draw. Mark and the younger Tripps insisted on an open bar, and I didn't fight them. No one wanted to face this night sober, least of all me.

I haven't spoken to most of the Tripps in years. To say I'm not close with my family might be the understatement of the decade. I've forgotten several of their names, in fact, and had no idea my cousin Samantha now has four children or that Uncle Frederick's hair implants finally took root after decades of fighting male pattern baldness.

Now, thanks to being corned by Frederick in line for the bar, I know more about hair plugs and his triumph over a bad case of gout than I ever hoped to.

Desperate for something to make the time pass more quickly, I do a lap of the room, fetching fresh drinks for the older set and holding the door for the caterer as he swaps out a keg. I help a tiny Tripp in a ridiculous little black suit clean cake off his shoe and fetch him another slice, settling him at one of the tables at the back of the room with half a dozen other sugar-smeared children.

I'm headed for the lobby afterwards, intending to hide in the bathroom and check my email for at least fifteen minutes, when Laura waylays me not far from the door.

"Oh, there you are, Weaver," she says, her red-rimmed eyes shining in her puffy face. She pats her hairspray-sticky updo, though I haven't seen her blond helmet shift a centimeter since I arrived. "I've been looking everywhere for you. We should talk. Before the funeral tomorrow."

"Of course," I say, about to suggest we step outside when she grips my arm with surprising strength and drags me to a couch not far from Rodger's body.

At least she elected for a closed casket. If I'd had to stare down Rodger's pale, doughy corpse while people sipped wine and snacked on canapés all around me, I doubt I would have lasted more than five minutes.

Still, I avert my eyes from the flower laden casket as I settle beside Laura. I don't want to think about my brother lying dead a few feet away. I didn't love him or respect him, but he has always been there, a fixture in my life. The fact that he's gone, forever, is...jarring.

I blame that off-kilter feeling for the fact that I don't see Laura's question coming before she asks it.

"It would mean so much if you'd speak at the graveside service tomorrow. I know you told Mark you'd rather not, but could you possibly reconsider? For me? And for your brother?" She dabs at her cheeks as more tears stream from her pink eyes. "It would mean so much to him. To both of us."

She looks like a miserable rabbit and is probably the only person in the room genuinely grieving. Rodger cheated on her and treated her like a prize as much as a person—a doll he'd trapped in his mansion of a dollhouse—but he'd denied her nothing. She was his most treasured possession.

I have no idea how she's going to function without him, but that isn't my problem. Her misery and grief aren't my problem, either, but I'm not as coldhearted as most people assume. I feel for her...just not enough to spew a bunch of lies at my brother's grave.

"I can't, Laura," I tell her gently, but firmly. "I didn't know Rodger well enough to deliver a eulogy with the integrity it deserves."

"But he was your brother!"

"A brother I've barely spoken to in over a decade," I say, hurrying on before she can voice the protest I can see forming on her lips. "But I could do a short reading.

97

I have a passage by Henry Scott Holland picked out that I think Rodger would have enjoyed. It was inspired by a sermon Holland gave at the funeral of King Edward VII."

She sniffs again and dabs at the corners of her eyes. "Well, that sounds nice." Her lips wobble into a smile. "He was our king, after all."

I suppress a grimace and rest a hand on her slim shoulder. "I'll speak to the minister now and see where to slot that into the service."

Laura reaches out, gripping my wrist as I start to rise. "Please, Weaver. Give Mark a chance to prove he can fill his father's shoes. I know he's young and still has so much to learn, but he loves this town and so desperately wants to make his father proud."

A part of me wants to remind her that Rodger is dead and no one will be making him feel pride—or anything else—ever again. Instead, I force patience into my tone as I remind her, "You knew Rodger better than anyone, Laura. Do you think he would have left me in charge if he wanted it to be any other way?"

Her brow furrows and her lips wobble again—down this time—but after a moment, she gives a slow, small shake of her head.

I rest a hand on her back. "I'll see you in the morning. Don't wait for me here. I'll meet you at the cemetery."

I rise, moving as quickly as possible through the crush of people to the minister sipping coffee at a corner table. We confer briefly, decide my poem should close the section of the service featuring speeches from family members, and I duck out the back door.

Dusk is falling but the children are still running wild through the grass, screaming with laughter, providing the cover I need to ignore Aunt Wendy's call for me to come say hello.

I have nothing to say to Aunt Wendy or any of these people. The only person I'd actually like to speak to isn't here. I scanned the crowd a hundred times, but there was no sign of wild, sandy blond hair or clear blue eyes.

None of the Sullivans were here.

Rodger would be pissed.

Or maybe he would have relished the fact that he was able to turn an entire family against him. Rodger didn't mind making enemies...a fact I've been learning the hard way. When I emerged from the trail this after-noon, one of my tires had been slashed in a way that made it pretty clear the damage was deliberate.

And now...

I scan the rental car, covered from hood to bumper in a thick, gloppy gray mess that stinks of sour cream and rotten fish, and sigh. I should have parked closer to the funeral home, but this spot farther down the street felt like a better bet for a fast getaway.

"Chowdah," a scratchy voice says from behind me.

I turn to see a couple as old as the sea sitting in the shadows on their sagging front porch. Their home is the same faded, dark beige as their skin and the man's shirt, but the woman's pink sweater draws my eye to their rocking chairs. "Excuse me?" I ask.

"He said it looks like chowdah," the woman says in a voice nearly as rough as her husband's, thick with an old-timer's New England brogue.

"Ayuh," the man says with a nod of his gray head. "Smells like it, too. Wicked awful when it starts to turn."

The woman hums in agreement. "That one's been off for a day or two, I'd wager. Gonna need a hose."

The husband grunts. "You can borrow ours. Look just 'round the corner. To your left from where you're standin'."

I nod. "Thank you." As I climb the steep lawn toward the house, I ask. "Did you happen to see who did this?"

"Nope," the man says so quickly that I know it's a lie. "Just got out a few minutes ago. Was havin' our supper."

"Ayuh. Just came out after supper," the woman seconds. "Seems like a lot of work, though, if you ask me. Totin' all that chowdah up from some restaurant down on Main. Probably a few hundred pounds of it, don't you think, Bran?"

I can't see the man's face—I'm already unwinding their neatly-stored hose and turning on the water—but I hear his grunt of agreement.

"Maybe more. You'd need a big truck to carry a load like that." As I reappear around the side of the house, he adds in a more pointed tone "If you start looking for suspects, you should start with somebody who drives a big truck."

"Thank you," I say with a tight smile, "but I don't plan on being in town long enough to bother."

It's the woman's turn to grunt this time. "But you ain't from away, Weaver Tripp. You belong here as much as anyone else, no matter how things have been with your brother and father in charge."

I look up, a little shocked that she recognized me. I haven't been in Sea Breeze since I was a very young man.

"Condolences on your loss," she adds, her dark eyes now barely visible in the dense shadows on the porch. "We would've come to give our respects, but we don't get around the way we used to."

"Thank you," I say, turning on the water and directing the spray at the hood of the rental.

The hose has excellent pressure. In just a few minutes, I have most of the soup off the car and the chunky parts guided into a storm drain. I'm sure old chowder isn't the best thing to send into the ocean a few blocks away, but it's better than leaving the mess on the road to draw animals and stink up the street.

By the time I turn off the water, the car is fine to drive. There's still a hazy gray cloud on the windows, but this will work until I can locate glass cleaner and a rag.

I return the hose to its holder and start back down the steep yard, intending to offer the couple payment for the use of their water. But when I reach the front of the home, they've vanished. The laugh track of some thirty-minute comedy echoes loudly from behind their closed doors, making it clear calling out to them would be pointless.

And unwelcome.

I know when I've been dismissed.

But they were kind first, a gift I'm not sure I deserve. No, I'm not my father or my brother, but I doubt they'll like my plans for the Tripp fleet any more than the way Rodger ran things. I intend to increase pay for anyone operating under the Tripp banner, but I can't disband the entire operation.

At least not right away. Too many families depend on things staying the way they are.

I've already been approached by several cousins concerned about losing their health insurance. There are sick kids and wives on the verge of giving birth to think about. And Rodger handled a lot of the red tape. He did so to keep our relatives dependent on him and continuing to cut him in on their profits without a fuss, but it will take time to educate them enough to see the benefit in taking control of those aspects of their lives themselves.

In the meantime, I'll be expected to keep greasing politicians' and regulators' palms to keep them from cracking down on our monopoly.

Dismantling any system is a difficult thing, but one this deeply entrenched has the power to suck us all up in its gravitational pull. The old ways might prove too difficult to change without a certain degree of pain for everyone involved.

And without my presence in Sea Breeze...

My firm has already made it clear they're open to

me working remotely—I'm their top mergers and acquisitions advisor and would be difficult to replace —but I can't stay here. I can already feel my hometown sinking its claws into me, doing its best to twist me back into the person I was before.

Sea Breeze will never allow me to be the man I truly am. Here, I'm an avatar, a storybook villain twirling his moustache or a prince on a stolen throne. I'm someone who inspires fear, awe, and contempt, but never just Weaver, a man who's created his own success, his own life.

I can't let that happen. I've worked too hard to put the past behind me to let the Tripp whirlpool suck me back in. I'll have to find a way to manage the transition into a new business model from the city.

I can't get back there fast enough. I've only been in Sea Breeze two days and look what a mess I've made. I've become the target of expensive adolescent pranks and developed a fascination with a woman I never should have laid a finger on.

I avert my gaze as I pass by the Sweet Pussy Cat Café, refusing to think about Gertrude Sullivan's sweet pussy or how much I'd like to have her under me again.

Back at the dock, I fetch the materials to clean the car and take care of the mess with just enough sunset glow left to lock up the yacht for the night without turning on the deck lights. Before I go below, I pull up the gangplank, just in case. I don't want any surprise visitors tonight, not even ones with killer curves and a plush mouth that fits perfectly against mine.

Not that I really think she'll show up, not after her

behavior today. She's clearly horrified by our connection.

As she should be.

I destroyed her family. I didn't intend to do so, but destruction is my superpower. Even in New York, far from the chaos of my clan, I have a knack for breaking things.

As a younger man, I chalked it up to being focused on my work, with no time to invest in romantic relationships. But as I aged, and forged connections with women I would have liked to keep in my life, longer term, it became clear there's something not quite right about my relationship style. I'm too blunt, too reserved, and demanding, too...something for most women.

I don't consider myself an unkind man, but I don't understand courting games and have no wish to engage in them.

Eventually, I quit trying to find "The One" and leaned into my identity as the cool, detached billionaire who's good for one thing. I'm the man you fuck for a month, maybe two, while you're in between better prospects. I can be trusted to deliver multiple O's and to pay for the car service back to your apartment and not much else.

There are no car services in Sea Breeze, only a single taxi that operates on its owner's random, sporadic schedule. There's very little public transportation, either. If you want out of this town, you have to drive, or wait in the pedestrian shelter by the old courthouse for hours until the bus trundles by on its undependable route.

It's logical to feel trapped here. Most people *are* trapped.

But I'm not. Not anymore.

I remind myself of that the next morning as I dress for the funeral and make the drive to the cemetery, arriving just seconds before the minister asks everyone to be seated for the service.

I take my place in an empty chair beside Laura. Mark leans forward from his position on her other side to shoot me a judgmental look, but I ignore him. I'm here, in a suitably somber black suit with the poem I promised committed to memory.

I don't owe Mark or anyone else at the funeral anything more.

Laura cries softly throughout the service, her tears reaching a fever pitch as Mark talks about what an inspiration his father was to him, but the rest of the crowd is notably unmoved. As we file past the coffin at the end of the service, dropping white roses onto my brother's casket, I'm struck by the sudden realization that my own funeral will probably look much the same from the outside.

None of the people I work with or my friends in New York would be secretly celebrating my death the way I suspect many of my family members are celebrating Rodger's, but there won't be tears. Even Bella, my closest ex-girlfriend, who's become a friend in recent years, will remain dry-eyed. She's learned to hold me at an emotional distance. Even Bella's abundant warmth couldn't melt the permafrost around my heart, so she stopped giving me access to that part of her.

She's a smart woman.

So is Sully. I realized that within a few minutes of meeting her.

So why is she waiting for me when I return to the yacht early that afternoon, after an equally uncomfortable post-funeral lunch? She leans against the ice cream shack in a striped sweater and yellow raincoat that make her look like the poster child for Sea Breeze's famous Seafood Seasoning Salt.

And cute. She's very fucking cute.

"Can I help you?" I ask, my voice rough from disuse. I didn't speak much after the last line of the poem. I didn't have anything else to say to my dead brother or the people gathered to say their goodbyes to him.

Sully pushes away from the faded wood behind her, sliding her hands into the pockets of baggy jeans that do nothing to disguise her strong legs and curvy hips. "Maybe. I have a few questions. Is now a good time? I know the funeral was this morning. I can come back later if—"

"It's fine," I cut in, nodding over my shoulder. "But we should go below."

"To talk," she says, emphasizing the word in a way that makes her meaning clear. "Just talk."

I incline my head. "Of course. My family will be driving this way. I doubt either of us wants to risk them seeing us chatting alone on deck."

She nods. "Agreed. I don't want my people to see anything, either. The quieter we keep this, the better."

Her words give me an idea...

"Want to get out of town?" I ask. "I haven't had the boat inspected, but Rodger's attorney assured me it was in sea-worthy shape. We could head up the coast, dock, and grab lunch somewhere?" I barely ate anything at the post-funeral luncheon and like the idea of treating her to a nice meal.

She hesitates only a moment before she shrugs. "Sure. I've never steered a yacht before."

"And you're not steering it now," I say as she moves past me to the gangplank.

Once I join her on deck, she pins me with a steady gaze. "Yes, I am. You've been in the city too long to be trusted on the water. I navigate this area five or six days a week. I'm the best choice for captain of this vessel."

I arch a brow as I stow the plank. "You think I haven't been out on the water since I moved to New York? I have a boat at my place in The Hamptons."

"That's cute, but the answer is still no," she says, propping her hands on her hips. "Either I drive or we stay docked."

"You're bossier than I remember," I say.

Her cheeks flush. "Yeah, well, that was *your* area of expertise. This is mine."

My lips curve. "Thanks for the compliment."

She rolls her eyes and exhales a flustered breath that makes me happier than it should. I shouldn't want to fluster this girl. I shouldn't want to take her to lunch or to kiss her again, but...I do.

So, I don't put up a fight as she collects the keys from the hook by the door of the cockpit and starts checking the controls.

I simply settle into the leather chair near the window and watch her work, doing my best not to find her capable handling of the yacht sexy as fuck.

I fail, of course.

But I try. I honestly do.

chapter 9

GERTIE

THE COCKPIT IS QUIETER than any I've experienced, swiftly killing my hopes that we won't have to talk until we're settled over a sandwich somewhere.

In the build-up to showing up on Weaver's dock, I'd convinced myself this conversation wouldn't be a big deal.

Yes, I slept with this man, but we're both grown-ups, and perfectly capable of having an adult conversation.

And, as expected, Weaver was cool about me wanting to "just talk."

Of course, he was. He's the epitome of cool. He's so cool, it burns a little. I feel his frosty gray eyes on me like an ice cube dragging slowly down my spine, making me shiver...and wish he would touch me.

I underestimated how much I would want him to touch me. But then, I've never slept with someone before. Maybe this is normal, this itching beneath the skin that grows worse with every moment I'm in this man's presence and not on top of him.

Or under him.

Or tangled with him against the wall.

That chair would also work. It's a big chair, wide and deep enough for even a large man like Weaver to sprawl out on its seat.

He's sprawled now, watching me as I guide the boat out of the tangle of boats and docks in the harbor and pick up speed, heading north.

Each time I glance his way out of the corner of my eyes, he's watching me, until I can't help shooting a pointed glance his way.

His lips curve. "Just enjoying watching a master at work. That was some impressive slow speed maneuvering, especially in this chop."

I roll my shoulders uncomfortably. "I've been steering since I was a kid. Gramps needed me to help out on the boat after his cataract surgery. He started teaching me when I was thirteen. I was good at it, so I stayed at the helm on the days I worked with him before school. It was technically against the law, but everyone knew I was better behind the wheel than Gramps. We were all safer with me in charge."

"Have you always worked with your grandfather?"

It's the perfect segue into the conversation I'm actually here to have. I could tell him "yes," and that I've lived with Gramps, too, since my family fell apart.

Since *he* helped it fall apart, that night he was caught with my mother...

But I can't bring myself to go there just yet. I'm

trapped on this boat with him for at least another hour before we reach another town large enough to have restaurants and room to dock a vessel this size.

Then, we'll be stuck together for lunch and the trip back.

There's plenty of time to get to the point, preferably once we're closer to being able to leave each other's company, so I say, "Yeah. I had the chance to join a bigger operation last year and potentially make more money, but I like working with Gramps. Maybe it's weird, but he's one of my best friends."

"That's not weird. It's nice," he says in that silky voice of his, the one I really wish was murmuring filthy things in my ear while he runs his hands over every burning inch of me.

Get a grip, Sullivan, I hiss silently to myself.

"Are you close with the rest of your family?" he asks, giving me yet another perfect opening. Still, I plan to avoid going there until he adds, "Your mother, for example?"

I glance sharply his way to find his glacier gaze already studying my face with the focus of a hawk watching an open field for mice.

Well...fuck.

I sigh and turn from the controls, which won't require as much attention from me now that we're in familiar open water.

"Did you know?" I ask. "That night? Before we...?"

He shakes his head. "No, but I suppose I should have. There's definitely a resemblance." My upper lip curls and his brows lift. "That wasn't intended as an insult. Your mother is a beautiful woman."

"She's a cheater," I say, trying to keep my tone as cool and level as his. This drama is old news. I'm not going to get upset about it now. I refuse to give my mother that kind of power over me. "And she wasn't too keen on being a mother, even before she got caught with another man. Afterward, she just...disappeared."

His mouth tightens. "What do you mean?"

"I mean she left," I say, waving a hand in the general direction of upstate New York. "After the night my dad caught her out at the bar with you, she never came home. I was alone at the house the next morning, freaking out, thinking my parents were dead or something, until Gramps came by to tell me that my dad was in the hospital."

I don't know what I expect his response to be—a wince of guilt, maybe—but it doesn't happen. His expression grows even more cool, more controlled, and his voice is steely as he asks, "How old were you?"

"Eight."

"And Tracy never came home?"

I cross my arms and shrug my shoulders. "Well, technically, I guess she did. When we got back from the hospital late that night, one of the big suitcases from the garage and a lot of her stuff was gone, but I didn't realize that until later. I was too upset. And too tired. A full day at the hospital, watching your battered father wheeze on a ventilator is a lot for a little kid. It wasn't until I was packing up my things to move in with

Gramps a few days later that I realized Mom's nice gray suitcase was gone."

His jaw clenches. "How long was it until you saw her again? Until she made contact?"

I huff out a humorless laugh. "Never. When I say never, I mean never. She never called or wrote an email or sent a card on my birthday. For a while, I thought she might be dead, but Elaina tracked her down when we were in junior high. She did a deep Google dive and found Mom in a posh town in upstate New York. She was remarried by then, to a horse breeder, and had a new last name, but somehow Elaina figured it out." My lips twist. "Thank God for good friends, right?"

"I'm not sure in this case," he says, his expression still unreadable.

I shake my head. "No, it was a good thing. After that, I could stop kidding myself that she was out there with amnesia or something and would come running home to me as soon as she remembered who she was. I could accept the fact that my mother was an asshole who didn't love me and move on."

"I'm sure it had more to do with your father than with you. She was very unhappy in her marriage." He pauses for a moment before continuing in a softer voice, "Not that that's any excuse. I'm sorry, Gertrude."

I laugh and roll my eyes. "What for? It wasn't your fault. You didn't make my family any promises or decide to have a kid. And call me Sully, please. I told you, most of my guy friends do. It's weird being called Gertrude by a man for some reason."

"Do you want to be friends?" He arches a brow. "With the man who traumatized you as a child?"

"You weren't much more than a kid, either. My mom basically cradle-robbed you," I say, uncomfortable with the directness of his gaze.

Does this man ever give casual eye contact? Or is it always this "looking through your skin to the secrets of your soul" thing, twenty-four seven?

"I was twenty-three, almost twenty-four," he says. "About the age you are now. Do you consider yourself a kid?"

I squirm a little before I shrug again. "No, but I'm a girl. A girl who had to grow up fast and started working part time on a lobster boat when she was thirteen. I'm sure privileged rich boys grow up slower." He stares at me, silently challenging my words until I feel forced to add, "And even if you were a full-fledged adult, it doesn't matter. It's still true that you didn't make my family any promises. My parents did and they both broke them—Mom by cheating and Dad by choosing the pub over his family every night." I turn, feigning the need to check in with the navigation system as I add, "Though beating the shit out of him probably wasn't called for."

"You're right," he says without missing a beat, surprising me. "I wasn't in control of my anger back then. He punched me and I…" He clears his throat before continuing. "I barely remember the fight. I just remember your mother pulling me away from him. I had another altercation like that not long after, when I was back in the city. I didn't remember much of that, either. I started therapy to get control of my anger afterward, and I've never hurt anyone like that again, but it doesn't excuse the things I did when I was younger. I owe your father an apology. I can arrange to give him one, if you'd like."

I snort, torn between being impressed with his willingness to apologize—that isn't a common trait in most of the rich men I've met, or men in general—and sad about the whole fucked up situation.

"Yeah, I don't think that's a good idea," I say, glancing his way as I guide the yacht a bit closer to shore, now that we're clear of the shallow water near town. "Dad isn't the same guy he was back then. The car wreck did a number on his head, and he never cut back on the drinking. If anything, it got worse after he was out of the hospital. He was living alone and Gramps was taking care of me and paying all of his bills. He had no responsibilities or reason to get his act together."

"You deserved so much more."

I sigh, rolling my eyes. "Please, don't. I don't want your pity. I don't deserve it. I've had a great life. My grandfather loves me to the moon and back and my friends' parents stepped in whenever I needed help with something he couldn't manage on his own. Maya's dad tutored me in math and Elaina's mom helped me through my first period and we all lived happily ever after."

"Except your father."

"But that wasn't your fault."

"I know," he says. "It wasn't yours, either."

My lips part on a protest, but I swallow it down. Obviously, it isn't my fault that my father's a drunk who failed his family, but there are times when I feel guilty for not doing more. I could have gone to see him after school more often as a kid or tried harder to get him into treatment. I already know he wouldn't have gone, but I could have doubled down on the effort.

I've had enough therapy to know that persistent guilt and fear that you're "not doing enough" are common feelings for adult children of alcoholics. But knowing the reason for a thing isn't always enough to keep the thing from making you feel like shit.

Which means it's time to change the subject. I've had enough feeling like shit in my life. I don't need any more of that, especially on my day off.

But I have one last shitty thing I need to ask first.

"So, were you and my mom..." I trail off, my throat tight. "Did you..."

"No," he says. "We'd only been out once before the night we ran into your father. Afterwards, it became clear Tracy Sullivan wasn't good for me. I didn't attempt to contact her again."

"She wasn't good for anyone," I say. "Well, I don't know. Maybe she's good for her new husband. They've been married a while now and she looks swanky in the photos on his company website. She's definitely had Botox and whatever else older women do to keep it tight. She looks like she could be my sister." I laugh. "I'll probably look older than she does, soon. If I stay out on the water and keep forgetting to wear sunscreen."

"You should wear sunscreen."

"I know," I say as I turn from the controls again, "but it's easy to forget at three-thirty in the morning, when you're stumbling out of the bathroom with your eyes barely open."

He considers me for a beat before he says, "You're an impressive, hardworking person, Sully."

My mouth twitches at the nickname. I like it on his lips. I like the friendly look in his eye, too, even if it does mean the steamy part of our relationship is over.

But that's for the best. Even if he didn't sleep with my mother, there's a lot of bad blood between our families and he's still a Tripp. He's also on his way out of town as soon as possible. It's obvious that he hates it here. The few glimpses I've caught of Weaver around Sea Breeze in the past two days, he's looked miserable, his permanent scowl enough to dull even his striking good looks.

"Thanks, but not really," I say. "All harvesters get up early. Our outfit gets up a little earlier because Gramps is hardcore, but it's just part of the job."

"A job you love?" he asks.

"Yeah," I say, ignoring the soft voice niggling at the back of my brain, insisting "love" is too strong a word. I love the sense of community and being my grandfather's right-hand woman, but if I'd had more options, this probably isn't the career I would have chosen.

But I didn't have options—Gramps needed me here —so there's no point thinking about that.

"I like being part of a legacy," I continue. "Sullivans

have been out on this water for over two hundred years. That feels pretty special."

He cocks his head. "You feel pride in your family."

"Yeah, don't you? The Tripps have been around just as long. And you've made a lot more money." I sweep my arm out to one side, encompassing the yacht bearing us smoothly northward.

This thing had to cost at least a million dollars, if not more, and according to Mark, his father has another one just like it down in South Carolina, docked at their vacation home.

"Maybe I should," Weaver says, rising from his seat and crossing to stand beside me at the wheel. He gazes out over the choppy water, churning beneath the clear blue sky. The hurricane passed by far enough out to sea that we didn't get much rain, but the ocean still shows signs of the recent storm. "Where are we headed?"

"I thought Saint Mary, right before you reach Canadian water," I say. "They'll have room to dock a larger boat and it's big enough we can disappear into the city and not be spotted by anyone we know."

"Perfect." He pulls his cell from his pocket. "I'll make a reservation for two. Any preferences on the restaurant? I was thinking French but I can look for something else if you'd like."

"French is good," I say, not wanting to tell him that I've never had French food before. I mean, I've had French onion soup down at the Moose Club—they always serve that and a side salad with the prime rib on Friday nights—but I'm pretty sure that's not the kind of French he's talking about.

Even more than the difference in our ages, the difference in our backgrounds and social status is something that makes this feel…a little strange. If we were actually dating, I'd be nervous all the time, afraid I was going to make a fool of myself by not knowing all the rich person rules.

I'm rough around the edges for a girl, even by Sea Breeze standards, let alone to a swanky New York investment banker. (And yes, I did an internet search on Weaver. I couldn't help myself. I also couldn't find much on the man. He's as private and reserved online as he is in person.)

"But we don't have to get lunch," I say, wanting to give him an out if he'd rather head for home now that we've had our talk. "That's all I really wanted to know."

He turns to me, the clean, fresh scent of his cologne stronger now that he's so close. It makes me want to lean into his neck and inhale. I love the way he smells, like a fancy hotel lobby and something masculine and raw that makes my mouth water a little. "You wanted to know if I'd slept with your mother?"

I force a tight smile. "Yep, that's about it. I was just wondering how grossed out about the other night I should actually be."

"Is that all?" He angles even closer, bracing his hand on the console behind me, until he's looming over me in a way that makes me feel unusually small.

I'm tall and broad through the shoulders for a woman. I'm strong and tough and can count the times I've felt "dainty" on one hand. Hell, on one finger. The first and only time was the other night, when Weaver pulled me up the mattress, showing off the unusually large muscles he keeps concealed under his well-fitted suits and dress shirts.

I tip my head back, bringing my face just inches from his, forcing myself to ignore the electricity flowing across my skin. "What other reason would I have?"

His mouth moves closer, sending my already speeding pulse into overdrive. "I don't know. Maybe you wanted to see if it would be okay to do it again."

"We shouldn't do it again," I say, my voice breathier, weaker than I would like. "Our families hate each other."

"They do," he agrees, close enough now that I can feel his heat on my lips.

"And I made out with your nephew. And you made out with my mother."

He smiles, what I sense is his real smile. There's no tightness around his mouth this time, just an easy swoop of his gorgeous lips and a mischievous flicker in his eyes as he whispers, "It's scandalous, I'll give you that. Are you afraid of scandal?"

"No," I say, dying to kiss him, to feel his strong arms around me showing me how much he wants my body close to his. "But if anyone in my family found out, it would kill them. They might never forgive me. I was worried about them finding out about Mark, but you..."

"I'm so much worse," he supplies, his hand settling on my hip for a beat before smoothing around to the small of my back with a confidence that makes me ache.

"So much worse," I whisper. My hands mold to his chest, but I don't push him away. My fingers curl around the lapels of his suit coat, holding him close.

"Well, then," he murmurs, the tip of his nose brushing against mine.

I lift my chin in anticipation of a kiss, but it doesn't come. Instead, his warmth abruptly vanishes as his coat slides from my fingers. My eyes fly open with a soft breath of surprise to find him already descending the stairs leading into the cabin below.

"Well, then, what?" I demand, propping a hand on my hip.

He grins up at me, his wicked eyes dancing. "Well, then, that's something you should think about before I do any of the things I'd like to do to you."

"You'd like to do things to me?" I ask, hating the slight hint of insecurity in my tone.

But I can't help it. This man is ridiculously good looking and I'm just...me, the tomboy who inherited her beautiful mother's genes, but has no idea what to do with them. I can't transform "cute" into drop-dead gorgeous the way she did. I've never had the time or the patience for girly stuff like expensive haircuts or makeup or dressing for my body type.

But I suddenly wish I'd made time. At least a little.

"Very much," Weaver confirms in a husky voice that makes my entire body tingle again. "Now, if you'll excuse me, I'm going to change into something more comfortable for lunch at a waterfront bistro."

I nod. "Okay. I'll um...steer."

His lips quirk again. "Excellent idea. Someone should stay on top of that."

And you can stay on top of me, I silently add, my cheeks flaming as I turn back to face the wheel.

"Get a grip, Gertie," I mumble beneath my breath as I tug the collar of my sweater away from my flushed throat.

It's only then that I realize I'm in one of my favorite comfy sweaters, my rain slicker, and jeans, with nothing on my face but the sunscreen I actually remembered today and berry-colored lip gloss. That must be the real reason Weaver is going to change, so that we won't look as mismatched as we do right now with him in a fancy suit and me dressed to cosplay as Paddington Bear.

It's thoughtful of him.

It was thoughtful of him to pull away, too, giving me the time and space to decide if I really want a repeat of the other night. But that bossy man who owned my body is still there, lurking beneath Weaver's excellent manners and self-control. I have a feeling all it would take is a word to bring that heart-palpitation-and-orgasm-inducing side of him to the surface.

And God, I want that, I really do.

But should I? Can I risk breaking my grandfather's heart for a one-night stand?

"It would technically be a two-night stand at that point," I whisper as the skyline of Saint Mary appears in the distance. "Or more, depending on how long he's in town."

It won't be long; I know that much. Maybe not even the couple weeks he mentioned on Friday.

It's clear he can't wait to get away from his family. He seems to dislike the rest of the Tripps nearly as much as Gramps does.

At least they have that in common.

It isn't enough to make me consider doing something as stupid as openly dating Weaver Tripp. But it's enough to think maybe, just maybe, I could justify what I've done to Gramps in the unlikely event we're discovered.

It would be *highly* unlikely. I'm good at sneaking around and I lied to my best friend for almost a decade about how I lost my virginity. And lies to protect the people I love will come even easier than lies to protect my pride.

"You're talking yourself into betrayal awfully quickly," I murmur, but the wave of guilt I'm expecting doesn't come.

There's no room for guilt inside me right now.

There's only longing and the sobering knowledge that Weaver can't get back from changing his clothes soon enough. No matter how off-balance he makes me feel sometimes, I already...miss him.

"You're so fucked," I murmur, earning a resounding, *Sure are*, from the inner voice.

Well, at least we agree on something.

chapter 10

WEAVER

IT'S SUCH A FUCKING CLICHÉ—THE girl who has no idea she's beautiful.

I can name three cheesy pop songs on the topic off the top of my head...but that doesn't stop me from being every bit as drawn in by the phenomenon as the teenaged members of One Direction.

As I watch Sully scan the menu in the autumn sunshine, her cheeks pink from the portable heater our waiter pulled closer to our table, and her hair a golden halo around her face, I'm moved by her beauty. Watching her run a finger over her lip as she thinks, the way she tilts her head with an unconscious sensuality...it's like standing in front of one of my favorite paintings at The Museum of Modern Art.

I go to MOMA at least once a month, usually right when they open on a Saturday, to take advantage of private member hours in the galleries. I didn't discover art until I was an adult—it wasn't something my parents had time for or encouraged an appreciation for in their children—but once I discovered the New York City museums, I was hooked.

Hooked on the sheer volume of genius on display, on the beauty and passion and creativity, but most of all, hooked on the way the art made me feel.

I wasn't encouraged to *feel* as a child, either. I certainly wasn't encouraged to give in to surges of emotion or dive deep into the mysteries of the human heart. The Tripps are old school New England, a stoic, solid, cynical lot who value the material over all else. I was taught that the material is all a man can count on.

In many ways, I still agree with that tenant of my childhood—it's a cruel world and acquiring wealth is one of the few paths to safety—but I don't want to imagine my life without what I found at the museums. Without awe, reverence, and that ache that hits in the center of my chest when I see clear evidence that an artist working hundreds of years before I was born felt the weight of the world the same way I do...

It's a kind of connection I never imagined I could experience, let alone crave.

I also never imagined a woman like Gertrude Sullivan would send that same ache winding around my ribs. I'm still not sure why she has this effect on me, why she softens my sharp edges and brings a genuine smile to my face in a way few people can, but I know it's about more than her beauty.

Or about more than the beauty that's skin deep, perhaps...

"You're staring at me again," she murmurs, her

eyes still on her menu. "Am I taking too long to decide if I'm monstrous enough to eat a rabbit?"

"Not at all," I say, smiling again. It's a problem, how much this girl makes me smile. "I'm sure the rabbit is delicious. The restaurant has impeccable reviews."

She glances toward the inside of the bistro, filled with older couples on vacation and a few businessmen scrolling through their phones. "I bet." She turns back to me, leaning closer as she whispers, "This place is fancy as fuck."

Again, with the smiling. "So, order the rabbit. If you've never had it, a fancy as fuck establishment is the way to go for your first time."

She makes a soft considering sound, glancing up at me through her long, sandy blond lashes as she murmurs, "I've heard that about first times. That fancy as fuck is best."

I hold her gaze, imagining all the things I'd like to do to her beautiful body if we have a second time. "Thank you. I'm flattered...I think."

"You should be," she says, her tongue sweeping across her bottom lip, making the swelling behind my fly more pronounced. "But here's the problem, Mr. Fancy, I don't actually want to eat a rabbit. It's just the only thing on the menu that isn't stuffed with spinach or comes with some kind of cheese sauce I can't pronounce."

"The mussels sound good. Just a white wine sauce, no cheese in sight."

"But I've eaten muscles my entire life," she says. "I

want to try something authentically French, expand my horizons and all that, but..." She glances back to her menu before casting a pleading look my way. "But there's no porn for eating French food."

I sputter and nearly choke on my sip of water. When I've regained control, I ask in a rough voice, "Excuse me?"

"That's how I had an idea what to do in the bedroom," she says, her cheeks pink with embarrassment. But she also looks pleased with herself for throwing me off-kilter. "Porn. The good stuff, though, not the angry, mean-to-women stuff." She waves the menu back and forth. "But they don't have that for French food."

"I'm pretty sure they do. It was called The French Chef and ran for ten years out of a public television studio in Boston in the sixties and early seventies."

"Before my time, old man," she teases.

My lips twist. "Before mine, too, young wench."

She laughs and the ache in my chest squeezes a little tighter. "Touché."

"Look at you, using French words like a natural," I say, wishing I could reach across the table, curl my fingers around the back of her neck, and pull her in for a kiss. Instead, I say, "Why don't you let me order for you? We can get a few things to share. Anything you don't like I can take care of. I didn't eat breakfast before the funeral and the luncheon was repulsive."

Her smile fades. "I'm sorry. I didn't even ask how it was."

"It's all right. It was sad, but not in the way it should have been."

Her brow furrows as she mulls that over. "Yeah, I can see that. Better to mourn the loss of a great person than mourn the loss of who that person could have been if they'd had more time."

My jaw tightens. "Exactly. Though I don't think Rodger would have become anything better than he was. Most people don't improve with age."

"But some do," she says, her robin's egg blue eyes studying me with an intensity that makes my empty stomach even more unsettled. "I already like you more than I did the first time we met. You should let your smiley side out more often. It's nice."

She's astute, perceptive, and deserves a taste of everything on this damned menu...even if I have no intention of embracing my "smiley" side.

She laughs, adding, "You should see your face. You look like you swallowed a shot of apple cider vinegar."

"Let me order for you?" I ask as I spot our waiter on his way through the mostly empty tables on the outdoor patio.

She nods, a secret smile on her lips. "Sure. But I can't do wine at lunch. If you were thinking about that. I don't drink before I get behind the wheel. Not even a little bit."

"Understandable," I say, the reminder of her father's car accident taking some of the shine off the moment.

I hurt this woman. Not directly, not on purpose or with malice of forethought, and the violence I doled out that night was absolutely provoked—Leon came at me first.

But still...I hurt her. And she was only a child at the time, a kid left alone in the world after her parents both abandoned her in their own shitty ways.

When she was telling her story, I could practically see her at eight, wandering around her childhood home, calling for a mother and father who would never be there for her again. It reminded me of my own childhood, of realizing that any thought, feeling, or opinion not approved of by my parents would lead to rejection.

Standing up for my mother when my father beat her led to the same.

My father used my "back talk" as an excuse to beat me, as well, then treat me like a ghost in my own home.

He didn't leave me alone—he sent me to my room and wouldn't allow anyone in the family to speak to me for days, no matter how I begged for forgiveness— but the end result was the same. I learned at a young age not to take safety for granted, and that I was the only person I could count on.

I want to tell Sully that I understand her better than she might think, but how can I? When I was part of the reason that she learned such hard, ugly lessons so young?

The only thing I hate more than a bully is a hypocrite. I refuse to be one, so once I've placed our order, I turn the conversation to other subjects.

"Tell me why you haven't tried French food," I say. "When you're so close to French Canada?"

She blinks as she sits back in her chair, relaxing now that all our decisions are made. "I don't know. I haven't been anywhere, really. I work too much, I guess. And Gramps isn't one for travelling. Everything he loves in the world is right there in Sea Breeze. Some girlfriends and I have been saving up for a trip to Iceland, though. I'm pretty excited about that. I'm dying to shoot the northern lights."

I arch a brow. "You're a photographer?"

She shrugs. "Not really. It's just a hobby. What about you? Have you been all over the world and seen all the things?"

"No. I've been to Europe several times, but I work a lot, too. And I'm not a fan of travelling alone." I'm shocked to hear that last sentence leave my mouth. I'm not usually the kind who confesses those sorts of things. Not even to myself.

Her brow furrows. "And why are you alone when you don't want to be?"

"What was the word you used the night we met? Bastard, I believe it was?"

"So you would have had me believe. But you also told me that we'd have to pretend not to know each other if we ran into each other in town," she shoots back without missing a beat. "And the very next morning you asked me to breakfast."

I grunt. "Touché."

She grins. "So why are you alone? The real reason?

133

Are you too picky? Too bossy? Stare too long at people with your icy vampire eyes?"

"Do vampires have icy eyes?" I ask, amused. "I thought they had eyes that glowed red in the dark. Like a wolf's."

"Well, Weaver," she says in an overly patient tone, "vampires aren't real." I smirk in acknowledgement of her joke and she continues, "but in the vampire movies Elaina made me watch in junior high, they all had icy eyes. Even if they were brown, they were still...cold looking. Like they'd been frozen and were only just starting to thaw."

"I don't know," I say, wondering if *I'm* starting to thaw, if that's the reason for this strange ache I feel with this woman. "Could be all three. Or maybe I'm defective in some other way."

"Like what?" she asks, proving she's still the brave, blunt girl who got under my skin the night she crept onto my yacht.

I shake my head. "I don't know. Maybe you can tell me, if you decide I'm worth a month of your time."

"A month, huh?" She presses her lips together. "That's longer than you said before."

"My family's affairs are proving more complicated than I anticipated." I ignore the inner voice taunting me for changing my mind about remote work so quickly. It really would be easier to manage the transitions I want to make to the Tripp business model from Sea Breeze. And if I had a compelling, enjoyable reason to stick around as well...

"What's your high-powered investment firm going

to say about that?" she asks. "Don't they want you back in the city, doing important things with money in your fancy suit?"

I couldn't stop the smile pulling at my lips if I tried. "I didn't tell you I worked for an investment firm."

She rolls her eyes with a self-conscious laugh. "Okay, fine, so maybe I did a little digging once I found out your name. Just to make sure you weren't a sociopath. Obviously."

"Obviously," I echo, still grinning.

She laughs again and reaches down to swat my leg under the table. "Stop. Stop looking so pleased with yourself. I'm not obsessed with you or anything. I'm just a naturally curious person."

"Oh yeah?" I ask, biting my lip as our waiter approaches with the first course. "We're about to put that to the test, Ms. Sullivan."

Our server sets the appetizers down, refills our water glasses, and leaves with a quick, "Bon appétit," that reminds me why I love French restaurants. I'd much rather have a server who's politely disinterested than one of those waiters who hover over you the entire meal, asking how everything's tasting.

"What is that?" Sully asks, eyeing the small cast-iron dish between us with suspicion. "It smells amaz-ing, but..."

"But?" I prompt after a moment, reaching for her appetizer plate.

"But I read the menu. I saw the appetizers," she says, the uncertainty in her gaze increasing as I slide a slice of toasted bread and two steaming hot escargots onto her plate. "There was nothing that sounded like anything I'd want to put in my mouth."

"You'll like this. They're drenched in butter, white wine, and garlic."

She hums beneath her breath as she takes the plate from me and lifts it closer to her face, examining the shining brown lumps beside the bread. "Okay, but what *are* they?"

"Snails," I say, suppressing a laugh at the gagging sound that bursts from her lips. I slide two onto my own plate and collect a slice of bread. "There's nothing to be afraid of."

"I'm not afraid," she says, setting her plate down in front of her, but making no move to reach for her fork. "I'm disturbed. Confused." She studies the plate for another beat before adding in a softer voice, "Vaguely repulsed."

"Oh, come on," I say, sliding a perfectly cooked snail onto my bread. "If you've eaten a mussel or an oyster, you can eat a snail. They all come out of a shell, and from a visual standpoint, oysters are far more repulsive."

"Yes, but they're also fifty cents apiece at happy hour at the Marina Point Grill on Thursdays," she says, wrinkling her nose. "And they never crawled through the dirt in my garden."

"Dirt isn't inherently dirty."

"Garden dirt is," she counters. "Gramps adds cow dung to ours as fertilizer."

"Well, as I said before, anything you don't care for,

I'm happy to put on my plate. But I didn't take you for a coward."

She bristles as she sits up straighter. "I'm not a coward. I'm just...confused by snails on a plate."

"Better than a bunny on a plate," I remind her. "No small, fluffy creatures were harmed in the making of our meal. And some might say working through one's confusion is an act of bravery, Sully."

"Ugh. Yuck. Fine. You're right. I may be many things, but I'm not a coward." She reaches for her fork, mimicking the way I've slid a single snail onto the edge of my bread. When it's ready, she lifts it to hover in front of her mouth. "On three? We go for it at the same time?"

"Sure," I say, humoring her though I've had snails enough times to know these are going to be incredible.

"One, two..." She pulls in a breath, letting it out in a rush as she adds, "Three."

We both bite down into crusty grilled bread and plump, perfectly seasoned snails.

She chews, her expression still tight with uncertainty, but after only a beat or two, the tension fades from her features.

"Oh, wow," she says, her mouth still full. She chews for another moment, moaning softly as her eyes slide closed. "Wow." She swallows and brings her napkin from her lap to her lips, sitting quietly for a moment.

"Good?"

Her eyes open. "I think I just had a food-induced orgasm," she whispers, making me smile. Again.

And not just smile, but laugh and assure her, "There's more where that came from. I ordered all the best things. Now try the pastry with pears and Gorgonzola. Quick, before it gets cold."

"Bossy, bossy," she mutters, but I can tell she doesn't mind. She's already loading a slice of the pastry onto her plate and warning me as I reach for another snail, "Leave me at least one more of those."

"I'll leave you two," I assure her before adding in a whisper loud enough for her to hear, "Now who's bossy?"

She laughs, her eyes crinkling in a way that makes it impossible not to return her grin. "It's me. I'm super bossy. All the time. If we're going to be hanging out, you'll have to get used to it, Mr. Fancy."

Oh, I could get used to it, all right. I could get used to a lot of things about this beautiful, vibrant woman.

But I can't let this ache get any more intense. She's not a painting in a museum; she's a human being, and they always let you down, sooner or later. At least, with Sully, however, I doubt the let-down would be intentional. She's a good, honest person. If she disappoints me, it will be because she's staying true to who she is, and you can't blame another human being for that. Living in integrity is an admirable thing, even if one person's version of integrity is very different than another's.

We move on to our second course and our third, both of us growing increasingly drunk on good food and better company, no bottle of wine required. By the time I pay the bill and we step out onto the boardwalk outside the hotel to walk off our meal, I can't resist reaching for her hand.

She casts a startled look my way, but after a beat, her fingers curl around mine. "You're full of surprises, Mr. Fancy."

"You can call me Weaver."

She seems to mull that over for a moment before she says, "Maybe I will. And maybe I'll come over tomorrow night. I have dinner with Gramps tonight at the lodge, but..."

"You would be very welcome tomorrow night," I say. "I'll look for you as soon as it's dark enough to sneak down to the dock."

She nods. "I'll be the one dressed all in black."

"But wear nice panties this time," I say, earning a glare from her.

"I don't own any nice panties," she shoots back. "I have cotton briefs. You'll just have to make due with those and be glad that you get the chance to take them off of me."

I tighten my grip on her fingers. "Oh, I will be. Very glad."

I'll be far more than "glad," but I don't tell her that. I just pull her against me in the shade of a beach shack that's closed for the season and kiss her, devouring her sweet mouth until she's moaning for me far louder than she moaned for the escargot.

Take that, snails.

chapter 11

GERTIE

CAN a person be considered a sex fiend for just *thinking* about sex twenty-four seven?

Or do you have to actually do the deed more than once to qualify?

This is the question front of mind from the moment my alarm blares at three-thirty Monday morning—interrupting a dream in which Weaver was feeding me exotic foods while slipping his hand between my legs beneath the table—until late Monday afternoon, as I'm zoning out on my favorite couch in the café with a chubby gray cat in my lap, pondering where I might be able to acquire "nice panties" in our one lobster town.

I don't want to change myself for a man in any way, even a small way.

But I *do* want Weaver to look at me the way he did after our kiss on the boardwalk yesterday, like I'm the sexiest thing he's ever seen. Like he can barely control the urge to rip my clothes off and—

"Earth to Gertie." Elaina's sharp words are followed by a snap of her fingers, inches from my face.

I do a full-body flinch, sending Maybe bolting for the cat climbing structure, where he was hiding in one of the bottom tubes when I arrived. "What, I'm awake, I'm awake. What?"

"I've been asking if you wanted a truffle with your espresso shot for at least two minutes." Elaina props her hands on her hips, making her orange velvet circle skirt poke out even more than it did before. For someone who professes to hate Halloween, she spends a large chunk of October dressed in orange and black. "What's up with you?"

"Nothing," I say, feeling bad about withholding information from my best friend, but the fewer people who know I'm seeing Weaver Tripp in a romantic capacity, the better. "I'm fine. Just tired from being out on the boat in the cold all day."

"You were humming to yourself," she accuses, her eyes narrowing on my face.

I plaster on what I hope is an innocent expression. "So?"

"And smiling."

I arch a brow. "I'm not allowed to smile?"

"Of course, you're allowed to smile. You're allowed to smile and hum and stare at the wall like you're watching a dreamy movie only you can see," she says, settling onto the cushion beside me. "But not when you refuse to share what has you on cloud nine." She points a finger at my chest, "Or *who*... It's a who, isn't it? And I'd bet a year's supply of fancy Himalayan salt that his name starts with a W."

"Hush!" My eyes fly wide as my gaze flits about what I can see of the café behind her, but thankfully, we appear to be alone.

"Relax, Monday afternoons are always dead," she says. "There's no one here but us. Well, us and the cats, but they know how to keep a secret." Her bottom lip pushes out in an exaggerated pout. "And I do, too. I promise. Please tell me what's going on. Maya's been busy shopping with her mom and Sydney's up to her armpits in moving boxes and no one has time for me. I'm lonely and need gossip."

"You should consider talking to someone about that," I say, only half kidding. "Being able to be alone for a day or two is an important skill."

Elaina kicks off her ballet flats, settling more fully onto the couch. "Yeah, yeah, or I can just keep being a chatty extrovert and living my one wild life the way I want to live it."

"Co-dependent and up in everyone's business?"

"Yes," she says seriously. "Now spill it. You talked to Weaver yesterday, right? What did he say? About your mom and dad and all the drama?"

"Not much," I say, briefly filling her in on what I learned on our trip up the coast.

She exhales a relieved sigh when I'm done. "Well, that's good news, right? I mean, the best news possible, in any event. He didn't bang your mom and he's willing to apologize to your dad. Not that it matters." She wiggles her perfectly shaped brows. "When he asks permission to marry you, he'll have to ask Gramps. That's only right. Gramps is the one who put in the hard work raising you to be the magnificent woman you are today."

I burst out laughing, then laugh harder at the annoyed expression on her face.

"What?" she asks. "What's so funny? Don't you want your forever guy to ask permission from your family?"

"No, and I wouldn't have thought you would, either. You're the most independent woman I know."

She tucks her legs beneath her. "Well, yes, but I'm also a romantic. I think asking permission is romantic. And practical. I mean, better to know up-front if your lady's family hates your guts, right?"

Her words send a pall over my dreamy, sex-obsessed thoughts. I already know Weaver's family hates my family and vice versa. Even if I wanted happily ever after with a guy who makes me as nervous as he does turned-on, there's no path forward for us.

This is a temporary thing. We have a month at most, maybe, and then he'll go back to his life and I'll go back to mine.

And that's fine. Better than fine. I don't want a long-term relationship right now, anyway. I just want to make the most of the time I have with this irresistible man.

Which is something Elaina might be able to help me out with...

"Do you have an idea where I might be able to get some sexy panties around here on short notice?" I ask.

She squeals, clapping her hands. "I knew it! I knew you wouldn't be able to resist banging him again. I have a feeling about you two, I swear."

I roll my eyes. "You've never even seen us together."

"But I've seen you separately, and you vibrate at the same frequency. And you're both fucking gorgeous and will make seriously beautiful babies that I can babysit every Friday so you can have a date night."

"The baby fever still making you insane? Or more insane than usual?"

Her lips turn down. "Yes. I don't know what's wrong with me. I'm not in any position to have a kid. I work all the time, and I don't have a fuck buddy, let alone a life partner. It's just stupid hormones, I guess." Her expression sobers. "Speaking of, you're using protection with Tall, Sexy, and Frosty, right?"

I nod. "Yeah. And I'm on the pill."

"Good." She nods. "Then you don't have to worry about anything except having fun and showing off your new panties. I have an adorable bra and panty set I bought in August and haven't had a chance to wear yet. If you'll watch the cash register, I can run up and grab them."

"I'm never going to fit into something in your size," I say, eyeing my tiny friend as she bounces to her feet.

"Of course, you will." She turns, slapping the back of her fluffy skirt. "I have a big butt for my height. And you're a C cup, right?"

I nod. "Yes, but—"

"Then you'll be fine. You'll probably have to put the strap on the widest clasps, because I'm a little smaller around the ribs, but it'll be fine." She winks as she sashays toward the staircase at the back of the café, leading to her apartment on the second floor. "It's not like you'll be wearing them that long anyway."

I try, but I can't fight the grin pulling at my cheeks. "You make a solid point."

She squeals again, calling out, "I'm so happy for you," as she dashes up the stairs.

It's nice. Supportive. And I know Elaina's mostly kidding about the marriage and baby stuff.

I don't even know if I want marriage or babies, especially babies. I love kids, but I don't think I want to raise one. Either way, it's never been something I've thought about too much. I've been so busy keeping our family business alive that the years have slipped away faster than I realized. But as a teenager fresh out of high school, determined to stay in my hometown and help Gramps the way he'd always helped me, I never would have imagined that one day I'd be almost twenty-five, still single, and living above my grandfather's garage.

Well, the garage part, maybe. Rent prices are insane in Sea Breeze. There just isn't enough housing to go around. There's no shame in living in an apartment on a relative's property, but I would have assumed I would have had someone sharing it with me by now. And I was positive I'd have my associate's degree in photography from the community college. I started online classes the spring after graduation, as soon as the most active part of lobstering season was over.

But sometime in my first two years of working full time on the boat, I started resenting the fact that I had to spend two evenings a week and a good chunk of my weekends on schoolwork. I busted my ass five to six days a week doing intense, physical labor. On my time off, I wanted to read for fun, go on a hike through the marsh or dancing at the Moose Club, and spend book club nights giggling with my girls.

I gave up on my degree with twelve credits left to graduate. It wasn't a conscious decision, time just... slipped away from me, and suddenly it had been two years since I'd signed up for classes.

Same thing with dating.

If Weaver hadn't shown up and shocked me out of my routine, who knows how much longer things would have clicked along the way they've been the past six years? Would I have been thirty by the time I finally realized I'd slipped into autopilot and was no longer actively guiding the course of my life?

I don't know, but the thought scares me a little. It reminds me too much of Dad, lost in the booze haze and only surfacing to take a hard look at his life every few years or so. During those brief episodes of clarity, he'll come around the house more, his eyes teary and his hands trembling from alcohol withdrawal, promising that he's going to get a job and help out around the house more.

He never does, though, and the thought of ending

up anything like him scares the shit out of me. Even if Weaver weren't proving to be a fun distraction from the status quo, I would be grateful to him. He's forced me to examine my life and realize it's time to make some changes.

I want to travel more, the way he has. I want to learn about other places, meet people outside my tiny hometown, and take pictures of things other than the ocean, lobsters, and sea birds stealing French fries from tourists on the pier.

Though the tourist pics are pretty funny...

"Here we go," Elaina says, stepping over the rope bearing a "Do Not Enter" sign that's draped across the stairwell leading up to her place. She holds up a scrap of blue satin and white lace in each hand. I glance over my shoulder again, and she laughs. "Relax, I told you, Mondays are dead." She stops in front of me with a grin. "What do you think?"

I reach out, touching the fabric. "Wow. It's softer than I thought."

"It's silk. The good shit," she says, but when I reach for the bra, she pulls it out of reach. "You're going to have to hand wash these in the sink. No throwing them in with the rest of your laundry. Can you do that?"

"Sure," I say, reaching for the lingerie again, only for Elaina to draw it away a second time.

"I'm serious. It hurts me to see beautiful things ruined. We must respect the beautiful things."

I fight an eye roll. "Yes, ma'am, I will respect the beautiful things. I pinky swear."

Her smile widens as she finally puddles the bra and

panties into my outstretched hands. "Good. I assume that means you'll have no problem with me closing early and doing your hair and makeup for you before you head over to meet your man? In the name of making beautiful things even more beautiful?"

"He's not my man," I say. "And I'm not meeting him until later, after it gets dark. I have to cook dinner with Gramps first and then pretend to head over to my place for the night. If he sees me all girlie, he'll know something is up."

Elaina gives a patronizing shake of her head. "Oh, Gert Gert, how can you be so smart and so clueless at the same time? Just tell Gramps you're having dinner with me tonight and then go straight to the yacht when it's dark. Easy peasy."

I bristle a little. "I can't."

"Why not? You've obviously already showered since you don't smell like bait." She wrinkles her nose. "Much, anyway. The smell never really leaves you completely, does it?"

I bristle more as I surge to my feet. "Thanks. Way to make a girl feel confident about heading over to see a guy who smells like the lobby of a fancy hotel and money." I start to move past her, muttering, "I should go take another shower, I guess."

"Oh, stop." She catches my elbow as I start toward the door, and I let her spin me back to face her. Her dark eyes stare imploringly into mine. "Please. Stay. I'm sorry. I didn't mean to make you feel self-conscious. The total opposite. I want you to feel confident and beautiful." She releases my arm and reaches up, guiding my wild hair over my shoulder. "Because you *are* beautiful. You're like a supermodel, Gertie, without even trying. I can't believe it took a man this long to notice how special you are and want to treat you like a queen."

I bite my lip before I say softly, "I'm not a supermodel. And Weaver doesn't want to treat me like a queen. He just wants a discreet booty call and maybe a few laughs. We had fun together yesterday. He took me to this amazing French restaurant in Saint Mary. And he's actually nice...and funny. When he wants to be."

Elaina's lips curve in a knowing smile. "Yeah, guys are like that when they have a crush."

I snort-laugh, shaking my head. "Oh my God, stop. You're making this out to be so much more than it is. He doesn't have a crush."

"Right, he just likes you enough to take you out to a swanky restaurant and want to see you two days in a row."

I huff again, but there's hope in my voice when I ask, "Really? Two days in a row is a big thing?"

"It is. I can't remember the last time I liked someone enough to want to see them two days in a row." Her lips scrunch to one side. "I can't remember when someone liked me enough to do that, either. I really need to expand my fishing zone. Continuing to cast my net around here is clearly a fruitless endeavor."

I arch a brow. "Well, if you hadn't overfished in the first place..."

"You're right. I hate you, but you are." Her nose joins the scrunch until her prune face makes us both laugh. When we've pulled ourselves together, she squeezes my arm, "Come on. Let me close up and pamper you a little. You deserve it. We can paint our nails, too. I have a home gel kit that keeps the paint from chipping for at least a week."

I tip my head to the side. "Okay." Before she can celebrate, I warn, "But not too much makeup. And you have to teach me how to do it. Just in case I want to put it on myself sometime."

She beams. "Yes. That will be perfect. *You* will be perfect. You don't need much. Just a little something to bring out the color in your cheeks and those gorgeous eyes."

While she closes up, I text Gramps—*Hey, gonna grab dinner with Elaina then head back to my place for an early bedtime. You need anything from town? I can grab you a plate from The Seafood Hut on my way back if you want.*

After a few moments, he texts back—*Nah. I'm good. I'll just have chili leftovers. Good for a fall night. The temperature's going to nosedive, so put out your warm socks for tomorrow and wear a base layer. See you in the morning.*

Okay, will do. See you then—I say, feeling guilty for lying to Gramps.

But lying is for the best and it's not like he hasn't had company today. We were out on the boat together until one-thirty and he hit the pub for a drink with some friends while I headed home to shower.

Still, I never lie to Gramps.

Well, almost never...

I might have lied a teeny tiny bit when I said I wasn't sad about giving up that scholarship to study photography at the college of Art and Design in Portland. I wanted to stay and help out on the boat...but I also wanted to spread my wings and fly. I wanted to be one of the first people in my family to go to college and work a job that didn't involve hauling traps into a boat or frying up food at the restaurant my grandmother owned before she died.

"Ready?" Elaina asks once she's drawn the curtains over the front windows, giving the cats privacy for the rest of the day.

I nod. "Yeah."

I am ready. Ready to make a change and maybe drag out some of those old dreams I've put on the shelf.

But first, I'm ready to spend the night with a man who makes me feel more alive than I have in a very long time.

chapter 12

AFTER A DAY SPENT WORKING REMOTELY, several phone calls from family members with boat maintenance concerns, and another conversation with a teary Laura about why I won't be turning the reins over to Mark any time in the near future, I'm desperate for something to take my mind off how much I wish I were anywhere but here.

Then I hear her soft footsteps on the deck. She appears at the top of the stairs, dressed in a fluffy black sweater and dark gray leggings. Her hair flows around her shoulders in silky waves, her eyes are even more arresting than usual, and I suddenly don't want to be anywhere else.

It's a problem, how quickly I'm becoming attached to this girl, irritating in an entirely different way than my needy relatives.

I blame that irritation for the harsh note in my voice as I say, "What have you done to your face?"

Her hand flies to hover beside her pink cheek,

uncertainty in her expression as she steps off the final stair to face me across the living room. I remain seated in the large leather armchair, not wanting her to see that I'm already pitching a tent in my pajama pants.

This is a problem, too, how just laying eyes on her is enough to make me desperate to fuck in a way I haven't experienced since I was in high school.

"Elaina did my makeup," she says, rubbing lightly at her cheek with the back of her hand. "Is it too much? I thought it was too much, but she said that was just because I wasn't used to wearing any."

"Stop, you're stunning," I grumble, annoyed with myself for making her doubt herself. "You're just more stunning without it."

Her darker-than-usual brows lift. "Seriously?"

I nod, "You look more...like you."

She cocks her head. "You mean that, don't you?"

"I do."

Her eyes narrow. "And you think you know me well enough to know when I look more like myself, Mr. Fancy?"

I hold her gaze, my cock getting even harder as the air between us fills with potential. "I know you better than you think, Ms. Sullivan. We're not so different. You and I."

She blinks, seemingly surprised, but after a moment, she nods. "Maybe we aren't. Not in the ways that count. But you still scare the shit out of me sometimes."

I stand and cross the distance between us, not caring if she sees what she does to me. I need to put her mind at ease, to assure her that she never has to be afraid when we're together. "I told you, Sully, I've done all the anger management. All of it. You don't have to worry about that."

She smiles, a fond smile I'm sure I don't deserve, but relish all the same. "I didn't mean scared in that way. I mean..." She chews on her berry-stained lip for a beat. "I've been thinking about you. A lot. Probably more than I should."

"I've been thinking about you, too." I lift a hand to cup her face. Fuck, she's beautiful, mesmerizing, better than any painting in any museum.

She tips her cheek closer to my hand, the trust in the gesture making me even more determined never to hurt her. At least, not any more than I have already.

"But that's normal," I add, sliding my fingers into her hair. "That happens when the sex is really good."

Her mouth hooks up on one side. "So, the sex was really good for you, too? Even though it wasn't your first time?"

"It was fucking incredible." I wrap my free arm around her waist, drawing her closer. "I've been dreaming about you ever since."

"Me, too," she says, her eyes widening as her hips brush against my borderline obscene erection. She grins, looking pleased with herself. "Last night, I dreamt you were fingering me under a table while you fed me exotic things."

"What kind of exotic things?" I ask, fighting a groan as she twines her arms around my neck and wiggles closer to where I ache for her.

"There was a fruit that looked like a star and caviar," she says, her eyes dancing as she adds. "And eggplant. Lots and lots of eggplant."

I arch a brow. "Eggplant. Seriously?"

She shakes her head, her laughter the sweetest sound I've heard all day. "No, but for some reason I'm having a hard time thinking about anything except eggplant right now. Go figure..." She pushes up on tiptoe, pressing a soft kiss to my lips before she whispers against my mouth, "I would like to suck your cock, Mr. Fancy. Would that be okay with you?"

My erection jerks in response, but when she starts to bend her knees, I capture her upper arms, holding her in place. "Only if you call me Weaver."

"Okay, Weaver," she says, my name intimate on her lips, just the way I hoped it would be. "And you can call me Goddess of your Loins, once I show you how good I am with my mouth."

For the first time in my life, I find myself smiling as a woman drops to her knees in front of me. I haven't had a lot of "playful" sex in my life, and things quickly lose their playful edge now as Sully curls her fingers around the top of my pants, guiding them down just far enough to sweep her tongue over the head of my cock.

But still...there's an ease with her. A familiarity.

It feels like I've known her so much longer than a few days, and like I'm far more familiar with her hot little mouth than I actually am. But that doesn't dull the thrill of watching her suck me between her lips. If anything, it makes it that much more intense.

I thread my fingers into her hair, making a light fist as she works me harder, taking me even deeper. "Relax your throat, beautiful. Yes, just like that." I tighten my grip at the back of her neck. "Can I fuck your pretty mouth?"

She moans low in her throat and gives a little nod, sending a fresh wave of arousal surging straight to my balls. I'm going to come faster than I usually would from something like this, but that's all right.

The faster I come, the sooner I can recover and be inside her again.

Fuck, I can't wait to be inside her. It's all I could think about last night, as I lay in bed, trying and failing to get to sleep, then jerking off to memories of her body writhing beneath mine.

The memory is almost enough to make me pull her to her feet, bend her over the couch, and jerk her pants down to her knees. But she's opened her throat so perfectly for me and she's so sexy like this, with her hands braced on my thighs and her lips wrapped around my cock.

"Touch my arm if you want me to stop," I murmur as I draw back and slowly glide into her mouth, holding her in place with a firm grip in her silky hair. I encounter the hint of resistance at the back of her throat, but then, she relaxes even more, giving me space to bury myself to the hilt. "Fuck, woman," I say, my voice shaking a little. "You're going to ruin me."

She moans and digs her nails deeper into my thighs as if agreeing with me. Then her eyes roll up to meet mine and I can't hold back any longer.

Holding her gaze, I move faster, until I'm stroking so deep into her mouth that her eyes start to water at the edges.

But she doesn't look away or grab my arm. She keeps her gaze locked on mine, the hunger in her deep blue eyes driving me on until I'm slamming my cock between her lips.

I come with a curse and a guttural cry, spilling myself down her throat. She swallows every drop, her tongue caressing the underside of my throbbing cock until my orgasm is finally finished with me.

Only then does she pull back, giving the head of my cock a final swirl goodbye with her tongue that makes my breath hiss out.

She looks up at me, still on her knees as she wipes the sides of her mouth. "You okay?"

"I'm fucking incredible."

"You twitched. Like you were in pain."

My lips curve. "Cocks are sensitive after you make them come like a fucking freight train."

"Yeah?"

"Yes," I say, my smile widening at the pleased expression on her face.

"Yes, what?" she asks, grinning.

"Yes, Mistress of my Loins," I say, making her laugh, a low, husky laugh I know I'll never get tired of.

"It was Goddess of my Loins," she corrects as she rises to her feet. "But close enough."

"Mistress, goddess," I say, pulling her closer. "Why settle for one when you can be both?"

She reaches up, pressing a hand to my lips before I

can kiss her. "Wait. I need to brush my teeth. I brought a toothbrush in my purse."

I frown. "Why?"

"Because I just...you know. Aren't you supposed to brush your teeth after?"

"You're supposed to do what makes you feel good and then, after that's covered, what makes me feel good. I don't care that you just swallowed my come. I still want your tongue in my mouth. I'd want your tongue in my mouth if you'd just eaten a plate full of onions."

Her smile is shy this time. "Yeah? You like kissing me that much?"

"Yes." I drop my hand to her ass, squeezing the muscled flesh as I pull her closer. "So, can I kiss you, Sully? Kiss you and get you out of these clothes and do very bad things to you in my bed?"

She sighs as she melts against me. "Yes, please. Please, please, please."

"You don't have to say please," I whisper, my lips brushing hers. "Unless you like it when a man makes you beg."

She smiles against my mouth as a shiver runs through her gorgeous body. "Well, Weaver, as you know, I don't have a lot of experience in that area. But I think I might like it. What are you going to make me beg for?"

"Everything," I promise.

And then I sweep her into my arms and carry her into the bedroom, where I deliver on that promise. First, I make her beg for my mouth on her clit, and then

I make her beg for my fingers in her pussy. Then, once I'm hard again, I tie her wrists to the bed frame with two of my silk neckties and make her beg for my cock.

"Come on, sweetheart," I say, teasing the tip of my erection down one side of her soaked, swollen sex and back up the other, my cock leaking pre-come as she squirms and moans beneath me. I should put on a condom before this gets any more dangerous than it is already, but I love the feel of her hot, silken skin against mine. "You can do better than that. Tell me how much you need me inside you. Make me believe it this time. Then, I'll put on the condom and fuck you. I promise."

"No," she says, bucking against me, trying to force me inside her. "No condom. It feels too good like this."

I can't argue with that, but, "No babies for me."

"I'm on the pill," she says, rolling her hips, making the urge to thrust inside her almost irresistible.

But I clench my jaw and grit out, "Still a no, I'm afraid. I can't risk it. I don't want children. Ever."

"Then you should have a vasectomy," she says, her words remarkably lucid considering her eyes are glassy and her cheeks flushed with frustrated desire. "That would take care of both of our problems."

I smile, despite the hunger rampaging through my bloodstream. "What's your problem again?"

"Being a newly minted sex fiend who wants you bare?" she says, moaning as I circle her hot little cunt with the head of my cock, so close to gliding inside her I can't breathe. "Please, Weaver. Fuck me like this. I want to feel you, just you, not latex."

"You're dangerous," I say as I force myself to pull back and reach for the condom on the bedside table. "Very dangerous."

"And very bad," she agrees, her glassy eyes glittering now with humor and a challenge I can't ignore. "Someone should probably teach me a lesson."

I exhale a soft laugh as I roll on the protection. "And how should one do that, my little sex fiend? Another spanking?"

She shakes her head slowly back and forth. "I like this," she says, glancing toward her bound hands. "But I'd like it better if it were your hands holding me down."

"Holding you down," I repeat, wondering if maybe I'm not as much of a bastard as I've always thought. I must have done something good in my life to earn this gem of a woman in my bed, even if it's only for a few weeks.

She nods. "Yes. Hard, please. And don't let me up, no matter how hard I fight you."

My balls tighten and a wave of desire so intense it's almost painful wrenches through my core. "We'd need a safe word for something like that, sweetheart."

"Eggplant," she says without hesitation. "That's what I'll say if I want you to stop, but...I won't want you to stop. I already know I won't."

And she doesn't. Ten minutes later, we're both covered in sweat and slamming together hard and fast, even as she twists and struggles to get free. It's frenzied, wild fucking at its finest, and when I finally come, it's with an intensity that puts even my first orgasm of the night to shame.

I come groaning and cursing and calling her name like a prayer.

And she does the same, until we're both lying limp and boneless in each other's arms.

Finally, I lift my head to stare down into her dreamy face. "Good?"

She sighs and nods. "I can't feel my toes."

"Then I'll move," I say, but she wraps her legs around my hips, holding me in place with a flex of her strong thighs.

"No. Stay. I'm memorizing you. You still smell like a fancy hotel, even after you've done sweaty, wonderful things to me."

"And you..." My words trail off as I spy the faint blue marks on her wrists. I curse again as I reach up, taking her arm gently in hand.

"What's wrong?" she asks.

"I bruised you. Why didn't you use your safe word?"

She drags her arm down, staring at it with an unconcerned expression. "It didn't hurt then. And it doesn't hurt now." She sighs again and loops her arm around my neck. "I like it. It's like...a souvenir. I can look at it tomorrow, while I'm working and wishing I were fucking you instead and feel smug about how great I am at being sexy." She frowns. "Which reminds me, you didn't even notice the effort I made to look delicious for you."

I return her frown. "Yes, I did. I told you that you were stunning, but I like you better without makeup."

"No, not that," she says with a huff. "The bra and panties. I wore fancy ones. Just for you. And you didn't even notice."

I blink, but she's right. I can't remember what I took off of her. I was in too much of a hurry to get to her skin. "You're right. I'm sorry."

"You should be," she says, grinning. "Now you can never complain about my cotton panties again."

"Would it make it better if I told you I ordered several hundred dollars' worth of lingerie this evening, while I was waiting for it to get dark, and wishing you were already here? They're arriving Wednesday."

Her smile widens. "Yeah, that does make things better, actually. Thank you."

"You're welcome. I'd also like to take you shopping on Friday. If you can take the afternoon off. I'd like to buy you something to wear to a fancy dinner out of town next week."

Her lips purse. "That's sweet, but Friday is Halloween. I have to be spooky on Halloween. The girls and I are having a book club Halloween party and then I'll probably hit the Moose Club's haunted house or something. Halloween must be celebrated."

"Must it?" I tease, even as my wheels spin, not willing to give up one of my nights with her so easily. "And what if I arranged for us to celebrate together, after your book club party? Somewhere we won't be seen by prying eyes? Could I tempt you away from the Moose Club for the evening?"

She brushes a gentle hand down my face, that fond smile on her lips again that makes my heart do borderline painful things in my chest. "Yes, you could. I'm pretty sure you could tempt me away from just about anything, Mr. Fancy. Thank you for being the best first lover a girl ever had."

Refusing to think about how much I want to be her last lover, as well, I turn my head, pressing a kiss to her palm. "My pleasure, beautiful."

And then I fuck her again, but it isn't fucking this time.

It's slower, softer, with her eyes locked on mine as she takes her first turn on top of me. And as her hands brace on my chest and her hips rock into me with a sensual rhythm that mimics the rise and fall of the sea, I know I'm losing something.

Something important.

I've never let my defenses fall like this. I've never dropped my guard or let anyone so deep into the secret places inside. But with Sully...

I have no choice.

She shows up with an authenticity that's humbling in its bravery. How can I do anything less? Anything less than a fearless woman like her deserves?

You're going to fall in love with her, the inner voice warns as we lie together after, her cheek resting over my heart.

Love...

I'm not sure I even know what it is.

But if I spend much more time with this incredible woman, I have a feeling I'm going to find out.

chapter 13

GERTIE

Four days later...

COME FRIDAY NIGHT, our Halloween book club is even more festive than usual.

Elaina made creepy sugar cookies to go along with the Young Adult horror novel she consented to read—even though it didn't have any sex and relatively little romance compared to our usual selections—and Sydney joins us via Zoom for the first part of the evening. She just visited ten days ago, so she couldn't make it back to town for the party, but having her here via laptop is better than nothing.

Her boyfriend, Gideon, also makes an appearance at the end to share his thoughts on the story. He read it because Sydney was reading it, and he wanted to be able to discuss it with her.

How adorable is that?

Very adorable. And Gideon makes Sydney so happy. She's glowing with excitement for the new chapter in her life and already loving her new job at Gideon's real estate development firm in Burlington. I can't imagine most of the couples I know wanting to work together *and* live together, but Gideon and Sydney are clearly loving every second of their twenty-four seven life together.

After book talk and saying goodbye to the love-birds, we dress the cats in their costumes and I take hundreds of pictures, while Maya and Elaina giggle and the cats shoot us looks that would foretell our doom if they had opposable thumbs and the ability to hold a weapon.

Maybe is the only feline who seems to enjoy his costume, a cozy lobster suit complete with giant claws bobbing around in the front. He dashes around the closed café, pouncing on the pinchers and rolling over to bat at them with his paws, purring the entire time.

"Get a shot of Pudge and me, will you, Gertie?" Maya asks, cuddling the giant orange tabby she finally adopted last month, after being in love with him for ages.

Pudge is dressed as a bat, and Maya is Lady Dracula, complete with fangs she pops in to grin for the camera as they cuddle on the couch. Pudge, as usual, is a sweet beast. Though he clearly isn't happy with his bat wings—he's been trying to rub them off against the wall for the past ten minutes—he adores Maya. He consents to several portrait shots, including one where he's perched on Maya's shoulder, before wiggling to be set free.

Maya sighs happily as she watches him waddle toward the catnip toys, her cheeks pink from the warmth in the café and two Imaginary Fiend cocktails. Elaina invented the rum-based drink to go along with the book about killer imaginary friends, but I stuck to cinnamon tea with my cookies.

Weaver made plans for us in Saint Mary at eight, and I want to be sure I'm still awake for our first night out on the town. I convinced Gramps to leave at five a.m. this morning instead of four, since I had plans for Halloween night and wanted to stay up late, but I'll still be asleep by nine if I start drinking too soon. I'm not a lightweight, but alcohol makes me way sleepier than it used to.

It's another sign that I'm a full-blown adult...along with the suitcase waiting by the back door.

I'm going on a romantic weekend getaway for the first time in my entire life!

Weaver seems as excited about it as I am. Last night, while we were eating strawberries and whipped cream after working up an appetite in his bed, he expressed how pleased he was to be the first man to take me on a trip, even if it is only to a hotel a few towns over.

The exact details of what we're doing are a surprise, but he insisted he was going to give me "a weekend you'll never forget," and then he did things with the whipped cream and his tongue that I'll also never forget.

I'm never going to forget a second of my time with Weaver. A part of me is already dreading our inevitable "goodbye" in a few weeks. But I push that voice to the back of my mind and enjoy my last few minutes with my girls.

When Weaver pulls up behind the café—the better for us to sneak away without being seen together—I hug Maya and Elaina, track down the lint roller to tidy up my dress, and dash out to the car, suitcase in one hand and a sugar cookie in the other.

"Wow." Weaver's lips part as he takes in the sexy black dress I found at the resale shop, my borrowed jacket, and shiny high heels. "You look..."

"Like I don't work on a lobster boat?" I ask with a laugh, the heat in his gaze assuring me the outfit is as "fire" as Elaina promised me it was.

I needed to bring the fire tonight. Weaver looks even more striking than usual in a dark gray three-piece suit with a silver shirt that brings out the steely color in his eyes. His dark hair is brushed back, showcasing the salt and pepper at his temples that I love, and he smells as divine as ever as he pulls me close.

"Like you've never been close to one." He bends, pressing a kiss to my cheek. "I'll have to beat the other men off you with a stick."

Shivering at the feel of his breath warm on my neck and his lips so close to my ear that they kiss my skin as he speaks, I say, "Nah, I'm tough, I can beat them off myself." Then I realize how that sounded and add as he laughs, "I didn't mean that the way it sounded."

He grins—that big, easy smile I've only ever seen

when we're alone, the one that makes him even sexier —and winks. "You'd better be. I'm not in the mood to share you with anyone, let alone other men."

Ignoring the fizzy bubbles his words send rushing through my blood—I can't take the romantic things he says too seriously, or I'll really be in trouble when he leaves—I let him take my suitcase and follow him around to the back of the Subaru.

Weaver pops the trunk and slides my bag in beside his much fancier leather one in the slightly funky-smelling storage area.

Someone dumped bait on his car Wednesday night, the one night I wasn't on his boat this week. We got lucky with that, and with no one seeing me leaving his place while they were trashing his rental, but Weaver had a hell of a time finding someone willing to detail the car.

Not only was the mess gross, but people in town seem to be taking sides between Weaver and Mark. Both auto mechanics in easy driving distance are Mark's friends.

But a few hundred dollars over the usual detail price convinced one of them to switch loyalties, and Weaver had a security system installed on the dock with a view of both his parking spot and the yacht earlier today. The next time someone comes to deface his property, he'll be able to see who's behind it and take the footage to the sheriff's department.

I would say I can't believe people are being so petty, but trashing Rodger Tripp's car was practically a town pastime. It got so bad in the past few years that he spent most of his time at his vacation home in South Carolina and only came to town for important meetings or family celebrations.

But Weaver isn't Rodger, a fact he proves by smiling as I present him with his cookie. Rodger hardly ever smiled and never over something as simple as a sugar cookie decorated to look like a dragon with giant teeth.

"And what's this?" he asks, holding it up to the light streaming from the bare bulb above the back door.

"It's a killer imaginary friend," I say. "That's what our club pick was about this time. Elaina always makes cookies to match the book on Halloween and Christmas. She made extra this time to be sure I had one to share."

His expression softens. At first, he wasn't sure about sharing our secret with both Elaina and Maya, but he came around.

Maybe because he trusts my judgement and taste in friends.

Or maybe because he doesn't care if we get caught as much as I do.

Yes, Weaver is a discreet person, but I'm the one whose entire family will turn against her if we're found out. Dad's disappointment, I could handle—it's not like he hasn't disappointed me more times than I can count—but I don't want to lose the respect of my extended family, and this could literally kill Gramps.

His cholesterol is high and he's been short of breath lately on more than one occasion. He needs to watch his diet, exercise more, and avoid flipping his lid because his granddaughter betrayed the family with a member of the evil Tripp clan.

Gramps now has multiple t-shirts he's had specially printed to express his ire with the Tripp family at dock meetings. "Tripp Lobsters Taste Like Oppression" was the first one, but I personally prefer, "Don't Tripp and Fail at Dinnertime. Get your lobster from a real indie fisherman!" The illustrated lobster giving a claws-up on the front is pretty darned cute, and I like the sketch of our family boat in the background.

"Should I eat it on the way or save it for later?" Weaver asks, circling around to open the passenger's door for me—another first.

I stop, staring at the open door, my stomach flipping.

He's changing everything. Pretty soon I won't be able to live my life without reminders of Weaver around every corner.

"What's wrong?" he asks. "Does the car still smell like herring?"

I shake my head and force a smile. "No. I just..." I lift my chin to meet his gaze. "No one's ever opened a car door for me before. Or any door, I don't think."

He rests his hand on my waist, fingers molding to the curve of my hip beneath my slinky black dress. Technically, I opted out of a costume for our Halloween party this year, since I had to be dressed for a fancy dinner right after, but these clothes feel as much like a costume as my Bigfoot suit from last year.

I've never worn anything like this before. The silky cotton of the dress hugs my every curve, with a deep V in the front that reveals a scandalous amount of cleavage and a slit up the right side, all the way to the thigh. Paired with a fake fur coat from Elaina's well-stocked closet and a pair of relatively sensible high heels from Maya's—she's seven inches shorter, but we wear the same size shoe—and I look like a completely different person.

I look glamorous, posh, expensive...

Staring at my reflection in the mirror earlier, I knew I should feel confident as hell in these clothes, but...I don't. This is just a costume, a disguise. The real me is the girl in oilskin pants and a waterproof slicker, with her hair up in a knot and Carmex caked on her lips to keep the worst of the chapping at bay.

He knows that. And he likes her, too, the inner voice whispers as Weaver bends to kiss me again, making my head spin.

The kiss is firm, but also careful. He's doing his best not to smear my lipstick, I realize, and for some reason that makes me feel better.

Weaver sees me, he really does, and so far, he seems to like every side of me— from the goofy girl who made him watch cartoons in bed, to the kinky woman who relishes making love like we're locked in a wrestling match between the sheets.

When he pulls away from the kiss, he murmurs, "I'm just getting started, woman. Tonight, I'm going to treat you the way you deserve to be treated."

I rest my hands on his strong chest and tilt my

head back. In my best flirty voice, the one I've only brought out for him, I ask, "Does that mean you won't be tying me to the headboard and spanking me if I come too soon?"

His gaze takes on that predatory quality I've come to love. "Oh no, I'll definitely be doing that. You deserve to be tied up for making me wait five extra minutes out here by the dumpster."

I smile. "It was Elaina's fault. It took a while to find the lint roller to get all the cat hair off my dress."

He shakes his head and mutters, "Excuses, excuses."

My grin widens. "You're right. And I promise to accept my punishment with a positive attitude." I pinch the taut skin at the side of his waist before adding in a whisper, "And plenty of screaming."

He laughs and swats my bottom before putting a hand to my elbow and helping me into the passenger's seat. I don't need the help—I'm steady on my feet, even in borrowed heels—but I enjoy it.

It's sort of like men in general. I don't *need* a boyfriend, but after this past week with Weaver...I really want one.

I want someone to talk to at the end of a long day, someone who makes me laugh, challenges my assumptions, and enjoys snacks at midnight as much as I do. I want orgasms and pleasure and the perfect ease I feel when I'm lying on Weaver's chest after we've made love.

I want someone to hold me the way he holds me, like I'm his favorite person in the world.

But I'm *not* his favorite person. Not really.

I'm a temporary distraction, a fuck buddy, and I can't forget that for a moment. If I do, I'm going to lose my heart to this man.

Glancing at his sexy profile as he guides the car out of the alley and onto the main road leading out of town, I fear it might already be too late. But I'm not going to let that ruin our night.

There will be plenty of time to regret falling head over heels for the wrong man when Weaver is gone.

But for now, he's here.

And he's mine.

I reach out, slipping my hand into his, loving the way he squeezes my palm tight as we gain speed, zooming past the city limits into the cool, starry night.

chapter 14

HER FACE...

It's so damned beautiful.

And it gives her every thought and feeling away.

As I pull up in front of The Royal Dunes, the premier luxury hotel in Saint Mary, Sully's jaw drops and her cheeks flush. "What have you done?"

"Exactly what I said I was going to do," I murmur. "This is one of the things you deserve."

"Are you sure? I think the people who work here are dressed better than I am," she whispers, tugging at the lapels of her coat as two tuxedoed valets approach the car.

"Not a chance." I take her hand, giving it a squeeze. "You look like a million bucks."

"My dress cost thirty dollars," she says in a rush. "Secondhand. And I didn't wash it because I was afraid that I'd ruin it because I'm bad at laundry. And yes, they probably washed it before they put it up for sale, and it smells clean, but there's a chance I'm wearing another woman's sweat as well as her dress."

"Doesn't matter," I say, holding her anxious gaze, loving that she lets me in like this. Even when it's embarrassing or hard. "You could be naked, and you'd still put every woman in this hotel to shame."

Her shoulders relax as her lips twitch into a crooked grin. "You're a liar, but I like it."

"I'm not a liar," I say, before turning to the valet opening my door. Another appears on Sully's side, welcoming her to the hotel.

I hand my valet the keys and a twenty before sliding out into the brisk evening air. I circle around to meet Sully on the passenger's side, offering her my arm and the other attendant a twenty, as well. I tell him the name on the reservation and he gives me a claim ticket and a big grin before moving toward the trunk.

Sully glances over her shoulder. "Do we need to get the bags?" she asks in a soft voice. "Or give them a room number once we have one or something?"

"No, they know where to take the bags. I checked in online this afternoon. The key to our room is already on my phone."

Her eyes widen. "Wow. I love an old-fashioned key, but that's swanky."

"And convenient." I tip my head to the uniformed men at the top of the steps, who leap to open the copper and glass doors as we approach. "It will give us time to do a little shopping before dinner."

Her brows lift. "Shopping for what?"

"Jewelry," I say. "You could use some."

Her nose wrinkles. "I know. But I didn't have anything that looked good with a dress like this, and Elaina's earrings are all enormous. I'm not a big earring girl."

"Absolutely not," I agree. She's far more understated than that, elegant though I know she doesn't think of herself that way. But she is, a fact proven when she selects a stunning, but discreet pair of diamond-and-pearl drop earrings from the gift shop beneath the grand staircase leading to the second floor.

"I can pay for them," she whispers, as I tell the clerk we'll take them and reach for my wallet.

"No, it's my treat, consider it an early birthday present."

"All right. Well, thank you." She smiles, but her grin vanishes when the clerk gives me the total before taking my extended card.

"Five thousand dollars?" she mouths when the clerk dips her head, her eyes wide and scandalized.

"It's fine," I mouth back. "You deserve it."

Her lips press into a thin line, but she leaves the earrings in her ears as I finish paying and takes my arm again as we leave the store. It isn't until we're halfway up the staircase that she says, "I had no idea they were real. I thought they were costume jewelry. We can take them back before we leave."

"We're not taking them back."

She scoffs. "You don't buy a five-thousand-dollar present for a friend."

"I buy whatever I want, whenever I want," I say, smiling down at her as we reach the top of the stairs.

"It's one of the benefits of being a heartless finance guy who invested wisely in his twenties."

She makes a considering sound beneath her breath. "The only thing I've invested in in my twenties is new traps when someone stole some of our old ones last season."

"We'll have to change that," I say, leading her toward the entrance to the ballroom on the far side of the impressive lobby. Soaring ceilings, two-story windows, and bronze Art Deco accents give the space an old-world feel. They also give me hope this party won't be the usual cheesy, skeletons-and-fake-spider-webs Halloween affair. "We'll get you set up with a retirement account that reflects your risk tolerance before I leave. Even a small monthly investment will grow with compound interest. It's not too late to make sure you're taken care of when you're older."

"Okay, that sounds smart," she says. "I'd appreciate that. Thank you."

The reminder that our time together is flying by dampens the mood for a moment, but by the time we reach the small line forming in front of a woman dressed in a gold ball gown, we're both smiling again.

"What is this?" Sully asks, her eyes shining as she reads the velvet banner draped across the top of the ballroom door. "Harvest of the Mystic Moon?"

"A Halloween party," I say, "but no costumes, thank God."

She snorts. "I can't imagine you in a costume, Mr. Fancy. Far too undignified for the likes of you."

"Damn straight," I agree, pulling my cell from my pocket and scrolling to the event app for our tickets.

She laughs and squeezes my arm. "But you'd make a great brooding Mr. Darcy. At least the Weaver I see around town would."

My brows draw together. "Yeah?"

She nods, glancing forward as the line starts to move. "Yeah. That Weaver never smiles. Which is a shame." She shifts her gaze back to mine. "Your smile is pretty special."

I want to tell her that *she's* special, that I wish I never had to be the Weaver I am in town, the one who has to walk around the world without her in his impenetrable shell. The realization hits hard, making my stomach tighten as we amble the final few feet to the check-in desk, and confirming the fear that's been sneaking up on me with every amazing night I've spent with Sully this past week.

I'm falling in love with this woman.

Hell, maybe I already *am* in love with her.

As I look down at her now, the outline of her profile and the faint freckles on her nose are enough to send an ache spiraling through my chest. I want to write a song for this girl, to paint her the way I see her— perfect and authentic and wildly, messily alive.

I'm a money guy, a *numbers* guy. I appreciate art, but I've never had the urge to do anything "artsy" in my life. The fact that now it's all I can think about half the time...

I'm screwed, so fucking screwed.

Even if I could find a way to fit into Sully's life, she

would never want to fit into mine. She made me pick her up next to a dumpster for God's sake. She was *that* worried about someone seeing us together.

I hold my phone out to the woman in the ball gown with only half of my mind present and accounted for. The other half is racing through the facts as I know them, trying to figure out a way to dismiss the emotion swelling behind my ribs.

It's just the sex. The sex has been better than I could have imagined when a virgin cat burglar crawled into my bed. Sully makes me feel things I haven't felt in so damned long. Maybe ever. I think about being inside her, about fucking her until she makes those husky, sexy-as-hell coming sounds at least two hundred times a day.

Fabulous sex is intoxicating, disorientating.

I've never mistaken a great lay for true love before, but there's a first time for everything.

Then there's the fact that I'm back in my home-town, dealing with my brother's death, surrounded by people who profess to love me even as they plot and scheme behind my back. As much as I hate to admit it, I'm in a weakened state, and Sully is a dangerous person to let your walls down around. She's too curious, too kind. If you let her, she'll crawl right over your defenses, pull you into a big hug, and convince you that don't need your armor anymore.

Not as long as you have someone like her watching your back...

That's all this is, a case of disparate, but powerful

outside forces combining to convince me I'm feeling things I couldn't possibly feel.

Not after a week.

Not when I know there's no future for me and this shining girl.

She *does* shine, like she's lit up from the inside. As we step into the ballroom, moving through a surprisingly realistic cornfield sprouting from the tile into a Stonehenge-type gathering of giant papier-mâché boulders positioned around the still empty dance floor, heads turn.

But Sully doesn't notice, she's too busy spinning in a slow circle, taking in the decorations.

"Wow," she says, with a soft laugh. "This is so cool." She motions toward the far right of the room, where several vintage wagons with brightly colored tents on top are parked in a row. In front of them, half a dozen women, wrapped in silk scarves, sit behind tables with tarot cards and crystal balls. "Fortune tellers, I assume?"

"Looks like it," I say, still feeling off-kilter. My voice sounds strange, even to my own ears, and it doesn't go unnoticed by my savvy companion.

Her brow furrows. "Are you okay?"

I nod. "I'm fine."

"We don't have to do the fortune-telling thing if you don't want. My friend Maya never will, not even in Portsmouth, where the ladies at the witchy store are always the sweetest. She has a phobia that a fortune teller is going to foretell her doom and she'll end up going insane and throwing herself into the sea."

"I don't have a phobia about a fortune teller fore-telling my doom," I say, forcing a smile. "I do need to go check in with the host in the dining area, however." I motion toward the long table set up in a clearing in the fake cornfield near the stage where the band will start playing at nine. The table is filled with other people in ball gowns and suits, sipping white wine and coffee as they tuck into their dessert course.

"Oh, okay. Sure thing." She starts that way, but I stop her with a hand on her arm.

"No, you go ahead, check out the fortune tellers. I'll touch base with the host and meet you there." I glance down at my watch. "We still have thirty minutes before they seat the second dinner service."

She considers me for a moment, looking like she's about to ask if I'm okay a second time. But in the end, she just nods and says, "Okay. I'll see you there."

I give her arm a light squeeze. "See you in a few."

Then, I turn and stride quickly away across the room.

I just need a few moments to pull myself together and remember that tonight is for good times, good company, and fantastic, no-strings-attached sex. It isn't for obsessing over what will happen when it's time to leave Sea Breeze or getting swept up in some ridiculous feeling that isn't even real.

It can't be real.

It's too fast, too intense. This surge of emotion is like a junk stock propped up by some Reddit chat board. It's surging like crazy right now but will plummet just as quickly. Things that are built on unsteady foundations always do.

And a foundation can't get much more unsteady than mine and Sully's...

I dated her mother, destroyed her father, and permanently altered the course of her childhood and life. Her people hate me, with good reason, and my "people," such that they are, consider her beneath them. I don't care what the other Tripps think, but she would.

With both of our families against us, we'd never last. We'd end up isolated on my yacht, turning on each other. She'd resent me for making her a pariah in her own hometown, and I'd resent her for forcing me to stay in a place I loathe.

The reminders of how pointless this longing is helps ease the feeling. By the time I check in with the host, get our seat assignment—the far end of the communal table, as requested—and start back across the room to rejoin my date, I'm feeling more grounded than I was before.

Then I see her, Sully, crouched in front of a striking older woman with a bountiful collection of smile lines and silver-white hair, taking her picture.

Instantly, my stomach starts to churn all over again. And it isn't even because Sully's skirt has ridden up, revealing one toned, sexy thigh, nearly to the hip.

It's the reverence on her face, the awed smile on her lips, the way she sees the beauty in this woman I know so many would have dismissed as unworthy of a second glance.

In an instant, I'm falling for her all over again, all my logical reasons for dismissing the emotion evaporating in the wave of warmth that fills my chest.

Looks like love isn't something that can be managed by logic.

I'm in uncharted territory, guided only by the burning certainty that this woman is worth striking out into a scary new world.

She's worth just about anything...

chapter 15

I'M SO busy snapping Effie's portrait—capturing her incredible face, crystal ball, and the blurred tent behind her from different angles, and wishing I had my camera with me, instead of just my phone—that I don't realize Weaver is behind me.

It isn't until Effie grins, showcasing her missing tooth on the upper right side, and says—"Well hello there, you must be Gertrude's fellow. What a lucky man."—that I emerge from my shot-hunting haze.

I glance over my shoulder as I stand, an apology on my lips for going into full feral photographer mode in the middle of a classy ballroom, but Weaver doesn't look annoyed.

He looks...moved, the same way I felt when I saw Effie sitting here with her peaceful smile and dark brown eyes full of all the secrets of the universe.

The realization makes me ridiculously happy, even though I've been around the man enough by now to know that he isn't nearly as cold as he pretends to be.

But I just love that he sees the beauty other people miss. I love that he sees it in Effie.

And I love that he sees it in me.

Heart thumping a little harder, I reach out, squeezing his hand as I smile. "No, he's not my fellow. We're just friends," I tell Effie.

It's true, he *is* my friend, and I hope he will be for a long time. A part of me would desperately love for this to be more, but that isn't in the cards for us. And maybe that's for the best. If Weaver were really my "fellow," I'd lose him eventually.

He'd get tired of being with a small-town girl who's never done anything or been anywhere. The charm of teaching me things I don't know would turn into annoyance that I'm so clueless, and then I'd be left alone with nothing but my regrets and several pissed off and betrayed relatives.

As friends, I can call him in New York whenever I want. I might even be able to go visit before Christmas, the way he said I should. I'd love to walk around the holiday markets and ice skate at Rockefeller Center with him. But then, I think I'd have fun doing just about anything with this man. He just makes me feel so alive, like I'm fully awake for the first time in years.

I'll always be grateful for that, no matter how long our connection lasts.

Effie hums beneath her breath, her wise eyes flicking back and forth between us. "Oh, I see. Well, that's a special thing, too." She smiles in a way that makes me think she isn't buying the "just friends" thing as she motions to the chair in front of her. "If

Gertrude doesn't mind, you're welcome to sit with us while I do her reading."

I shake my head. "Oh no, I don't need a reading."

"You paid for one," she says, casting a pointed glance toward the blue bowl on the corner of the table, where I placed my twenty-dollar bill.

"That was for the chance to take your picture," I say, lifting my cell. "And I did, and I think I got some beautiful shots. Thank you so much."

"May I see?" Weaver asks, extending his hand toward my phone as Effie insists, "Nonsense, you'll have a reading. I don't charge for my picture. I have a firm grip on my soul. I'm not worried about someone stealing it with a photo." She smiles again, shooing me into the chair with sweeps of her wrinkled hands.

Torn, I pass my phone reluctantly into Weaver's palm, warning him, "I haven't had the time to process them, so don't judge. They'll look much better once I take them into the editing software on my computer and adjust things."

He nods.

"And don't look at the cat pictures," I add. "Most of them aren't good, but I haven't had the chance to delete the bad ones. I prefer to do that on my computer, too. Sometimes you see something in a photo on the large screen that you can't see on a small one."

He nods again, the hint of a smile on his lips. "I understand. Sit down. Have your reading. I'll give you your privacy."

He steps away with my phone and for a second, I'm

possessed by the urge to run after him and snatch my cell back into my hot little hand. I never show raw photos to anyone. Not even my best friends. I only show processed pictures when I'm certain they're something special.

I don't want to be that annoying amateur photographer who's always showing off my mediocre shots, desperate for attention I don't deserve. I have a certain amount of talent—if I didn't, I wouldn't have been accepted into the college of Art and Design right out of high school—but I haven't developed it nearly enough.

But before I can spazz out, Effie pats the top of the table and says, "Sit now, love. You need this reading. I can feel it. Your spirit is unsettled."

My brows lift. "Really?"

She nods, her kind eyes filled with compassion, but also a steely resolve. "Really. I'm no charlatan, darling. I wouldn't lie, especially not to a sweet new soul like yours."

Intrigued, I cast one last glance over my shoulder at Weaver, who is leaning against a pillar wrapped in fake vines a short distance away, scrolling slowly through my camera roll with an unreadable expression.

Shoving aside my anxiety, I sit down in the cushioned chair opposite Effie, and exhale a nervous breath, "Okay, I guess. Tell me everything."

She laughs, a rusty sound that's still nice in my ears. Kind of like a cat's purr. "Oh, sweetheart, we don't have time for that. And you wouldn't want it anyway. There's such a thing as too much information." She curls her fingers. "Give me your dominant hand. We won't worry about the tarot cards or crystal ball with you. I have a feeling I'll be able to read everything we need to know right on your palm."

I hold out my left hand and she gives a knowing grin. "A south paw. I'm not surprised. Creative people often are."

I'm about to tell her that I'm not really a "creative" person—I work on a lobster boat—but something stops me. I may not be a professional photographer, but it's definitely a creative outlet, and it could have been my career if my life had taken a different turn.

A long-neglected part of me likes being called creative. It likes it a lot.

So, I keep my mouth shut as she takes my hand in both of hers. Her skin is so dry it feels like paper against mine, but her touch is comforting as she prods at my palm. "Yes, this is all we need," she murmurs before falling silent for several moments.

"What do you see?" I finally ask, more curious than I've been about something like this before. I've had my tarot cards read several times, but never my palm, and never by someone like Effie.

If she isn't the real deal, I don't know who is, and it isn't just the fact that she looks the part more than anyone else offering their services here tonight. It's her energy.

She projects an air of complete confidence, kindness, and wisdom as she says, "As I thought, you're a new soul. It's your first time here in a human body." She clucks her tongue sympathetically. "Which means a lot of pain and ugly surprises. People will let you down. Not because they're bad people, necessarily, but because you're so innocent and new."

I frown. "I don't know about that. I mean, I wouldn't say I'm a bad person, but I have dark thoughts every now and then."

"We all do, darling," she says, unphased as she moves her prodding fingers closer to the center of my palm. "But your dark thoughts are pale, peachy gray in a world of midnight black." She exhales a soft laugh. "Trust me on that." She lifts her chin, her eyes brighter now. "But that's a blessing to the world. And to the people who love you. Of which there are many. I see wonderful friends who treasure you for exactly who you are and a family member..." She looks down again, humming softly. "Not a parent... Maybe an older relative?"

"My grandfather," I supply.

She nods. "Yes, a grandfather, but he's like your parent. He loves you desperately. He'd do anything for you. Even if he seems cranky or closed off at times, his heart is as soft and devoted as yours." She looks up, holding my gaze as she adds in a more pointed tone, "He will never abandon you or stand in the way of your dreams. Not for a moment. He only wants your happiness. He might put up a fight at first, if there's something he doesn't understand, but in the end..." She glances past me toward where Weaver stands by the pillar. "He'll learn to love what you love. Whatever and...whoever that happens to be."

I pull in a breath and let it out with a shake of my head. "I'm not so sure about that."

"That's all right." She smiles. "I am."

"But he's..." I clear my throat and glance quickly over my shoulder, ensuring Weaver is still distracted before adding in a softer voice, "My family would hate him, Effie. Our families have ugly, awful history between us, and Gramps..." I shake my head again, more firmly this time. "Gramps would never be okay with me being romantically involved with a Tripp. Not even someone my age, let alone a man who's so much older. The age difference doesn't bother me, but it would bother him. A lot. I know it would."

Her expression sobers. "Sacrifices will have to be made to build a life with an older man, but your family won't be one of them. They might be upset or hurt at first, but they'll come back to you." She taps her thumb to the center of my palm. "I see a happy family life in your future. And a happy marriage."

My jaw clenches. "That's a nice thought, but...it can't happen. Not with Weaver. It just can't. There are too many things standing in our way."

She smiles, sadly this time. "Well, you know best, I'm sure. I read what I see, but futures are never set in stone." She releases my hand. "If you're determined to push happiness away, you'll succeed. You have that power. All you have to do is keep believing that other people's dreams are more important than your own."

My lips part as pain flashes through my chest.

She gives my wrist a gentle squeeze. "I'm sorry if that isn't what you wanted to hear, sweetheart. I can assure you, however, that everything will be okay. It always is. You'll get where you're going eventually. There's no rush, no finish line, no goal except to live as fully as you can each time you get the chance, and learn your heart lessons along the way."

She looks up, shooting Weaver a wide grin as he appears at my side. "And what about you, handsome? Would you like your palm read? Or do you still think you have it all figured out?"

I jerk my attention Weaver's way, uncertain how he'll handle Effie's challenging words. But he doesn't seem offended.

His lips actually tilt up as he says, "Not right now, thank you. We have dinner reservations in five minutes. But perhaps later. I certainly don't have everything figured out. I thought I did." He glances my way, his smile fading as he adds, "But I think those days are behind me."

"Excellent," Effie says, as I take Weaver's offered hand and let him draw me to my feet beside him. "Go bravely into the unknown. You'll be glad you did."

"Thank you, have a good night." I lift a hand in farewell as we move away, leaving Effie sitting peacefully in her big purple chair, waiting for her next customer.

"How was that?" Weaver asks, his hand at the small of my back as we cross the room.

"Good." I purse my lips. "Or bad? Or sad? Maybe all three? I can't really tell. I think I need some time to digest everything she said."

He grunts. "I wouldn't take any of it too seriously.

People like that don't have any more knowledge about the future than we do. They say frightening things to prey on people's insecurities and keep them coming back for more."

I shake my head. "I don't think so. Not Effie, anyway. She didn't say anything scary. She said good things, actually...assuming I don't fuck them up."

"As far as I can see, you're not the type to fuck things up." He passes my phone over. "Your pictures are incredible, by the way. You have serious talent, Ms. Sullivan."

"Thank you." My cheeks heat with pleasure as I tuck my cell back into my small purse. "But seriously, they'll be way better once they're processed. Editing is almost as important as getting the right shot in the first place."

"Then I'd like to see them when they're edited," he says. "And to send a few shots of your choosing to Makai, a friend of mine in New York. He runs a photography gallery in the East Village. I think he'd be interested in your pieces. Especially the portraits of the old men down by the lobster boats."

I look up at him, my eyes wide. "You went back that far?"

"I went back to the start of last summer," he says. "The shots of your friends around the beach fire are stunning, too. You've captured the New England coast with an intimacy I haven't seen before. It's beautiful."

My throat tightens as we join the line of people waiting to be seated for dinner. "Thank you." I lean closer, brushing his hand with mine as I ask, "You really think my stuff is good enough to send to a gallery? You're not just saying that to be nice?"

"I'm not nice," he says bluntly. "I thought you would have realized that by now."

"But you are," I say, my pulse picking up as I hold his piercing gaze. "You're very nice and you make me feel..."

I trail off, my anxiety levels rising until my heart is pounding against my ribs and I'm on the verge of saying things I shouldn't. I try to swallow, but my tongue is suddenly dry and feels too fat in my throat.

What was I thinking? Now isn't the time to tell Weaver that I count the minutes until I get to see him again, that I think about him all the time, and that my first thought when something good happens lately, is that I can't wait to share it with him.

He's not stupid. He'll know what all that means.

He'll know that I'm falling in love with him.

I'm on the verge of faking a laugh and making a lame joke about being ready for a drink after the stress of knowing he's scrolled through half my camera roll.

But before I can, his fingers curl around mine. "You make me feel, too."

My throat squeezes even tighter, but I manage to force out a soft, "I do?"

"You do," he confirms. "More than I have in a long time."

And then we're at the host stand, being guided down the long table to two seats at the very end, where another couple is already settled and private conversation is impossible.

But his words linger between us, charging the air every time our eyes meet.

We make small talk with the other diners and share our mutual appreciation of the lobster bisque and fantastic seafood risotto, but there's something simmering beneath the words that wasn't there before, an awareness that things are about to change.

If we're brave enough to let them...

chapter 16

AS SOON AS we're done eating, I want to drag Sully out of the ballroom and up to our suite on the top floor, with the view of the harbor and a bathtub big enough for two. I've been fantasizing about having my way with her in that tub since I saw it on the hotel website.

But this isn't something I want to rush.

This night...

The possibilities arising between us...

I don't want to do anything to scare her away or dim the warmth in her eyes.

So, once we're finished eating, I draw her onto the dance floor and into my arms, swaying with her to a Celtic ballad sung by the band's witchy-looking singer. I can't understand the words—they're in Gaelic—but I understand the longing behind them all too well.

The song swells and dips and aches, the way I ache for this woman.

She curls her fingers around mine and rests her

head on my chest, sending a twist of longing through me that's painful. And for the first time in my forty years of life, I understand why so many songs talk about how much love hurts. Even if there wasn't a single obstacle standing in our way, it hurts to want someone this much, to realize too late that you might not be okay without them.

I'm a survivor, I always have been, but I don't like the idea of surviving Sully.

I don't want to lose her. Hell, I don't want to spend another day without her. I want her in my bed when I go to sleep and when I get up in the morning. I want to make her dreams come true and to celebrate her successes and to watch her grow into an even more powerful, impressive woman than she is already.

There isn't anyone else like her, not even close. And though we come from different worlds in so many ways, being with someone has never felt this right, this...necessary.

I bend my head, pressing a kiss to her forehead, the ache in my chest growing almost unbearable when she sighs and clings tighter to my neck. I'm about to do it, to tell her that I don't want to dance with anyone else tonight—or ever again—when the sound of a horn blaring cuts through the air.

Sully jerks away, apologizing to the couples swaying around us as she quickly fetches her cell from her purse and silences the sound.

"Sorry," she says again, this time to me as she glances down at the screen with a worried expression. She's already moving toward the front of the ballroom as she says, "It's Aunt Cathy. She only calls if there's a family emergency. I have to take this."

"Of course," I assure her. "I'll get your coat from the check, in case we need to leave."

Relief in her eyes, she mouths, "thank you," before accepting the call. She turns, pressing her cell to her ear as she hurries through the cornfield toward the exit. I only hear her say, "Cathy? Hey, what's up?" before her voice fades away.

I step into the line for the coat check, where late-comers are just dropping off their things and only the over sixty set are looking to pick up. Watching the slightly stooped older couple in front of me shouting loudly into each other's hearing aids, I think about the age gap between Sully and myself in a different context than I have before...

For now, it doesn't matter. I'm a man in my prime. I have no trouble keeping up with or besting younger men in the gym or at the office and keeping up with Sully isn't an issue, either.

But there will come a day when my body will begin to deteriorate, no matter how hard I fight it. When this thing with Sully had no future, I wasn't concerned about that.

But now...

Will the beautiful woman striding toward me with a relieved expression still look at me like she can't get my clothes off fast enough when she's a woman in *her* prime, and I qualify for the senior discount and can't stay up past ten o'clock?

She lifts her cell in the air, rocking it back and forth

as she comes to stand beside me. "False alarm." She sighs, rolling her eyes. "Well, not a false alarm to the crazy people in my family, but nothing we need to worry about. My cousin Jennifer is in labor. It looks like the baby is coming in the next hour or two, but her grandmother, my great aunt, is the crazy kind of Catholic, so..."

I arch a brow, trying to push the vision of myself stooped over and asking a still strong, gorgeous Sully to shout into my hearing aid from my head. "And that means...?"

She laughs. "Sorry. I forgot your family isn't very churchy. It's Halloween. Great Aunt Sue thinks Halloween is the devil's day. So, if the baby is born tonight it might end up being the Antichrist, or something. And she's worked way too hard to keep the Sullivan clan on God's good side for that."

She shoots me a wry smile as we shift forward in line. "She's in the hospital chapel, praying for the baby to hold out until after midnight, so it can be born on All Saints' Day instead. Aunt Cathy's worried she's going to give herself a heart attack, but I told her it would be okay. Aunt Sue is in incredible shape. She was the only eighty-year-old to finish the town 5K last year. She'll still be here, stressing out about our immortal souls and making her horrible onion dip for the church picnic when the rest of us are six feet under."

She glances at the older couple in front of us, smiling as she watches them laugh at a shared joke. She clearly isn't haunted by the specter of her future self.

But why should she be? She has her entire life ahead of her, decades before she's even middle-aged, let alone approaching her dotage.

I'm the problem here. I'm the one with the age and experience to know how quickly the years fly by, moving faster and faster, until you blink and suddenly a decade's passed and you're no longer the person you were before.

Until now, I've leveled up with the passing years, but constant, unrelenting growth isn't sustainable. Or natural. It's something I tell my clients—that no matter what capitalism and the modern market might demand, all companies experience times when profits are down. It's important to acknowledge that, and to prepare for seasons of scarcity as well as plenty.

"Are you all right?" Sully asks softly, her fingers plucking at the sleeve of my shirt.

I blink, dragging myself from my progressively depressing thoughts. "Yes, why?"

"You didn't say anything about my story."

I pull in a breath, exhaling with a shake of my head. "Sorry. I guess I didn't know what to say. Are we Team Antichrist or Team All Saints' Day?"

She laughs. "I mean, not to be a jerk, but I'd love a Halloween cousin. Either way, I'm buying him a devil costume for baby's first Halloween next year. Just to mess with Aunt Sue."

I force a smile. "As you should."

She nods toward the people ahead of as we shift forward again. "Do we still want to be in this line? We don't have to leave if you don't want to. Though we *have* already danced and eaten and had one of our palms read..."

I cock my head. "But it's only ten o'clock."

She shrugs. "That's okay. I'm used to going to bed early, hazard of the lobstering lifestyle."

The mention of her dead-end job sends a flash of heat through my chest. It was bad enough, watching her throw her life away on a grueling career with no chance of advancement or a pay raise, when I didn't know she had real talent.

But now that's different, too.

"We should talk about your job," I say, stepping forward again. We're nearly at the claim window now, and I'm grateful. This room, with its crush of people and haunting music, is starting to make me feel claustrophobic.

Or maybe that's just my own skin...

She frowns. "What about my job?"

"You're wasting your potential."

The furrow between her brows deepens. "What? Where is this coming from?"

"It's coming from concern for your welfare and your future, not to mention your body. Most twenty-four-year-olds don't have a shoulder injury that aches when it rains."

Her chin hitches up, and her eyes take on that stubborn gleam I haven't seen since Tuesday, when she refused to try the duck-liver pâté I bought at the gourmet shop in town. But we're aren't half-naked, laughing over a plate of crackers right now.

"Well, I do," she says. "And that's from playing rugby in high school, not working on the boat."

"But if you didn't work on the boat, it might have had time to heal," I counter. "And don't you want a job where you don't have to hose off the stink of salted herring at the end of every day? Don't you want to make something of yourself? To honor the talent that you've been given?"

She crosses her arms over her chest. "What's gotten into you all of a sudden?"

I clench my jaw, feigning ignorance. "I don't know what you mean."

"Oh, yes you do," she shoots back. "Don't pull that Mr. Ice in My Veins thing with me. I don't buy it anymore. Just put your normal face back on and talk to me."

I frown, doubling down on my impenetrable stare. "Excuse me?"

She reaches up, poking a finger into my cheek. "Your face. Put the real one back on."

I clench my jaw harder, fighting to maintain control as she pokes me again, this time on the other cheek.

"That's right," she says, poking my forehead, between my eyes, and finally, the tip of my nose. I huff out a soft laugh and her lips curve into a victorious smile. "There it is. I knew the real Mr. Fancy was in there somewhere." Her grin fades, concern filling her eyes as she says, "Should we head up to the room and talk about what's *really* bothering you?"

I glance down at the floor, ashamed of myself. I'm

supposed to be the older, wiser person in this situation. Instead, I'm lashing out like a fucking teenager.

"I'm sorry," I say.

She takes my hand. "Don't be. You don't have to be perfect all the time. God knows, I'm not." We step forward, until only the happy older couple stands between us and the coat check window. "And you aren't the first person to say something like that to me. Elaina and Maya have both expressed similar things, but...that was a long time ago. At this point, most of the people in my life have learned to respect my choices."

I'm about to apologize again and promise that I'll do my best to respect them, as well—even if I want a better, easier life for her—when she adds, "But maybe that's not necessarily a good thing."

I arch a brow. "No?"

She shakes her head. "No. I've been thinking a lot this week about time and that thing..." She bites her lip, searching for a word. "You know, that thing where matter stays stuck in a pattern unless it's disturbed by an external force?"

"Inertia?" I supply.

"Yes! That." She nods, seeming to chew on the concept for a moment. "I've been stuck in the inertia zone for a while, longer than I realized until you came along. I guess I needed an external force to get me thinking about the big picture again." She squeezes my hand. "So...thanks."

"I'll be your external force anytime," I whisper, wanting to tell her so much more.

I want to tell her that I don't want to say goodbye.

That I don't want a future without her in it.

That I'm in love with her.

But it's our turn at the coat check and I hand over our claim tickets and a ten-dollar bill, instead.

When we're outside the ballroom with our coats, Sully loops her arm through mine, and whispers, "Take me upstairs?"

"Always," I say, wishing it was a promise I could keep.

chapter 17

SOMETHING'S UP WITH WEAVER.

I felt it even before our little fight in the coat check line.

The way he looked at me after he saw my photos, the way he held me on the dance floor, his lips brushing my forehead as we swayed to the haunting melody drifting through the air...

It was all so damned bitter-sweet.

He feels it, too, how special we could be. I'd bet my hands on it. But I'm just as sure that he's about to end things. I can feel him pulling back, looking for reasons to bail.

And he won't have to look far.

There's the age gap, the wealth gap, the lifestyle differences, our families, the distance between us once he returns home...we have at least half a dozen obstacles that would make a long-term relationship very difficult. If he's thinking it's time to cut bait before this

215

"casual" thing gets any less casual than it is already, now is the time.

But for some reason, I'm not afraid.

Something's up with me, too, something that's been shifting the past few days and finally slid into place somewhere between having my palm read and holding Weaver's gaze across the table at the best meal of my life.

I love this man. I love him with every piece of my heart. And despite all the times I've watched love crash and burn in my life, that's the least scary thing in the world.

It doesn't matter that I've only known him a week. Being with him feels so right and real, not scary at all. Even if he leaves, I'll never regret falling in love with him. It's the best thing ever, like the world is suddenly in technicolor and every beautiful thing is more beautiful, because I get to share them with him, my Ice Prince.

Though now I know he isn't nearly as cool and untouchable as he pretends to be.

As he taps his phone to the sensor on the door of our room, I study his profile, seeing him with new eyes. He isn't cold. He's one of the most passionate people I know. He cares so much more than he lets on and is more vulnerable than he'd like the world to believe.

The sensor hums and he pushes on the handle, pausing with the door cracked a sliver to glance my way. "Yes?"

I smile. "Nothing. I just like looking at you."

He doesn't return my grin, and his tone as he says, "I like looking at you, too," sounds like he's reading the first lines of a eulogy.

Ouch. This is going to hurt. Whether he ends it tonight or waits until he drops me off in Sea Breeze on Sunday, the pain of saying goodbye to the only man I've ever loved is going to kill me a little.

But I *still* don't want to run. I want to stay and soak up every second with him. If all I'll ever have of Weaver is memories, then I want as many of them as I can get.

Inside the room, there's soft jazz music playing on the large, old-fashioned radio by the door. As Weaver empties his pockets on top of the smooth wood, I kick off my heels and wander across the thick carpet, my jaw dropping as I take in the space.

The room is round and enormous, with a high ceiling featuring a tasteful chandelier. In the center of the space, there's a cream-colored sofa and a coffee table topped with fresh flowers, flanked by two gray lounge chairs. Behind them, closer to the gently sloped wall, is a formal dining table with seats for six, topped with more fresh flowers, and to the left is the entrance to a galley kitchen bigger than my kitchenette at my apartment.

"Wow." I spin in a slow circle, taking it all in before pausing in front of the coffee table to stare out at the view. The windows curve all the way around from the kitchen to this side of the room, creating a ninety-degree view of the harbor and the ocean beyond.

"The room meets with your approval?" he asks, his voice a soft rumble from behind me.

I turn, watching him cross the carpet with my heart in my throat. "Yes. I don't even care that there's not a bed."

His lips twitch. "There's a bed." He nods to his right. "It's in there. In the bedroom. Through the door."

"I know," I say, keeping my eyes locked on his, certain that if I look away for a second, I'll lose him for good. "I was joking. I'm not that backwoods."

"You're not backwoods at all," he says, closing the last of the distance between us. He reaches up, skimming his fingertips across my forehead, brushing over the place he kissed on the dance floor before tucking a few loose strands behind my ear. "You're a proper Downeaster Maniac with saltwater in your veins."

I search his face, trying to guess where this is going, but his expression is back to the unreadable mask I encountered that first night in his bedroom. "Thank you? I guess?"

"It was meant as a compliment," he says, his voice still sad. "You belong here. You love everything about being from Sea Breeze and Sea Breeze loves everything about you."

"Oh," I say, my throat tightening. "I see."

"What do you see?" He scans my face, as if trying to memorize it before he walks out the door.

"That's the deal-breaker," I say, a little wobble in my voice. "You've decided I'm happy where I am and it's best to leave me there. Like a pig in shit."

His brows lift. "I never said that."

"No, you said I should pull myself up by my boot-straps and do something with my life instead throwing it away hauling lobster traps," I say, motioning toward the door behind him. "What happened to that? That was like...five minutes ago. What changed between down there and up here?"

"I didn't say that, either."

"You did," I say. "Maybe not in those exact words, but that was the underlying message. I can read subtext, you know. I may be dumb dock trash, but I got pretty good grades in school."

His gaze grows frostier. "Decided it's your turn to pick a fight?"

I press my lips together, forcing away the stinging sensation pricking at the back of my nose. "No, I just..." I swallow and force the heat from my tone. "But like I said, I'm not stupid. I can feel it."

"Feel what?"

"You pulling away." I shrug and drop my gaze to the lush carpet, not wanting him to see the shine in my eyes as I add, "And I really don't want you to. Because I..."

I dampen my lips with the tip of my tongue, gathering my courage as my heart beats frantically in my chest. It feels like I'm about to stand up in front of a firing squad, but my logical mind knows that's not true. Losing the people you love hurts like a killing blow, but it doesn't actually kill you. If Weaver turns his back on me and walks away, or worse, tries to let me down easy, I'll be okay.

Maybe not tomorrow or the next day or the next, but eventually, time will pass and I'll forget how it felt to stand at the edge of this cliff, desperate to take the leap, if only my person would jump with me.

He *is* my person.

He may not see that, but I do, and that certainty gives me the guts to lift my chin and look him straight in the eye as I say, "I love you. I didn't mean to love you. I didn't expect to love you. You were a real piece of work that first night. And you're bossy and fussy and you have pretentious rich person snacks that don't taste as good as normal snacks. But..."

I pull in another breath, feeling like I might vomit as he continues to stand there staring as I puke my heart out onto the floor between us. "But you're also a smartass and an art lover and kinder than you want anyone to realize. You're thoughtful and compassionate and take genuine pleasure in making other people happy. And you continue to be patient with your family long after a saint would have thrown up their hands and run."

"I did run," he says softly. "I ran all the way to New York City and I almost never came back."

"But you did come back. When they needed you."

"They might need me, but they don't want me," he says, still holding my gaze, giving me hope that all isn't lost. "They'd be happy to keep things just as they were before Rodger died, until they eventually run into a politician who can't be bribed, and the Tripp empire sinks into the sand. No one wants me here."

"I want you here," I say. "And there are more of us. I'm sure Elaina and Maya would love you once they got to know you."

His lips quirk up on one side in a humorless smile. "And how would that work? We'd sneak into the café after dark through the back door? I'd get to socialize with a group of much younger women with the curtains drawn like some kind of cult leader? Or maybe I could hide in the back of your pickup truck on the way to the beach party and come out once you'd made sure the coast was clear and no Sullivans were there to see me."

Taking his meaning, I exhale a frustrated breath. "You don't want your family to know, either. You said so. Hell, you said you didn't want anyone in town to know. You wanted me to sneak onto your boat after dark and leave before morning, like some shameful secret."

"Things change," he says, his voice rough as he steps closer, his entire body suddenly vibrating with energy. "You aren't a shameful secret. You're..."

"I'm what?" I ask, the tears slipping down my cheeks no matter how hard I try to stop them.

"You're all I want," he says, the wall behind his eyes finally falling away, revealing the pain beneath. "All I think about. Every moment of every day, no matter what I'm doing, if you're not there, it feels hollow. An exercise in fucking futility. Step after step down the wrong path. Nothing feels real or good until I share it with you."

I gulp, my tears falling faster as he wraps his hands around my upper arms.

"I crave the sound of your voice in my ears," he rasps. "I dream about your mouth, your laughter, your hand in mine. I dream about holding your damned hand, Sully. Not fucking you or your mouth wrapped around my dick." I'm shocked to see tears shining in his eyes as he adds, "I dream about walking through Central Park with you and...knowing you're mine."

"Come here," I whisper, trying to reach for him.

But he holds me at a distance, shaking his head. "But I can't kidnap you from your life like some Viking on a raid." His hands slide down to grip my wrists. "You would have to want it. Truly want it, with every part of you. And you'd have to be open to change, whether we can make this work for the long term or not."

He hesitates, despair tinging his voice again as he says, "And you don't want it. You don't want to leave this town or your friends or family. You don't want to change careers or go back to school in the city." He releases my wrists. "Hell, you don't even want to tell the people you love that I'm part of your life. I'm the one who's the shameful secret, not you. It's never been you."

"You don't want to leave your life, either," I shoot back, but there's no heat in my voice.

I'm too soggy to sound angry. And I'm *not* angry, not with him anyway. A part of me is overjoyed that he feels the way I do. But the other part is still thinking logically, the way it has since I was that kid who woke up to find her parents were gone and taking care of herself was now her full-time job.

This isn't me versus Weaver.

This is me and Weaver versus Fate, and Fate is proving to be a real bitch.

"You don't want to move back to Sea Breeze and get an apartment with me or hang out with my 'much younger' friends," I say, using his own words against him. "You would be bored to tears in a month. You'd get sick of how early I get up to go to work and probably hate whatever job you'd be able to get here and eventually you'd—"

"I wouldn't have to get a new job," he cuts in, startling me.

"What?"

"I already spoke to my superiors," he says, but still with that hopeless note in his voice. "I can work remotely for as long as I need or want to do so. I would have to make trips into the city every once and a while for meetings, but I could live in Sea Breeze full time or... anywhere else, really."

I sniff and take a breath, rolling his words over in my head. "You... You really did that? You asked about staying?"

He nods. "I did. And if that were the only issue, I would. But it's not."

Fuck. He'd move to Sea Breeze. For me. He would give up his Mr. Fancy lifestyle and come back to a hometown he hates. *For me.*

No one's ever inconvenienced themselves in the slightest to be my man. And here Weaver is, ready to abandon everything for a chance with me, Gertie from the docks, a woman with biceps larger than those of half the men downstairs and nothing to offer him but myself.

Tears threaten again as I whisper, "I don't know what to say. No one's ever loved me like this before. No one's ever loved me...period."

His features soften, and Weaver steps in, wrapping me in his arms.

I rest my face on his chest and let it crumple, clinging to him tight as I cry.

"Everyone loves you," he murmurs to the top of my head as his big hand smooths up and down my back. "It's impossible not to love you. Believe me, I tried."

I look up, not caring that my face is puffy and my nose is starting to run. "You did? You tried not to love me?"

He nods. "For about ten minutes."

I sniff again. "Liar. You didn't love me after ten minutes. You were still holding me down on your bed and threatening to call the police at that point. Or to rough me up. I don't remember."

"I never threatened to rough you up."

I arch a brow. "Except I'm pretty sure you did."

His lips curve. "Maybe. But I didn't mean it." His hand drifts lower, until it rests at the base of my spine, right above where my bottom begins to curve. "And holding you down on beds is one of the ways I show my love. You should realize that by now."

"I do." I smile, even as fresh tears threaten. This night... It's the hardest, sweetest, scariest, most thrilling night of my life, and I honestly have no idea how it's going to end. "But..."

224

"But?" he prompts after a beat, his hand sliding lower, making heat pool between my hips. It would be so easy to give in to our chemistry, to make love on that couch or in the bedroom or out on the balcony with the cold ocean wind swirling around us, and forget about the heavy stuff until later.

But I'm no coward. And neither is he.

So, I answer him in a wobbly voice, "But I can't see you here. It doesn't make sense. You'd be miserable and..." I slip my hands under his vest, relishing the feel of his warm skin through the thinner cotton shirt beneath. "And well, I think I'd actually like New York. I like cities."

His brows lift. "You do?"

"Well, I like Portland. That's the only big city I've ever been to, but I liked it. I was really excited to go to school there before I decided I needed to stay home."

His eyes narrow. "Because you felt you had to sacrifice what you wanted to take care of your grandfather."

I start to deny it, but what's the point. "Yes. But I don't regret it. These past six years, working the boat with Gramps...they've been good times. And we've been able to put away a lot more for his retirement than we would have if I'd gone to school, and he'd been alone on the boat. I honestly don't know if he could have managed things by himself. His shoulders are so messed up, half the time I have to haul all the traps in by myself. And if I got a decent job in the city, I could send enough money back for him to hire someone to take my place."

Weaver shakes his head, but with affection. "Or

you could just let me set your grandfather up with a pension for all his years of service to the community, and you could focus on taking care of yourself for once."

I roll my eyes. "Even if I felt comfortable with that, Gramps would never allow it. Like...never. He'd throw himself into the sea before he took a Tripp's money."

"You wouldn't have to tell him where it came from. You could say that you've come into an inheritance."

I snort. "From who? He knows everyone I'm related to and most of them are even worse off than we are financially."

"Make up a relative from your mother's side of the family. Or tell him you won the lottery or found sunken treasure off the coast. Whatever you need to say to give you both a fresh start. He's too old to be working his body this hard, and you're too young to accept that this is all your life will ever be. Not if you want more."

I press my lips together and give a little nod.

But inside, it feels like I'm out on a boat in the middle of a storm.

Can I really do this?

Can I leave Sea Breeze and everything I love behind for a shot at making love work with Weaver? I can't, can I? It would be stupid to bet it all on a man I've known for a week, a man who comes with enough baggage to ensure the path forward won't be easy for either of us.

But when I lift my gaze to his, I don't feel scared or worried.

I feel like someone is finally seeing me, all of me, for the first time, and he thinks I'm special.

Precious. Irreplaceable.

"I've never been in love like this, either," he says, showing the soft underbelly I love just as much as his strength and confidence. "But I promise I won't let you down, Cat Burglar. If you trust me, I'll do everything I can to make sure you don't regret it. We can set up a bank account for you that I don't have access to. I'll put enough money in there to make sure you can leave the city whenever you want. You won't be tied to me in any way if you feel homesick or want to leave for any reason."

I smile and shake my head. "I don't want your money. Or need it. If I were ever stranded in New York City, I would have tons of places to stay. My friend Sydney's boyfriend has a penthouse he said I could use, and Sydney's dad is there. So is her friend Noel from high school. I'm sure one of them would have room for me. I'd be fine until I could get a train back home."

I slide my hands up his chest, looping them behind his neck, loving the feel of his arms wrapping tight around my waist as he pulls me close. "But I'm not worried about that. I'm more worried about what happens when I don't want to leave."

"I'm not."

"You're not?" I ask. "You don't think you'll get sick of me?"

He shakes his head as his lips drift closer to mine. "No, I think this is just going to get worse."

"Worse?" I murmur, my eyes sliding closed. "Don't you mean better?"

"Only if you stay with me," he whispers. "Forever."

Forever. He wants *forever*.

Before I can assimilate the awe-inspiring amazingness of that, his lips are on mine, and he's kissing me in a way that makes me believe him.

This is for keeps.

And after tonight, nothing will ever be the same.

chapter 18

WEAVER

I KISS her across the room before losing patience with the speed of our progress and picking her up to carry her into the bedroom.

Then I see the bathroom out of the corner of my eye and remember my plans for her.

"I want to give you a bath," I say, setting her on her feet by the open door next to the giant en suite.

She pulls back, her brows lifting. "Give me a bath? Like...a sexy bath?"

"A very sexy bath," I assure her, reaching for the button at the back of her neck.

She bites her lip, holding my gaze as the front of her dress falls forward, baring her gorgeous breasts. "Only if you join me. I want to give you a sexy bath, too. I think you need one, honestly," she says, reaching for my belt and drawing it through the clasp. "You're a filthy man."

My lips curve. "Am I?"

She nods. "So filthy. Especially here. This part is as

dirty as they come." She molds her hand to my erection through my pants. I return the favor by cupping her breasts and dragging my thumbs across her nipples.

Her breath catches and I take advantage of her open mouth, kissing her hard and deep. I slide my tongue against hers, promising with every stroke that I meant what I said—I love her. And I'm going to move heaven and earth to prove it, starting by making her come at least half a dozen times before we sleep tonight.

Lifting her into my arms again, this time with her ass in my hands and her legs wrapped around my waist, I carry her into the bathroom. I sit on the edge of the tub, still kissing her as I turn on the water.

"This is the biggest bathtub I've seen in my entire life," she says when we finally come up for air long enough to start stripping out of our clothes.

I watch her shimmy the dress over her hips, enjoying the way her breasts bounce lightly as she moves. She notices me watching and shoots me a crooked smile, "So I guess you'd call yourself a breast man?"

"I'm a you man," I say, tossing my shirt to the floor and finishing the job she started with my belt. "I enjoy your ass just as much."

Her eyes rake over me as I shove my pants to the floor. "I enjoy all your parts." She wrinkles her nose as her gaze moves lower. "Except maybe your knees. I think you might have weird knees."

I huff out a laugh. "Well, there had to be something

wrong with me. I mean, aside from being emotionally unavailable, cranky, and bossy."

Her eyes return to mine, her brow furrowing. "Don't say that. You're not any of those things, and I was kidding about your knees."

I smile as I pull her against me. "I know."

She smiles. "So you were just messing with me?"

"Turnabout is fair play." I squeeze the firm globes of her ass in each hand. "And I *am* bossy. And I was cranky tonight. I'm sorry."

"Don't apologize," she says, cupping my face in her hands. "We ended up where we needed to be. Sometimes you have to fight a little to work things out." She bites her lip, moaning softly as she rocks against my cock, pinned between our now naked bodies. "And I think making up is going to be a lot of fun."

"The most fun. We should get in while the water's running. I have a plan."

Her brows lift. "A plan?"

I nod toward the tub. "Get in. I just need to grab something from my bag, and I'll join you."

Fetching the silicone lube and condoms from my suitcase on the stand by the wall—water sex is always better with a waterproof lube—I return to find her stretched out against the back of the tub, already flushed pink and looking good enough to eat.

"You are so damned sexy," I say, setting the lube and protection within easy reach.

"You, too," she says, scooting forward to make room for me as I step into the water and settle myself behind her. She reaches back, caressing my swollen cock. "Getting you turned on is one of my favorite things in the entire world."

"Same." I kiss her shoulder as my hands return to her breasts, rolling her tight nipples lightly between my fingers. "Ever used water as a vibrator before?"

Breath coming faster, she digs her hands into my thighs beneath the still shallow water. "As a vibrator? You mean..."

"Yes," I assure her. "Want to try it?" I pinch her nipples, making her squirm against me.

"I guess," she says, sounding a little uncertain.

But I'm confident she'll change her mind once she feels the water flowing over her clit while I finger her into an orgasm she won't forget.

"We'll try it. If you don't like it, you know what to say."

"Eggplant," she says, arching into my touch as I continue to tease her nipples.

"That's right." I reach over, testing the water. "Is that too hot?"

She extends her foot, letting the water flow over her toes. "No, it's fine."

"Good, just lie back against me. Let me do all the work." I glide my hands lower, hooking my hands beneath her knees. I spread her wide as I shift forward, until her calves are dangling over the end of the tub and the water is flowing between her thighs.

Crossing my legs for better leverage—and to fit beneath the faucet—I shift forward that final inch.

The moment the water hits her clit, Sully stiffens with a gasp. But a beat later, her head is thrown back, resting on my shoulder as she wiggles her hips beneath the stream.

"Holy shit," she says, her breath already coming in shallow pants. "Oh my God, I'm going to come so fast. So crazy fast."

"Not yet," I say, reaching between her thighs, blocking some of the spray with my hand as I slide two fingers inside her. She groans and her head falls farther back as she puts herself in my control with a trust that humbles me.

My beautiful, sexy girl. She's come a long way since losing her virginity a week ago.

Which reminds me...

"You know what makes me really crazy? Thinking about another man fucking you," I whisper as I finger her slick pussy, still shielding her clit from the majority of the water, wanting to draw this out for her. For both of us. "Even that first night, thinking about Mark having his hands on you... It made me want to hunt him down and toss him into the sea without a life jacket."

"I don't want anyone else's hands on me," she pants, thrusting against me as I push my fingers deeper, curling against her inner walls as I rock back out again. "God, Weaver. You make me crazy. I want to do everything with you."

"Everything?" I drop my other hand under the water, teasing the tight ring of her ass.

She sucks in a breath, but doesn't stiffen as I apply pressure. Instead, she turns her head to kiss my cheek before whispering, "Everything."

I pull back, reaching for the lube. Spreading a good amount on my finger, I lift my hips, leveraging her higher in the water before returning my finger to her tightly puckered ring. "Just relax," I say, teasing at her sensitive flesh as I continue to finger her pussy, shielding her almost completely from the spray. I don't want to overwhelm her with too much sensation, too soon. "And tell me if you want me to stop."

I breach her entrance, and she tenses for a beat, before exhaling a ragged breath. "Weaver..."

"Yes, beautiful?" I say, finding a slow, sensual rhythm, penetrating her with both hands as she opens for me like a flower.

"I... I'm..." She trembles against me, gripping my knees beneath the water as her breath comes faster.

"Not yet, don't come yet, sweetheart. Not until I tell you to come for me," I say, fucking her a little faster, a little deeper. "I want you to feel this first." I move my hand, letting some of the water pour over her clit.

She cries out and her spine bows, but she doesn't come, she pants and moans and clings to me, but she doesn't come.

"Good girl," I murmur into her ear, so turned on by her mixture of abandon and control that my cock is leaking pre-come against her back. "You're so fucking sexy, Sully. I love feeling your pussy and ass tight on my fingers, love feeling how close you are to losing your mind."

She whimpers and wiggles closer to my hand,

clearly desperate for the release that's just out of reach. "Please," she finally begs. "Oh please."

"Just one more second, baby," I say, wanting her orgasm to be something she'll never forget. "One more second. Yes, almost there, almost..." I move my hand, letting the full force of the water run between her legs.

She comes almost instantly, her hips bucking into the air as I give her the resistance she craves, driving my fingers even deeper inside her.

And then, somehow the water's off, and I have a condom on, though I don't remember shifting positions. Sully straddles me, her breasts brushing my face as I rub lube between her slick folds and she lowers herself onto me beneath the water.

"Oh yes," she says, gasping as I fill her. "There you are. I need you like this. I need it so bad, all the time."

I grip her ass, squeezing tight as she seats herself fully. Looking up, my gaze crashes into hers with an even deeper intimacy than before, but that makes perfect sense. There's nothing to hide now, it's all on the table between us.

Holding her pinned tight to my cock, I whisper, "I love you."

"I love you, too," she says.

"I'm going to have my bathroom in the city remodeled to fit a larger tub. I need to fuck you like this at least once a week."

Her lips parting and excitement sparking in her eyes, she breathes, "We're really going to do this, aren't we? We're going to live together in the city and have sex all the time?"

"All the time," I say, grinning at the smile that stretches wide across her pretty face. "Now ride me, sweetheart, while I suck your tits. I need to show your nipples how much I love *them*, too."

Bracing her hands on my shoulders, she gives me exactly what I asked for and more, taking her pleasure from me, but giving me so much more in return. When I finally allow myself to come—after she's come twice, and we've shifted positions so I can take her from behind—I silently promise Fate that I'll never take the gift of this woman for granted.

I will treasure her and pleasure her and adore her every single day until my last day.

I come with a groan that echoes throughout the tiled room as I dig my teeth into the firm flesh on her shoulder. She cries out a beat later, giving me her fourth orgasm of the night.

But I need more...

"Two more," I say, as we're lying in the cooling water, catching our breath. "I need to make you come two more times before we sleep."

She sighs. "I can't. I'm tapped out. I'm going to need to train to work up to something like that."

But thirty minutes later, after we're dressed in our pajamas and snuggled in bed, my hand finds its way between her legs and she finds her second wind. Or maybe third at this point.

Whatever it is, it's perfect. We glide together slowly, almost gently this time, coming within seconds of each other as I rock into her on top, in plain old missionary position.

But nothing's ever plain or ordinary with her.

Nothing will be plain or ordinary again, because I get to take this incredible woman home with me. It's quite possibly the best night of my life, and I sleep like the fucking dead, too tired and happy to dream.

Then I'm awoken by Sully's panicked voice at six a.m. the next morning saying, "Weaver, wake up. We have to go. Gramps had a heart attack and they're taking him to the hospital," and the real world comes crashing down around us.

chapter 19

GERTIE

I'M USUALLY good in a crisis, but not when it comes to Gramps.

Weaver may turn out to be the love of my life, but Gramps is also my person.

We fuss over how to run the business, what to eat for dinner, and whether he's actually allergic to cats on a regular basis, but he's the only human in the world who's never let me down. He's like my mom and dad and grandfather and best friend all wrapped up into one salty old man package.

If I lose him, I will lose a piece of myself.

"I can't believe I didn't check on him," I say, throwing my toiletries into my bag in the bathroom as tears stream down my cheeks. "I should have checked. I should have been the one. Not Aunt Cathy."

Weaver appears behind me, squeezing the tops of my shoulders. "You had no reason to worry. You were on the boat with him yesterday and he was fine."

I sniff and squirm away from his comforting touch.

I don't deserve comfort.

Not when I'm the worst granddaughter on earth.

"Yes, but Cathy told me last night that she couldn't get ahold of him," I say. "I assumed he was just dodging her calls because talking on the phone annoys him, but I should have called to be sure. Or texted or... something." I sniff and swipe at my wet cheeks. "If he dies, and I don't even get to say goodbye, I'll never forgive myself."

"Baby," Weaver begins, but I cut him off with a swift shake of my head.

"No, don't be sweet to me. I can't take it. If you're sweet, I'll fall completely apart, and we'll never get to the hospital. I need cold, logical Weaver. Just tell me to pull myself together, get dressed, and get my ass down to the car."

He sighs, but straightens behind me, the softness fading from his expression. "All right, if you're sure that's what you need."

I nod faster and toss my toothpaste into the bag. "Yes. That's what I need."

His hand closes around my wrist, stopping me before I can reach for another toiletry. "Then, that's what I'll give you. Stop packing and get into the shower. Right now."

My jaw drops and an outraged squawk emerges from the back of my throat.

Before I can protest that we have to get going, however, Weaver says, "Look at yourself. Do it," he insists. "Take a breath and look at yourself in the mirror."

I do and blanche at the sight of my hair in a wild sex tangle and my tear-puffy face.

But I don't care what I look like right now.

I tell Weaver as much, adding, "I just need to be with him. Now. Five minutes ago."

"I've already called to have the car brought up to the front," he says, still holding onto my wrist. "But the parking garage is several blocks away. The valet said it's going to take fifteen minutes. Take ten of that to grab a quick shower and put on clean clothes. I'll leave some outside the door for you. While you're doing that, I'll pack our things and run downstairs to get breakfast and coffee for the road. That way we can leave as soon as you're dressed."

I swallow, my frantic brain parsing quickly through his plan and realizing it's solid. And a shower will help clear my thoughts after a long night filled with high emotion and not much sleep.

"Okay," I say, sniffing again as I shoo him out of the bathroom. "Go. Hurry. I'll be ready when you get back."

As soon as the door shuts behind him, I crank on the water and strip out of the t-shirt and panties I slept in. I take the world's fastest shower, run oil through my hair to keep my waves from frizzing, and rub lotion onto my face, before tossing all my toiletries back into the bag. A beat later, I throw open the door and snatch a pile of neatly folded clothes from the floor.

Weaver chose the "going home" outfit I intended to wear on Sunday—a comfy pair of baggy jeans and a sky-blue sweatshirt—and I'm so glad. The thought of putting on the clingy sweater dress and boots I packed for today in an attempt to be fashionable makes me want to claw my skin off.

I've just finished dressing and am tying my shoes in the living area when Weaver swings back through the door, a delicious-smelling bag in hand. My stomach growls, and I instantly feel guilty again.

How can I be hungry at a time like this? Gramps could be dying. He might never eat a bacon, egg, and cheese sandwich again.

"Even if he lives, he shouldn't eat bacon, egg, and cheese again," I say, tears stinging into my eyes. "His cholesterol is too high. I've been telling him that for years, but he wouldn't listen. He said life wasn't worth living without cheese."

Weaver crosses the room, pressing the bag of food and the small carrier holding our coffees into my hands. "You can google healthy cheese alternatives on the way to the hospital. Go call the elevator. I'll get our bags."

"No, I'll help, you can't handle all of it—"

He leans down, capturing my chin in his hand as he whispers inches from my face. "I absolutely can handle all of it by myself. And take care of you at the same time. Go call the elevator, Sullivan, and don't back talk again until we're at the hospital."

Grateful tears in my eyes, I whisper, "Okay. Thank you."

"I love you," he says, making the stinging at the back of my nose even worse. "Taking care of you when you need help is my job. You never have to say thank you for that." Then, he presses a swift, but firm, kiss to my lips and disappears into the bedroom to collect the bags.

Three minutes later—two minutes ahead of schedule thanks to the speedy valet—Weaver is pulling out of the hotel driveway and onto the road.

"Do you need me to navigate?" I ask, chewing on my lip, my anxiety spiking higher now that there's nothing to do but sit and wait.

I wanted to drive, but I knew better than to ask. Weaver is an excellent driver and he's the safer choice. I wouldn't want someone as panicked as I am driving me anywhere. That's for sure.

"No, it's all set." He nods toward the map on the dashboard's screen, which is already guiding us in the right direction.

"Oh," I say, feeling dumb. "Sorry. I should have seen that."

"Stop apologizing." He reaches over, resting his hand on my thigh for a beat, waiting until I relax beneath his touch before giving it a gentle squeeze. "Eat your sandwich and have some coffee." He shoots me a sympathetic glance before returning his attention to the road. "But maybe not too much coffee. You're already pretty wired."

"I am," I agree, forcing my muscles to relax into the warm leather seat. Exhausting myself with fear and worry before we even get to the hospital isn't going to accomplish anything. I need to save my energy to be there for Gramps and the rest of my family. "But coffee still sounds good, and I'm actually starving. We had five courses last night. How am I this hungry?"

I reach for the bag at my feet, fetching the sandwich with the "G" written on the foil for myself and passing the one with "W" on it over to Weaver. Mine is bacon, egg, and cheese. His will be just bacon and cheese because he likes his eggs scrambled and alone on a plate.

I know these things about him already. And he knows so many things about me. It's crazy how comfortable I feel with him after only a week, but I'm so grateful I do. I wouldn't want to be making this drive with someone who didn't make me feel completely safe and supported.

Hell, I wouldn't want to be making this drive with anyone else, I realize, not even Maya or Elaina. I love my besties, but they're both even more emotional than I am. Weaver's cool, calm, bossy side comes in handy in lots of situations, but especially in a crisis.

"I'm hungry, too," he says as he unwraps his sandwich. "We did a fair amount of cardio after dinner."

I sigh, both at the memory of that amazing cardio and how hopeful I felt. Last night, I was on the verge of walking through a portal into a thrilling new world.

This morning, real life is bringing me back down to earth with a vengeance.

My stomach lurches and my throat squeezes so tight, I can barely swallow my next bite.

I can't leave Sea Breeze with Weaver the way we planned. I can't. Not now, and maybe not ever. What if Gramps needs long-term care? I couldn't leave him with Cathy or anyone else. He would be miserable. I'm the only person he can stand underfoot more than a couple hours a day.

I press my lips together, fighting the waves of grief and guilt as they hit, one after the other.

After a few moments, Weaver asks, "Sandwich not up to snuff?"

"What?" I croak, fighting tears for the hundredth time since I hung up with Cathy.

"Your sandwich. Is it bad?" he asks. "You only took two bites before you stopped eating. If it's bad, I can get you something else from the hospital cafeteria."

I jerk my attention his way, the vice around my throat giving way as shock frees up my airway. "What? You can't come in."

"I can, and I will," he says, adjusting the rim of his simple beige ballcap. "That's why I bought this disguise at the gift shop while you were showering."

I let my gaze skim down his body, taking in his outfit for the first time. He's wearing a white "Saint Mary Yacht Club" sweatshirt that totally isn't his style. He still has on gray suit pants—Weaver isn't a khakis or jeans kind of guy—but his overall look is much more casual than usual. The baggy sweatshirt conceals his chiseled upper body and the cap sits low enough on his face to cast half of it in shadow.

But still...

He's still *obviously* Weaver Tripp and my family is going to know him on sight.

I shake my head. "I'm sorry, but no, you can't. This is going to be hard enough without having to answer questions from my family about why I was out of town with a Tripp. Especially you." I shudder as another realization dawns. "And my dad might be there. He's not into family stuff most of the time, but if he was remotely sober when Cathy called him, I'm sure he's on his way to the hospital. He loves Gramps."

"Does he?" Weaver asks, his voice cooling. "Or does he just love that his father still pays his bills?"

I bristle. "Stop. My dad loves Gramps. He does. Truly."

"Last night you were talking about how much more you were able to save for your grandfather's retirement because you stayed in Sea Breeze and sacrificed your chance to go to college. I'm sure your grandfather would have been able to save just as much by simply cutting your father off. Leon is a grown man and should be paying his own way, not cannibalizing his daughter's future and his father's golden years."

I exhale and wrap the foil back around my sandwich. It's actually delicious, but my appetite is gone. "I don't want to talk about this."

"You don't want to talk about it? Or you don't want to admit to yourself that for your entire life, your family has been putting your welfare last, when it should have been first?"

I huff and shake my head. "Why should it be first? Because I'm young? Family is family. We all help each other and—"

"Because you're the only innocent person in the situation," Weaver cuts in, his tone still calm, but the words making my blood boil all the same. "You did nothing wrong. You aren't an alcoholic, and you didn't decide to enable an alcoholic at the cost of your own livelihood. You were a child born into a dysfunctional situation, but instead of doing everything they could to get you out, your family is doing their best to suck you down with them."

My cheeks burning, I shoot back, "So, what should we have done? Let Dad starve and die?"

"Maybe," Weaver says, making me flinch. "If that was the only way to keep the rest of you safe. Paying for rehab or some form of treatment is one thing, something I would personally support. But paying his bills while he sits around getting drunk and destroying himself? How is that helping anyone? Even him? But especially you, the daughter *he* should be taking care of?"

I rub at the tight place in my jaw, hating that a part of me agrees with him. "You don't understand. You don't have a family like mine. We help each other. It's what we do."

"Like I said, the situation doesn't seem 'helpful' to me. Not to anyone. Your father is drowning, but instead of reaching for a life preserver, he's wrapped his arms around his father and his daughter. You've been treading water as hard as you could with dead weight hanging from your shoulders, but it's time to stop, Sully. For yourself and for your grandfather. Think how much less he'll need to live on if he cuts your dad off and focuses on taking care of himself?"

"I can't think about this now," I say, digging my fingers into my temples. I never get headaches, but right now an ugly one is clawing into my skull. "And you can't come in to the hospital. That's final."

He sighs, as frustrated as I am.

Maybe more so, since he clearly doesn't understand why what he's suggesting would be so hard.

I love my dad, really love him, no matter how many times he's let me down or how strained our relationship has become over the years. I still remember the way he'd push me on the swings as a kid, the way he'd buy me a snow cone from the cart on the pier or a stuffed animal from the toy store, even when Mom said we needed to save money. I remember lying on his strong chest in the sun on the beach when I was so tiny that my hair was still white as it blew around my face, feeling so safe and loved because my daddy was there to take my nap with me.

Those things are still true and real. They live inside me even though that version of my father is gone, probably forever.

But I can't turn my back on the man in that memory. It would be like setting the last of the goodness between us on fire.

The fact that Weaver can't understand that makes me wonder if we're really meant for each other, after all. I mean, I knew he didn't have a good relationship with most of his family, but isn't there anyone he would go that extra mile for? One person he would help no matter what? No matter how many times they failed to rise to the occasion and needed his help again?

I'm about to ask him when he says, "What if I stay

in the cafeteria? I'll grab a cup of coffee, find a dark corner, and keep my hat pulled down low. Then, if you need me, you can text, and we'll find somewhere private to meet. I don't want to leave you there alone. I should have thought of that before I offered my unsolicited advice at a difficult time."

Instantly, I melt.

Maybe there *is* someone Weaver is willing to go that extra mile for.

And maybe it's...me.

Chest aching at the thought, I nod. "Okay. That sounds good. Thank you."

I don't tell him that I wouldn't really be alone at the hospital, not with my entire family there. I don't want to seem ungrateful for his support, and there's a part of me that *is* starting to feel "alone" without Weaver.

We don't pull any punches with each other. We haven't from the beginning. But with my family? I pull punches all the time. I keep secrets and soften blows and sometimes, I just lie.

I don't like to, but when it's the kindest choice, I do.

I lie to Gramps about how quickly I can see him slowing down. I lie to my cousin, Henna, about how many days a week I see her husband lingering at the pub for another drink, when she's been at home alone all day with their two kids. I lie to Elaina about what the mean people in town say about her "raunchy" café and raunchier habits, and I lie to Maya about that the fact that not one of the men I hang out with has ever asked about my shy best friend.

I tell Maya tons of guys are interested, whenever she's ready. I tell Elaina that Sweet Pussy Cafe is a great name for her bakery and she should keep it.

And I tell myself that the way the Sullivans do things is the best way because I *want* it to be the best. I want to believe that all the sacrifices I've made are because I'm a good daughter and granddaughter and niece and cousin, not because I'm a shmuck who's let myself be used and abused by people too distracted by their own drama to have my best interests at heart.

My family doesn't want to hurt me, I know that with every bone in my body. But have they hurt me without meaning to? Without even realizing what they were doing?

I honestly...don't know.

There's enough doubt inside that I'm not about to kick Weaver out of my life for saying the things he said. Especially when it's obvious he was saying those things because he cares about me.

He really does care. This successful, gorgeous, supportive, sexy as hell man really does seem to love me. And I feel the same way about him. He's everything I wasn't brave enough to want until I met him.

But if it comes down to a choice between Weaver and my family—a very real possibility—which will I choose?

I don't know the answer to that, either.

I only know that I need Gramps to be okay. After that, maybe I'll have the bandwidth to take a closer look at the rest of my messed-up life.

I push the bigger questions aside as best I can, eat

my now-cold sandwich, and brace myself for the worst as Weaver gets on the highway headed south toward the hospital.

But not even in my wildest fever dreams could I have imagined the shit show that awaits us just outside of Bangor...

chapter 20

I DROP Sully by the entrance to the emergency room and circle around to park in the guest lot.

I dispose of our breakfast trash in a nearby bin and am headed back to the car to fetch my laptop case—might as well get some work done while I'm lurking in the cafeteria—when my gaze is drawn to a man stumbling out of a bus by the hospital's main entrance.

The man is balding, with dark under eye circles, an unkempt beard, and a sizeable paunch beneath his gray hooded sweatshirt. He looks nothing like the sandy haired guy in a red tee and jeans who took a swing at me in a bar parking lot sixteen years ago, but somehow, I know it's Leon, Sully's father.

And he's clearly still drunk from last night...

Or maybe he hits the bottle first thing in the morning, who knows? Whatever the case, he's obviously impaired. He trips on the curb and nearly goes down twice more as he wobbles unsteadily toward the sliding glass doors.

I freeze, my stomach balling into a knot as I predict how this ends. Best-case scenario, the hospital staff stops him at the entrance and turns him away for public drunkenness. Worst-case scenario, he finds his way to his father's hospital bed in his wasted state and causes a scene that makes a difficult time even worse for the rest of the family and imperils his father's already ailing health.

And yes, the hospital staff would surely take care of that, too, but only after he's upset grieving people and given his daughter another terrible memory for her collection.

I can't let that happen.

Not if I can prevent it. Sully's been through enough.

Leaving my laptop case in the trunk, I lock the car and cross the parking lot. Keeping my distance and the brim of my hat pulled low on my forehead, I tail Leon past the reception desk and into the wide, open space beyond. The center of the hospital is one large room, with floor-to-ceiling windows stretching four stories into the air and exposed staircases leading to other floors.

The first floating staircase is on the left, about fifteen feet from the entrance, but he weaves past that, as well as a bank of elevators. He passes a sitting area filled with couches, where several people read books or scroll on their phones while waiting near a door with "Inpatient Surgery" painted above it.

Past the inpatient waiting area, Leon pauses to get a drink from a fountain. Water dribbles down into his beard as he stands, sucking in a deep breath. He closes his eyes, swaying on his feet. For a moment, I think he might be about to pass out—a best-case scenario I hadn't considered—but a beat later, he swipes the back of his sleeve across his damp face and stumbles onward.

Trailing one hand along the wall, he tracks onward toward another large desk at the back of the hospital. I'm not sure what this desk is for, but the hallway to the left bears signs pointing the way to the East Wing and various lab stations. Behind the desk is a door labeled "Radiology," and to the right is the entrance to the cafeteria.

The tension in my jaw eases a bit. Maybe Leon realizes he needs to sober up before he sees his family and is on his way to buy some breakfast.

If that's the case, I'll find another place to lay low, and text Sully to let her know where she can find me. There appear to be several waiting areas scattered throughout the hospital and, according to the signs by the elevators, a chapel and yoga room on the fourth floor.

I haven't set foot in a church since I was in high school, but I know enough yoga to pass as a practitioner. I can spread out a borrowed mat in a corner, lie down in corpse pose, and savasana until my phone vibrates. After too little sleep last night and a stressful morning, a nap wouldn't be an unwelcome thing.

Fuck, I'm actually craving a *nap*.

Maybe I'm becoming an old man faster than I think.

I'm still meditating on the horrors of my sleepy,

weakening body when Leon veers left instead of right, headed down the hallway toward the East Wing. I have no idea where he's going, but no one stops him, or me, as I trail him down a narrower hallway. The ceilings here are only twelve feet high and there's a lot more traffic.

Most of the people approaching from the opposite direction see Leon weaving toward them and veer out of his path, but the old woman with a walker just ahead has her back to him.

She has no idea she's about to be mowed over from behind.

I'm about to call out a warning, when Leon suddenly careens to the left, bumping into the opposite wall and a teenager with a wad of cotton taped to the crook of his arm.

"Hey, watch it," the kid calls out, his Adam's apple bobbing in his skinny throat as he turns to glare at Leon.

But Leon only lifts a hand and stumbles forward.

I glance around to see if any staff members have noticed the interaction and are calling security. But the only nurse in the hallway is talking to a distraught elderly woman in a wheelchair, who seems confused about where she is and why she has to have her blood drawn.

Cursing understaffing, I circle around the woman in the walker and hurry after Leon, who's moving faster now. Wherever he's going, he seems to know the way. But then, Sully said her father spent a lot of time in the hospital after his drunk driving accident. If it was *this* hospital, he's probably fairly familiar with the layout.

At the end of the hall, the building opens up into another atrium, this one with trees planted throughout and tables and chairs arranged in the center. Here, several people work on laptops or take calls on their cell phones beneath signs that read, "No calls, please. This is a Quiet Zone."

But no one's policing that policy, the same way no one's policing the clearly inebriated man cruising toward the glass elevator on the right side of the space.

The elevator is the same size as our luxurious bathroom at the hotel last night, with streak-free glass that makes it easy to see inside.

I spot Sully and the older woman she's speaking to as the car descends from the third floor to the first. I reach for my phone to text her a warning, but it's too late. I watch helplessly as she steps out of the car—still distracted by what looks like a tense conversation with the other woman—and practically runs into her father.

Or rather, he runs into *her*.

As she moves past him, he lunges for her, grabbing her elbow and holding on tight as he slips and falls on the tile.

Sully cries out in pain as she's dragged to the floor by a sharp jerk of her arm, sending the people waiting for the elevator scurrying backward with sounds of surprise.

And that's all it takes.

Before I make a conscious decision to break my

promise, I'm on the move. It's instinctive. I can't watch the woman I love be physically assaulted and sit on my fucking hands. Even if the man assaulting her is her dad, even if he clearly didn't mean to hurt her.

Leon's intentions don't matter. What matters is that he's drunk, causing a scene, and hurting Sully.

Her eyes are shining, and she winces in pain as she detangles herself from her father and sits up. She's still on the floor, clutching her wounded arm to her chest when I arrive beside them.

She looks up, the pain in her eyes transforming to fear as her gaze meets mine.

Her lips part, presumably on a warning, but before she can say a word, a fist slams into the side of my head, sending agony flooding through my jaw and ringing into my ears.

chapter 21

FUCK, *oh fuck. Fuck, fuck, fuck!*

My inner monologue is a stream of panicked, pain-filled obscenities as I struggle to get off the floor with only one functioning arm. I'm pretty sure my dad jerked my shoulder completely out of the socket when he dragged me to the ground—I can't move it and the burning in the joint is excruciating—but that doesn't matter now.

What matters is that my father is trying to kill my boyfriend before he's even officially become my boyfriend.

We didn't label things last night after we confessed our feelings. I assume professions of love and offers to set me up with a key to his place and a bank account in New York City are enough to take the boyfriend part for granted, but I don't *want* to take it for granted.

I want to have that conversation with Weaver. I want to get excited about the first serious, committed relationship of my adult life. I want to relish every brilliant beautiful thing about being in love and taking the next steps with my person.

But, of course, none of that is going to happen.

It never was. Weaver and I were doomed from the start. This run-in with my father is just speeding along the inevitable ruin of the happiness I stupidly thought could be mine.

"Stop!" I cry out as my dad slams Weaver against the exterior of the elevator, sending a shudder through the glass encasing the shaft. "Dad, stop!"

But he just keeps slamming his fists into Weaver's stomach with a speed and ferocity I didn't realize my father still had in him.

As a younger man, he was one of the best boxers in the area. Before I was born, he used to win prize money in the amateur fights up and down the coast, and use it to take my mom out to fancy dinners. He still has a picture of them out at their favorite Italian place in Bangor on his mantle—Mom in a slinky gold dress and him with a black eye and a big grin.

But Dad hasn't been that fit, powerful man in a long time.

This intensity isn't a result of training or excelling at a sport; it's rage, pure and simple. He's running on adrenaline and hatred, and I can only hope he'll run out of both before he does serious damage to Weaver's body.

Because Weaver isn't fighting back. He's deflecting the blows as best he can, but he isn't even trying to land a punch. He's letting my father beat the hell out of him.

Maybe because he feels guilty for what he did years ago, maybe out of concern for me, but either way, it's not right.

My dad is the one to blame. He's the one who's drunk at seven in the morning—I could smell the whiskey on him as he stumbled and dragged me down —and he's the one who attacked Weaver.

"Stop!" I scream again, crying out in pain as I force myself to my feet, sending my useless arm swaying in an agonizing arc before it returns to my side.

I glance around, but there isn't a member of the hospital staff to be found, and the rest of the bystanders are backing away from the violence. Poor Aunt Cathy is the only one trying to get through to Dad —screeching at him from a few feet away—but she's shaking so hard I can't understand what she's saying.

There's no one here to intervene.

No one but me.

So, I do what I've always done. I step up. I walk up to my father, channeling the bravest version of myself, and grab a handful of his hoodie with my good hand. I start to pull him backward, but he spins and slams his fist into my stomach so hard I swear I feel his knuckles connect with my spine.

"Oh fuck, Gertie," my dad slurs, his clenched fists releasing with a spasm. "I didn't see, I didn't know it was you."

My breath rushes out and stays out as I clutch at my midsection. Pain blooms deep in my core, spreading like a fast-moving cancer. A second later, my knees buckle and hit the ground.

"Oh no, oh, Gertie, I'm sorry," Dad says, sinking down beside me as I fight for a breath. "Come on, honey, let me help."

"Get away from her," Weaver grunts from behind him.

"You get the fuck away!" Dad screams like the lunatic he is, adding a heaping helping of shame to the misery roiling through my belly. "This is your fault, you piece of shit. You ruined my life. You ruined everything! You're a fucking devil."

"This isn't about you or me. She's hurt," Weaver says, his voice thick-sounding. "She could have internal injuries. We need to get her to the emergency room."

I finally manage to wheeze in a breath, but before I can speak my dad shouts, "Fuck you! Don't you dare tell me how to take care of my family."

I look up, my heart shattering as I see the blood pouring from Weaver's nose and down the front of his Yacht Club sweatshirt. He's clutching his stomach, too.

I want to tell him how sorry I am. I want to tell him to run, to get away from my toxic father, but suddenly I'm bent over, vomiting watery streams of coffee onto the shining white tile as my internal organs continue to throb.

"Oh honey, oh no," my dad sobs, his words barely audible over his blubbering. He puts his hands on my back, and I instinctively flinch away, which only makes him cry harder.

From my hunched position, I see two hospital employees with walkie-talkies and security uniforms running across the atrium, and know this nightmare is almost over. But the thought doesn't bring much comfort.

The damage has already been done.

Everything is ruined. Even if Weaver still wants to be with me, my father has basically guaranteed that it will tear our family apart. As awful as Dad is, he's still a Sullivan, and the Sullivans are a tribal lot.

As the guards grab Dad by each arm, dragging him away from me while he shouts and cries, I'm already making a mental list of all the relatives I'm pretty sure will side with him. There won't be any more Christmas craft beer bingo at Great Uncle Charlie's for me, no summer sleepovers at Aunt Emma's little island cabin, and maybe not Thanksgiving dinner, either. Aunt Cathy loves me, but Dad's her baby brother. There's at least a fifty percent chance she'll choose him.

Or choose neither of us.

The Sullivans might decide this entire branch of the family should be cut off in a clean break. If Gramps dies, there won't be anyone with real influence to advocate for us. Gramps is our patriarch, our leader, and he's lying in an operating room on the third floor having stints put into his heart.

"Oh God," Aunt Cathy says as she crouches down beside me, breathing so fast I'm afraid she's going to hyperventilate and pass out. "Oh God, honey. Are you okay?"

I shake my head, tears sliding quietly from my eyes as I watch Dad being tasered by a third guard who's appeared on the scene. Or maybe he's a police officer.

Maybe they all are. I can't really tell. Whatever they are, they're efficient. Once they've tasered Dad, they have him flat on his stomach with his hands zip-tied behind him in seconds.

"Oh no, oh no," Aunt Cathy says, continuing to babble something about how she should have known better than to call my dad with bad news as Weaver appears on my other side, resting a gentle hand on my hip.

"Can I help you up?" he asks, his words still muffled by the blood in his nose. I thought Dad mostly got him in the stomach, but he clearly hit his face at least once, too.

"I'm sorry," I manage to mumble, the tears coming faster, hotter.

"Don't you dare apologize for him," Weaver says, squeezing my thigh. "He doesn't matter. You matter. Can I help you up and carry you to the ER? Do you want me to find a nurse and a wheelchair?"

"I can walk," I say, even though I'm not sure I can. I've never experienced pain like this before. It feels like someone put a hot coal in my guts and left it there to burn.

"All right, let's take this nice and slow," Weaver says, guiding my good arm around his shoulders. Then, with his arm around my waist, he lifts me to my feet as gently as he can.

I know he's being gentle, but the shift of my dislocated arm causes another blinding wave of pain to shoot from my shoulder straight into the base of my neck. Bright light flashes behind my eyes and for a second, I'm afraid I might pass out.

I'm not that girl, the swoony kind. I'm the girl who hoists my bestie across my shoulders and carries her off the beach when she's had too much to drink. I'm the girl who finished a ten-mile hike with a twisted ankle and not a word of complaint.

I'm the girl who does the saving, not the one being swooped into a man's arms.

But apparently, today, I *am* that girl.

Even though Weaver is probably hurting every bit as much as I am, he scoops me up, cradling me close as he whispers, "I've got you, Sully. I've got you."

"Oh, thank you," Aunt Cathy says, mincing along beside us as Weaver starts down the long hallway, leading to the older part of the hospital. "Thank you so much."

"Sir, we need to speak with you," a male voice calls from behind us. "We need to get your statement about what happened here."

"Then follow us to the emergency room," Weaver shoots back without slowing his pace or so much as glancing over his shoulder. "She's hurt and needs to be checked out. Now."

"You too," I wheeze, curling my good hand into his shirt, where the fabric is tacky with cooling blood. "You're hurt. You shouldn't be carrying me. Put me down, I can walk now."

"I'm fine," Weaver says softly. "Don't worry about me."

"I'm sorry," I murmur again, fresh tears in my eyes.

"We're both so sorry," Aunt Cathy pipes up, turning to the guard who appears beside her with a nervous flap of her hands. "Oh, please, just let him take my niece to the emergency room. I can talk to you. I was there. I saw everything. This man did nothing wrong. It was all my brother, the man your friends took away. He's not well. He's sick. In the head. He has been for years, the poor man. He didn't realize what he was doing."

The poor man...

Guess Cathy won't be choosing me in the big family break-up, either. She's being sweet to Weaver now, but once she realizes Weaver and I are more than just casual acquaintances, that will change, I'm sure. Cathy isn't as anti-Tripp as my grandfather, but she proudly wears her "Tripp Lobsters Stick in my Craw" shirt when she hits the local pub with Uncle Tom.

"And our dad is having open heart surgery right now. Leon's just out of his head with grief," she continues, tears pooling in her faded blue eyes. She swipes at them with the sleeve of her flannel as we emerge from the hallway and Weaver takes a right.

The security guard or policeman, or whatever he is, still trails along beside her, and soon he's joined by another guard. I catch a glimpse of the larger man, wearing what looks like a bulletproof vest, as Weaver stops in front of the elevator bank and hits the down button. We've acquired quite a following, but at least no one is trying to stop us and they seem to realize that Weaver isn't to blame.

"Your brother still assaulted two people, ma'am,"

the larger man says. "Once they've been treated in the ER, I'll need to get their statements, and they'll have the option to press charges."

"No," I say, shaking my head as the elevator doors open and our entire caravan of chaos files inside, causing the older couple waiting by the door to scuttle to the back of the car. "I don't want to press charges. He didn't mean to hit me. He's never hit me before. It was an accident."

The larger man sighs, his eyes sad and understanding and disappointed, all at the same time. "He's your dad?" he asks, gently.

I nod. "Yeah. And Cathy's right, he isn't well. He has a drinking problem. A bad one. He has for a long time."

"And what's your connection to the assailant, sir?" the man asks, shifting his attention Weaver's way as the elevator dings its arrival on the basement level.

"No connection," Weaver says in his ice-cold voice. "And I *will* be pressing charges."

Before the man can reply, Weaver's hurrying through the open doors, aiming himself for the check-in desk across the large waiting room.

chapter 22

GERTIE

SHIT.

This day just keeps getting worse with every passing second.

I press a hand to Weaver's chest, not knowing what to say. I can't blame him for wanting to hold my father accountable, but...he's my dad. As disappointed and angry as I am with him, I don't want to see him in prison.

"I'm sorry," Weaver murmurs beneath his breath, clearly sensing that I'm upset. "But I can't let him get away with this. If you won't stand up for yourself, I'll do it for you."

I swallow but don't say a word. I don't know what to say, I only know that assault charges are going to make an already awful situation even worse. By the time we're done, we'll be lucky if the Tripps and Sullivans aren't warring in the streets of Sea Breeze.

The thought is so sickening, I'm honestly not sure if it's my injury or my misery making my stomach roil as Weaver sets me on my feet by the desk, and I fight to give the woman my insurance information without getting sick again.

"Listen, she's in a lot of pain and vomited right after the assault," Weaver says to the woman in blue scrubs with bright pink glasses perched on the end of her nose. His voice is tight but respectful as he adds, "Isn't this paperwork something she can do while she's in the exam room lying down, waiting to be seen? Or after the CT scan? She was hit hard enough that I'm concerned about internal bleeding and organ damage."

The woman nods, her expression compassionate as she taps the bottom line of the form on the counter in front of us. "Of course, you poor thing. I'll call for wheelchair transport. Just sign the bottom to indicate you'll take responsibility for the charges, and we'll get the rest sorted out when you check out." She shifts her focus back to Weaver. "And what about you, sir? Do you need to be seen?"

"No, I'm fine," Weaver says at the same time I say, "Yes, he does."

"You need to be seen," I say when Weaver insists that he isn't seriously injured. "I saw what happened. He hit you at least a dozen times. He only hit me once."

"But he was closer to me," Weaver says. "He didn't have time to build up any momentum, and I saw him coming and locked my muscles. You didn't have time for that before you were sucker punched in the gut."

His eyes glitter with a cold fire that I know means a truce between my father and my boyfriend is never going to happen. Not if we all live for a thousand years and go to therapy every single day.

"He didn't know it was me," I remind him.

"He didn't know who it was," Weaver counters. "And he didn't care. He's dangerous."

He's right, I know he is, but I can't help wishing...

Fuck, I don't even know what to wish for at this point, not with my entire life turning into a shit show at a breathless pace.

"Just, please," I beg. "Get checked out. For me. For *my* peace of mind?"

Weaver hesitates another beat, but after a hum of agreement from the woman at the front desk, he relents. "All right. But I'll go to the urgent care near Sea Breeze later. I don't want to waste emergency room resources."

"But—" I start, only for Aunt Cathy, who I'd honestly forgotten was standing behind us, to pipe up, "That might not be a bad idea. They get to people so fast over there. Even on the weekends."

"Go now, then. I'm fine, and I have family here if I need someone." I don't want him to leave, but it's probably for the best. I have no idea where my dad is or what's going to happen when the rest of my family hears what went down by the elevators. They might be grateful to Weaver for carrying me to the ER or they might decide to come take a swing at him themselves.

I never should have let him come here. I knew it was a bad idea, though I never could have dreamed it would end this badly.

"You're sure?" Weaver asks, and I nod again.

LILI VALENTE

"Please. Yes. I just want to know you're okay," I say, ignoring Aunt Cathy's increasingly wide eyes as she apparently gets the memo that Weaver and I care about each other's welfare a little too much for complete strangers.

"I'd like to talk to you before you leave, sir. Get your statement if you have time or at least a phone number I can use to follow up," the large man in the vest says. I can read the "BPD" emblazoned across the front of it now. He's definitely a cop.

Ugh. I'm sure he'll want to talk to me, too.

But thankfully a nurse appears beside the desk with a wheelchair at that moment, calling my name. I tell Weaver goodbye and assure Cathy I'm fine to go back alone while she returns to the rest of the family with those snacks we were fetching before everything went to hell.

And then I'm gone, zooming through cool, antiseptic-scented air down a short hallway. I'm then steered into a larger open room, divided into exam areas by pastel bubble print curtains that are far too cheery for the ER.

Once I'm settled in my bed, I'm left alone to listen to the old man moaning across from me, the gunshot victim cursing about his "fucking leg" next door, and what sounds like a two or three-year-old screaming bloody murder in between bouts of vomiting a few curtains down.

"Happy bubble" is definitely not the vibe here.

I feel like I'm in a nightmare.

A nightmare that continues as I'm poked and

prodded by a nurse, then poked and prodded by a frazzled young doctor with freezing fingers, who pops my shoulder back into place amidst much air-sucking and nearly passing out on my end. Afterward, the nurse helps me into a sling she says I'll need to wear for at least four days and gives me an ice pack to hold on my stomach while I wait for someone to fetch me for the CT scan.

Eventually, I'm sent to lie in a terrible vibrating coffin for what seems like hours before once again being returned to my curtained bed, where the only improvement is that the puking baby has apparently been treated and discharged.

Cathy checks in on me via text from upstairs on the third floor with the rest of the family, but there's still no news about Gramp's surgery.

Her only significant update comes in the form of a text promising—*I'll keep my mouth shut about you and that man, but you need to take care of that, Gertie. Whatever's going on there, it's no good for anyone. Especially not your father. Hasn't he been through enough with Weaver Tripp?*

I lie back with a sigh, resting my head on the scratchy little pillow. I'm the one lying in a hospital bed, waiting to find out if my father damaged my internal organs when he punched me, but *he's* the one Aunt Cathy's worried about.

I might cry about it if I had any energy left.

But I don't. I'm so beaten down and exhausted by the insanity of the morning that I'm almost asleep when my phone rings. I startle out of my near-slumber, shifting the ice pack on my stomach to the table as I fumble to fetch my cell from beneath the thin blanket.

When I hold it up, the screen says the call is coming from a local police station. I move my thumb away from the answer button and silence the call, waiting for it to go to voicemail. I don't have it in me to give my statement right now. The officer can leave a number, and I'll get back to him once I'm out of the emergency room and know Weaver and Gramps are going to be okay.

It's definitely a "one crisis at a time" kind of day.

A few moments later, the voicemail notification pops through. I tap the play button and put my cell to my ear, only to be surprised by the sound of my father's voice.

He sounds like absolute hell...

"I'm so sorry, honey. You have no idea how sorry. If I could go back and redo one thing in my life, it would be what happened this morning." He clears his throat before continuing, "That's why I'm using my one call to call you, not a lawyer. I need you to know how sorry I am. And that I'm going to make a change. It's time. Past time. You deserve a father you can trust, one you know is never going to hurt you, not even by accident." He pauses, exhaling a breath that hitches into a sob.

I press my fist to my lips, fighting tears.

"I'm just so sorry, baby girl," he wheezes. "I swear, I'm going to get better. I'm going to be the dad you deserve. Even if I have to do it in prison. I'm going to get sober and stay sober. I love you, and I always will, even if you decide you never want to talk to me again, which...I would understand. You're a good person, Gertie. You're so funny and you work so damn hard. And you've got the best heart. If you didn't, you wouldn't have put up with a deadbeat like me for so long. Whatever you decide, just know I'm so proud of you."

The call ends, and I let my phone fall into my lap.

My dad has never expressed any interest in getting sober. Not once. He isn't that kind of alcoholic. He would never admit he had a problem in the first place, let alone think about getting help. He always made other excuses for why he couldn't work or function like other human beings—the accident, his brain injury, his back pain, his depression, his untreated ADD, even.

To hear him actually owning the disease and expressing a desire to get better is huge, though I know it won't be that simple. Dad's in so deep that he'll need medical care to survive getting off alcohol without killing himself. He'll start going into withdrawal in a few hours and be in bad shape by tomorrow morning.

But I've already vetted several local rehabilitation centers. I did a deep dive back when I was sixteen and still believed helping Dad was just a matter of getting him through a pair of sliding glass doors and into the care of medical professionals. There's even one that takes patients on a sliding scale. They'll probably treat Dad for close to free if they have a bed available.

I could text him, give him some names of places and their phone numbers...but he won't be able to see the text or claim a rehab bed if he's in jail.

"Shit," I mutter, my stomach starting to ache again at the thought of what I have to do.

But I have to do it. I won't be able to live with myself if I don't at least try to help Dad now that he's finally asked for it.

So, I lift my phone and send a message that might very well destroy what's left of my budding romance.

chapter 23

I'M NEARLY BACK to the yacht with a clean bill of health for my internal organs, a painkiller prescription for my swollen nose, and advice to ice my bruised ribs several times a day, when the texts come through from Sully.

I hit the play button on the car's screen, listening to the robotic voice relay her message—

Hey, I know this is a big favor to ask, but is there any way you would reconsider pressing charges against my dad? I know he absolutely deserves to be punished for what he's done, but I think he has been.

He's really upset, Weaver, and really sorry. He used his one call to leave a message for me, promising that he was going to get sober.

That's the first time he's ever done that.

It's a big deal. And I think he means it.

If I can get him into a bed at a rehab in the next twenty-four hours, before the withdrawal gets too bad, this might be the chance I've been waiting for my entire life.

283

Maybe he's finally hit rock bottom and is ready to make a real change. If so, I...I might get my dad back, the one I remember from when I was little.

But there's no chance of that happening if he stays in jail waiting to be arraigned or for bail to be set or whatever happens when you're facing assault charges.

She sighs and I brace myself for the rest of the message.

I can see your face right now in my head. I bet your jaw is all clenched and the muscle is bunched up into a ball under your skin.

I reach up, touching the muscle.

It is indeed a tight ball beneath my stubble.

And you're right to have doubts. I have doubts, too. But I also believe in helping people when they ask for it. This is the first time he's actually asked. I don't want to let him down, and you did say you would be supportive of helping pay for treatment for a relative more than rent or food or whatever, so...

Maybe you can see how this makes sense? If so, I would be so grateful. And if not, I understand. It would hurt, but... I would.

Hurt.

She said the magic word.

I can't hurt her. That's why I stood there, doing my best to deflect Leon's beating without fighting back. If you'd asked me ahead of time, I would have sworn I'd never do such a thing.

But in the moment, with Sully on the floor watching it all go down...

I couldn't hurt her father, even though he absolutely deserved it, because I couldn't risk hurting her.

And I won't risk hurting her now. She's been through enough. If I can spare her even a little bit of pain, I'll do it, even though I don't think Leon's going to change. He's too far gone, too set in his ways. It takes one hell of a person to turn their life around in their fifties, and Leon isn't one hell of anything.

Except for one hell of a violent pain in my ass...

Turning onto Main Street, I intend to text Sully back as soon as I swing into my parking spot at the edge of the marina's lot.

But there's someone in my reserved spot—a familiar red Jeep that signals the presence of the last person I want to deal with after the day I've had.

It's Mark, probably here to whine about how unfair his life is, yet again.

But as I park in a free community space a few spots down and slam out of the car, I realize that it's still Saturday, not Sunday. Mark knows I planned on being out of town until Sunday afternoon.

Or, he should. I told Laura, in case she needed me for some reason, and Mark and Laura have always been close. He wants to be like his father, but he depends on his mother to keep his life running smoothly.

But maybe Laura neglected to tell him that I wouldn't be here today. She is genuinely grieving, maybe the only person truly sad my brother is no longer above ground.

I brace for another uncomfortable conversation,

promising myself I'll get rid of Mark as quickly as possible so I can turn my attention to the things that really matter—namely, Sully. I need to text her back about her father, contact the police station to withdraw the charges against Leon, and set a few other things in motion that will hopefully make her life easier. Her shoulder is going to take time to heal. Neither she nor her grandfather—even if he makes it through surgery —are going to be up to lobstering for a while.

I'm thinking of people I know in town who might have extra hands to spare on their boat when I pass the ice cream shack and stop dead.

Mark isn't waiting for me on the dock. No, the gangplank I know I stowed before I left town is down and the yacht is filled with twenty-something kids drinking beer and...pouring it all over the deck.

There are four of them that I can see—two boys and two girls. Mark isn't topside, but I'm sure he's around somewhere. I recognize at least one member of his lobstering crew, and I'm pretty sure he used to date the skinny blond humming to herself as she pulls stuffing from the ripped cushions of the deck furniture. Meanwhile, the large boy with the buzz cut, who works with Mark, has his pocketknife out, carving something in the deck railing.

I watch, my blood simmering toward a boil, as a guy with bright red hair and a sunburned nose take a final swig of his beer before hurling the bottle against the already cracked window of the cockpit.

He snorts with laughter before shouting, "We're going to need more beer, Mark."

The girl next to him, a pale thing in a yellow sweat-shirt with greasy brown pigtails emerging from her orange sock hat giggles and hugs him around the waist. "And music. Something fun. It's too quiet out here."

"That's because I told you we have to be quiet," Mark says, emerging from below deck with another member of his lobstering team, our cousin, Barry, behind him. "So, keep it down, will you? We don't want anyone to hear us and come over to see what's up."

"That won't matter," I say flatly, causing all their heads to swivel my way. Most of them have the sense to look shocked and guilty, but the red-haired kid only smirks and opens another beer.

I smile, imagining how much I'm going to enjoy calling the authorities on him, in particular.

Looks like I'll get to press charges today, after all.

I point to the telephone pole near the edge of the water, still smiling as I say, "I had cameras installed. Everything you've done has been recorded. All I have to do is contact the sheriff's department with the footage."

Greasy Pigtails curses, her already pale face now marble white as she lifts her hands in the air. "I didn't do nothing, sir. I promise. I'm just here with my boyfriend."

"Then maybe you'll only be charged as an acces-sory to aggravated criminal mischief," I say, ambling closer to the boat, my hands sliding into my pockets. "That's the charge for damages over two thousand dollars. You've easily racked up that much from what I can see aboveboard. And who knows what you've done down below." Mark's face blanches, confirming my suspicion that he didn't confine his petty destruction to the deck.

"I looked it up after someone vandalized my car not once, but twice in the past week," I continue, cocking my head. "Are any of you familiar with the penalty for aggravated criminal mischief?"

"Uncle Weaver, please, I—"

"Quiet, Mark, a grown-up is talking," I say, still grinning as I glance from face to stunned, increasingly worried face. "No? None of you? Well, no worries. If convicted, it's up to five years in prison and five thousand dollars in fines. Five *years*." I chuckle. "That's a long time. And I don't think the prosecutor will have any problem getting a conviction with video evidence and all of you caught in the act, do you?"

"Please," the blonde begs, her voice wavering like she's about to cry. "My dad will kill me. Like, maybe for real. He kicked my brother out of the house when he was only seventeen for selling marijuana and that's not even really a crime anymore. I'm so sorry, Mr. Tripp. I promise I'll never do anything like this again."

Ignoring her, I scan the rest of the group. Red doesn't look so smug now. He looks angry.

Good, let him get angry. I don't mind making another enemy.

I already have plenty in this town.

"So," I say, motioning toward the parking lot, "I

suggest you all hurry home and start shopping for lawyers. Good luck and thank you for stopping by."

"We can clean it all up," the blonde sputters, her arms shaking visibly as she motions toward the ruined deck furniture. "I can sew these and I can get beer out of anything. I was in a sorority in college."

"Yeah, we'll clean it up," Greasy Pigtails says, ignoring her boyfriend when he nudges her in the side with his elbow. "We will," she doubles down. "I work at the daycare, Mr. Tripp. If I get in trouble with the cops, even just for being here while bad things happened, they'll fire me. I need that job, sir. Please, it's the only thing I could find where they'd let me bring my son to work with me."

A son, another innocent child, caught up in adult drama. It should make a difference, but maybe I've exhausted my empathy for the day.

Or maybe I'm just sick of this place.

Sick of its petty drama and sad grudges and the way this fucking town does its best to drag us all down to our own personal rock bottoms.

I certainly won't be sticking around to watch my family reach theirs...

And that's it. I've suddenly had it.

I'm done.

Done with Sea Breeze and done with facilitating the Tripps' continued dominance of the fishing trade here. Done with coddling my nephew and done with trying to be the bigger man.

I'd rather burn it all to the ground than be trapped in this cage for another second.

"Then I suggest you find a way to pay for a good lawyer," I tell the girl, not feeling the slightest twinge of conscience when her face falls. If she were mother of the year, she wouldn't be trespassing or destroying property, and she wouldn't be dating the red-headed piece of shit who's currently glaring at me like he'd like to start something.

Let him try.

I won't be pulling any punches this time, and I've had enough medication that I would feel no pain as I pounded his scrawny ass into a wad of pulp on the pier.

"As for you..." I shift my gaze to my nephew. "I suggest you start looking for another job. As of Monday morning, you no longer work on a Tripp lobster boat."

Mark's mouth falls open so wide that one of the seagulls reeling overhead could pop its entire mouth inside to clean the back of his gums.

He sucks in air, gasping like a landed fish as he shakes his head. "No. No, Weaver, please. You can't do that."

"I can do whatever I want," I snap. "I inherited control of the fleet. Which means it's mine to staff, mine to organize, and mine to sell off if I so choose. And I so choose." I stand taller, feeling a weight being lifted from my shoulders as I mentally run through next steps.

My more innocent family members will be punished along with the bad eggs if I do a mass sell-off of the fleet, but I can eliminate their suffering easily enough with a cash settlement from the sale and what's left of Rodger's estate. I don't need or want my brother's money. I'll happily divide it among the people who deserve help, put them on the path to independence, and let the spoiled brats like Mark figure out the future on their own.

He's due for some suffering in his charmed life. It's past time he dealt with the consequences for his bad behavior.

Mark's face is red now, and getting redder by the minute. "You won't really sell, you can't," he says as his band of losers makes their way down the gangplank and scurries past me.

The blonde isn't the only one in tears now. The big guy with the buzz cut and Tripp Lobster sweatshirt also has shining eyes and shame oozing from his every pore.

My conscience tries to rise from the cold depths where I've shoved it, but I remind myself that I was busting my ass at business school at this boy's age, not vandalizing property, and ignore it. Besides, if this is the first infraction for any of them, they shouldn't be punished too harshly. Likely, they'll get off with a fine and a stern warning not to trespass or destroy property again.

"It doesn't make sense," Mark continues, his arm sweeping out to encompass the rest of the docks behind me. "This is what our family has worked generations for. You wouldn't tear that all down for nothing."

"That legacy means nothing to me. It never did." I

291

meet Mark's cold gaze with a colder one. If he's looking for a "who can be a bigger bastard" fight, I'm going to win. I always do. "As I see it, selling is best for everyone involved—a fresh start for our family and the town. And I walk away without any ties to a place, or people, I can no longer stomach."

"You can't do this," Mark says, sweat beading on his forehead. "We won't let you. Mom's already hired a lawyer to contest the will. We'll prove Dad wasn't in his right mind when he wrote it, and get it reversed. Then, everything will be mine, and you'll be fucking sorry you treated me this way."

I huff out a soft laugh, eyes narrowing to slits as Red passes by, Greasy Pigtails sobbing beside him.

He pauses in front of me before shuffling on and, for a moment, he looks vaguely familiar. But then, everyone in this town does. I probably know his mom or uncle or sister. He probably has family ties going back nearly as far as ours do. Sea Breeze isn't a place that lets people fly off to chase their dreams. It's hungrier than that. It will hold you here and suck you dry if you let it.

I won't let it pull me back in, and I won't let it have Sully. Not if I can do anything to prevent it.

Which gives me an idea...

When Red steps off the dock, tugged along by his less confrontational girlfriend, I shift my attention back to my nephew. "Rodger set up the trust several years ago. There were no signs of his being in mental decline at that time or at any time after. You don't have a case." I pause. "You do, however, have one chance to get back in my good graces and earn a share of the profits once I've sold the fleet. If you decide this life is still what you want, it should be enough for you to start your own lobstering operation. If not, you can move on and start over somewhere else, somewhere you'll be forced to stand on your own two feet instead of on the shoulders of the crooked men who came before you."

Mark crosses his arms tight over his chest, his cheeks still bright red with anger. But I can see the wheels turning behind his eyes. My nephew is spoiled and entitled, but he isn't stupid. He knows I'm right about the strength of his case and he knows I rarely change my mind once it's made up.

He clears his throat, swallows, and finally asks, "What do you want me to do? Beg?"

I shake my head. "No, I have no interest in debasing you further than you've already debased yourself. I want you to track down and hire an excellent three-man replacement crew for Gertrude Sullivan's boat for the rest of the season. Her grandfather is in the hospital after a heart attack. They don't know if he's going to make it, but if he does, he won't be able to work for a very long time, if ever. And Gertrude was injured today and will also be unable to work for at least a month, maybe more."

Mark's expression softens. "Is she okay? What happened?"

"She's fine and that's irrelevant. Can you take care of that? If you can, and if you manage to have a trust-worthy crew in place by Monday, you'll be on my list of family members slated to receive a portion of your father's estate."

His brow furrows again. "Yeah, I can do it. But we'll have to pay them well to make up for them leaving their own operations."

"Pay them whatever they want," I say. "I'll cover the salaries. I just want it done. And make sure they're able to stay on through the end of December or whenever the haul starts tapering off for the season."

"Okay." Mark squeezes his arms tighter as he nods toward the entrance to the living quarters. "Do you want me to clean this up first? Before I leave?"

"No,' I say. "The Sullivan boat is a higher priority. You can hire one of the housekeeping services in town to take care of this tomorrow morning, assuming the authorities are finished with their documentation of the scene by then. I'll let you know, and I'll stay somewhere else tonight." I turn to go, but glance back at my pink-cheeked nephew. "You can pay for the cleaning service. Pay them well, and add a tip for the deep cleaning they'll need to do on the deck and whatever else you tried to ruin. If I hear you've short-changed them, our deal is null and void. From here on out, you will be on your best behavior with everyone in town, do I make myself clear?"

His jaw clenches, but he nods. "Yes. Though I'm not sure why you care."

I arch a brow. "Why I care about what?"

"About the Sullivans or the housekeeping crew or anyone else in town. You hate Sea Breeze. You always have. We all know it."

I ponder his words for a beat. "Yes, I do. But maybe I would hate it less if my family wasn't such a big part of the problem."

"Don't you think you're part of the problem, too?" he asks. "Especially if you press charges against my friends? They were only doing what I asked them to do. They never would have stepped foot on this boat without me."

"And the car?" I ask, curious. "Did you ask them to vandalize my vehicle, too?"

He has the grace to look ashamed of himself as he drops his gaze to the water between us. "I was just...so angry. It was all so unfair."

"Was it? Or was it just not what you wanted?" Before he can answer, I add, "Either way, the conse-quences of your actions aren't my problem. They're something you'll have to live with and make amends for. You could start with apologizing to your friends and offering to pay for their legal representation as well as you own."

His eyes widen again. "My own? But I thought—"

"You thought wrong." He pulls in a breath, but before he can speak, I turn away. I stride swiftly toward my car, ignoring the—"Weaver, please!"—shouted at my back as I go.

"By Monday morning," I call over my shoulder. "Have the Sullivan situation taken care of or you won't see a penny, Mark."

He doesn't say anything to that. It seems my nephew has finally realized that the time for begging and bargaining has passed. We've entered the last chance, "actions speak louder than words" phase of our relationship.

I honestly hope he'll do the right thing and take care of his friends, but that isn't my primary concern. Taking care of Sully and getting out of this town—preferably with her in a seat beside me on the plane—are all that matters to me now.

As soon as I'm back in my car, out of the cold sea wind, I send her a voice memo, "I got your message. I'll call to have the charges against your father reversed now. And if you want to give me the names of the rehabs you've vetted, I can call to reserve a space for Leon and arrange to have him transported straight from the jail to the facility. I hope the fact that you're advocating for him means that you've been discharged with a clean bill of health. I'm fine. Nothing but some bruises and swelling. I was given a painkiller and sent on my way. Please let me know how you are as soon as possible." I sigh. "I hope the surgery is going well for your grandfather. I'm going to get a hotel room close to the hospital. When you're ready for a break, let me know, and I can arrange for a car to take you there, as well. I want you to have a safe place to rest, while still being close to your family." I hesitate for a beat before adding, "They're lucky to have you. I hope they know that. Talk soon. I love you."

I do. I love this woman. I adore her, worship her, would slaughter hordes of barbarians for her.

But can I save her from the grips of a dysfunctional family system?

I don't know.

I would like to think so, but I'm old enough to know that in the end, we all have to save ourselves. Friends, therapists and lovers can help us out along the way, but we have to do the hard work on our own. We have to want to become a better, more functional person. We have to believe we deserve to see our dreams come true.

I don't know if Sully's there yet. I have no doubt she will be someday, but that day might not be any day soon, and I can't wait for her to come around to seeing how much she matters. It would kill me, to watch her family use and abuse and take her for granted, sucking up her youth and vitality like vampires who feel entitled to her blood because they share the same DNA.

I set my cell in the cupholder, hoping to hear from her, but I'm not really surprised when I emerge from the sheriff's station ninety minutes later to find no messages on my phone.

I check into a hotel across the highway from the hospital, but come six o'clock, when I order dinner delivered, there's still no response from Sully. I consider messaging her again, but decide the ball is in her court.

I want her to choose me more than I want to get on the next plane to New York, but I don't want to bully her into it. I want her here with me because it's where she wants to be, because she doesn't want to think about a future without me in it.

I certainly can't imagine one without her...

Or, I can, I guess, but it isn't pretty.

That bleak return to my old lonely life—made even

lonelier now that I know how incredible it feels to love one amazing woman—plays out behind my closed eyes as I try to sleep.

Call me, Sully. Just call, text, something, I beg, willing her to hear my mental plea across the highway and pick up her phone.

But she doesn't and eventually, I fall asleep, haunted by dreams of watching Sully guiding a lobster boat out to sea, never to return.

chapter **24**

THE AFTERNOON PASSES IN A BLUR.

I've just been discharged from the ER with assurances that my internal organs are in one piece and instructions to wear my sling for four to seven days and to avoid heavy lifting for twelve weeks—catastrophic news I barely have time to absorb when Aunt Cathy starts blowing up my phone.

Gramps is out of surgery and doing well, so well they might let a few of us in to see him in the next hour!

I hustle to the hospital gift shop as fast as my sore body will allow, possessed by the need to have something tangible to give to my grandfather to show him how much I need him to stick around. I settle on a stuffed lobster wearing a t-shirt that says "You're Claw-some" and head for the elevator.

As I'm stepping off, Weaver's voice message pops through. I listen to it, relief flooding my body, but before I can respond, Cathy is at my elbow, talking a mile a minute.

"Your dad just called!" she says, beaming. "The charges were dropped. Weaver must have changed his mind, thank God. Leon asked me to come pick him up. Can you keep an eye on everyone here while I go? Murray and Steven need to eat something and Henna needs someone to watch the kids while she runs Jennifer's baby present over to the maternity ward. Poor Jen. The baby kind of took a back seat in all the worry over your grandad."

She heaves a heavy sigh, laughing as she pats my good arm and leads me toward the waiting room our clan has taken over. "But all's well that ends well. The baby wasn't born until one a.m. Did I tell you that? So, Aunt Sue is happy. And Jen had a boy so David is happy, too."

I roll my eyes. "Whatever, David. How is it okay to say shit like that anymore? He should just be happy to have a healthy baby."

Cathy shoos my concerns away with a flick of her heavily-ringed hand. "Oh, come on. It's normal for a man to want a son."

"Is it? Why?" I grumble. "Because they'll 'have more in common?' What if his son turns out to be an artist who doesn't want to set foot on a boat? Or hates football? Or likes to dress up in vintage ball gowns and kiss boys? What's he going to think then?"

Cathy stops a few feet from the waiting room, turning to shoot me a concerned look as she hisses, "What's eating you all of a sudden? We've got nothing but good news here. Dad's out of surgery and doing well, your father's not going to jail, and Jen has a healthy baby. All reasons to be happy and grateful."

"Where does Dad want you to take him after you pick him up?' I ask, ignoring her questions. "Because he left me a message a couple hours ago about wanting to go to rehab. I can call around now, try to find him a bed before you go get him. That way he can go straight to the facility before he has a chance to get cold feet."

"Oh, I don't know," Cathy says, plucking at the collar of her cowl neck sweater. "He didn't say. I was assuming he wanted a ride home or...a ride here, if that was okay with you."

I snort. "You've got to be kidding me."

She lifts her hands in mock surrender, even as she lobs her next volley. "I don't know, Gertie. I don't know what you're thinking lately. First, you're getting involved with the man who ruined your family. Now, you don't want your dad around when—"

"He sent me to the ER, Cathy!" I say in a voice too loud for her liking. She shushes me, trying to drag me farther from the waiting room by my good arm. But I pull away, adding in an only slightly softer voice, "I'm in a sling for a week because of him, and I'll be out of work for at least twelve weeks. Maybe more if my shoulder doesn't heal as quickly as expected since I have a pre-existing issue in that joint. Unless Dad's planning to get on the boat and do mine and Gramp's work for us while we're out of commission, I don't see that he has anything worthwhile to offer this family. Certainly nothing better than going to rehab."

Cathy's lips turn down hard at the edges. "That's not what family's about. It's not about what you can take, it's about what you give."

"That's exactly what I'm saying!" An outraged laugh bursts from my chest. "All he's done is take, Cathy. And take and take and take. Even if he wanted to take over on the boat for us, he couldn't. He's too sick. The best thing he can do for everyone is go to rehab. And the best thing you can do for him is help him get there." I tug my cell from my purse. "I'll start calling places now. Text Dad and tell him you'll touch base about picking him up in a little while. And tell him that he'll be going straight to treatment, do not pass go or stop at the pub for a farewell whiskey."

Her lips press into a puckered line. "I don't know if he's going to go for it, Gertie. He wanted to see Dad. He loves your grandfather as much as you do, you know."

"I doubt it," I say, my patience way thinner than normal. Whether it's the pain in my abdomen and shoulder or Weaver's outsider's perspective making me see the dysfunction of my family in a new light, I can't say. I only know that I don't hesitate before I add, "Love is about showing up for people, and he hasn't shown up for me or Gramps in a long time. But we've shown up for him, and I'm ready to show up again by paying for his treatment from my savings. Tell him that." I start to walk away, only to turn back at the last minute and add, "And tell him that if he doesn't go, if he didn't mean what he said in the message that he left for me, then he can forget he has a daughter."

Cathy's jaw drops, but I don't stick around to see

what she's going to stay when she stops sputtering. I pull up the website for the rehab center with income-adjusted admission and place my call, moving toward the railing overlooking the atrium for privacy.

Twenty minutes later, I have a bed reserved for Dad at the second place I called, which thankfully takes Dad's insurance. It won't pay for everything—we'll still have to pay the three-thousand-dollar deductible —but they have room to take him tonight and a successful six-week program that has solid online reviews.

I tell them I'll call back when I know Dad's esti-mated arrival time and head into the waiting room to rejoin the family.

Cathy's sitting in the corner, looking like the cat who got sprayed with water and denied her daily dose of catnip, but when I tell her I found a bed for Dad, she nods.

"Okay," she says, waving her phone in the air. "He said he's ready to go as soon as I come get him, but I know he'd like to see his dad first. So, we'll just swing by here on our way and—"

"No, he should go straight to the center," I cut in, my gut assuring me this is the best way. The less time Dad has to worry about what rehab is going to be like before he's there, the better.

And selfishly, I don't want to see him again right now. I'm in too much pain—emotional and physical— and I'm not sure I would be able to hold back all the angry things I want to say. That wouldn't be good for me or Dad, and sometimes, it's okay to be selfish.

It isn't even "selfish," I realize as I stand firm throughout Aunt Cathy's second attempt to wheedle me into changing my mind. This is self-preservation. My father has probably sobered up by now, but there's no doubt he's still exhausted from his drunken run-in with the law and the fight with Weaver. Not to mention craving a drink. He's in no place to handle a stressful situation like seeing his father fresh out of surgery.

Besides, as I remind Cathy, "He was kicked out of the hospital. They're not going to let him walk back in. Not if they see him coming, and I don't see how they could miss him in a blood-spattered shirt." Cathy's lips part, and I quickly add, "Don't say you can take him home to change or buy him a shirt or whatever you were going to say. He's going to rehab. That's it. If you don't want to take him, I can order a car service."

Weaver offered to arrange for the service, but I don't feel right asking him to help any more than he has already.

He's already done enough for the man who assaulted him by giving him a chance to clean up his act. From now on, I intend to do my damnedest to make sure my family drama doesn't touch Weaver in any way. He's been so understanding and wonderful, but I know everyone has a limit to how much crazy they'll tolerate from their significant other's family, and I don't want to push Weaver's.

Because hearing him say "I love you" at the end of his message?

It was by far the best thing to happen to me today.

Even in the midst of all the insanity and pain and disappointment and fear for Gramps, those three words made me feel like I was sixteen again and Henry Chandler just asked me to the prom after the first beach volleyball game of the summer.

It also made me feel like a grown ass woman for the first time in my life.

I've been "grown" for a while now, but working with family means I'm still treated like a kid most of the time. To Gramps, I'll always be that ratty haired little girl he brought home after her parents abandoned her. As far as he's concerned, all my problems can be solved by ordering pizza and letting me watch cartoons, and it's inappropriate to go any deeper than saying "your dad tries" when discussing the failures of the man who helped bring me into this world.

But it's high time we had a real talk and decided how to move forward with Dad. Things need to change. If rehab works and Dad's able to start working again—amazing. If not, we have to deal with the reality that maybe we aren't doing what's best for him by continuing to make it so easy for him to flush his life down the toilet.

"All right, fine," Cathy says, shaking her head as she lifts both hands in surrender. "I'll take him straight there. But can I at least grab him some fast food on the way? I'm sure he's starving after spending the day in the drunk tank."

"Sure," I say. "That would be nice, and I'm sure he'd appreciate it." I nod toward her cell. "Why don't you tell him you'll be there in thirty minutes? And I'll call the center and tell them to expect you in about an hour. I'll send you a link to the location. It's only about twenty minutes outside of Bangor, between here and Sea Breeze."

"All right, and you'll take care of everything here?" Cathy asks, glancing around at the rest of the family, most of whom are pretending to be on their phones.

In reality, of course, they're shamelessly eavesdropping, a fact Uncle Murray proves by saying, "Go take care of Leon, we can take care of ourselves, Cathy. We aren't retarded."

"You shouldn't say that, Dad," my cousin Steven pipes up. "It's insensitive to disabled people."

Uncle Murray grunts as he makes a show of looking around the room. "So? There aren't any retarded people around to hear me. That's what I was just saying, that we *aren't* retarded."

Cousin Steven rolls his eyes to the ceiling, muttering beneath his breath in what I suspect is a prayer for strength.

"Or maybe I got it wrong," Murray continues. "You always were a little soft in the head. That's probably why you're so concerned about what words people are using, while I'm the one actually down at the rec center volunteering to teach the retards how to fish."

"Oh, my fucking God," Steven mutters, rising from his chair and making a beeline my way.

"Don't take the Lord's name in vain," Great Aunt Sue croaks from the sofa where she seemed to be asleep until a hot second ago.

"You want to get out of here? Take a walk or something?" Steven asks.

"Or you two can be the first to see Grandpa," his brother, Seth, says from the doorway, a big grin on his face. "The nurse said he's ready for his first visitors and we can go in two at a time until he gets tired."

"Yes, please," I say, my heart leaping as I grab the bag with my gift in it from a nearby table. "I'm dying to see him."

The rest of the family calls out for us to tell Gramps how happy we are that's he's okay—just in case he's too tired to see all of us in person—and Steven and I head toward the entrance to the intensive care unit.

As soon as we're clear of the waiting room, Steven asks in a soft voice, "So what's up with you and Weaver Tripp?"

I cut a surprised glance his way.

"Cathy was saying something to Aunt Sue about March women having a weakness for Weaver Tripp," he adds, answering my unspoken question.

"March" women. So, I'm a Sullivan when they need me to toe the line for the clan, but a "March," my mother's maiden name, as soon as I do something Cathy isn't happy about?

Good to know.

Meanwhile, I haven't talked to my mother in well over a decade and never met the March side of my family, aside from sweet Grammy March who passed when I was in kindergarten.

"Cathy's a menace," I mutter.

"Oh, for sure," Steven agrees, "but she's not wrong about Weaver Tripp. He's dangerous."

I sigh. "He's not, Steven. I...I know him. He's actually a pretty great guy."

Steven grunts. "Yeah? Tell that to Chris. Cops just showed up at his place to arrest him for aggravated criminal mischief for getting on Weaver's bad side."

I grind to a halt several feet from the intensive care unit, causing two nurses behind us to trip over themselves to avoid stepping on the backs of our feet.

"Sorry," I apologize to them as I grab Steven's shirt and tug him toward the railing overlooking the atrium. "So sorry."

Once they've moved on with irritated assurances that "it's fine," I turn back to my cousin and hiss, "What? How is that even possible? What did he do?"

"He didn't do anything," Steven says, running a hand over his close-cropped brown hair. "Mark invited him to party on the yacht, so he and Stella went. But apparently, Mark's not allowed to use the yacht anymore. I guess Weaver got it in the will after Mark's dad died or whatever."

"Yeah, he did," I say. "So?"

"So, Weaver showed up, saw them drinking beers on his fancy boat, and flipped out. He called the police and had everyone arrested. And then Chris called me to beg for a loan to pay for his lawyer." Steven's upper lip curls. "Though I'm sure Mark isn't shopping for lawyers. That little shit always wiggles his way out of trouble. I told Chris not to hang out with him, but he wouldn't listen."

"Shit," I say, remembering the camera I encouraged Weaver to set up. With video evidence, he won't have any trouble proving my cousin and his friends were trespassing.

But is that really their fault if they were just following Mark's lead? If he told them that it was fine? After all, we've all hung out on the yacht with Mark at one point or another. He wasn't supposed to use it when it belonged to his father, either, but he always did, and no one ever got arrested.

"Yeah," Steven agrees. "And Stella is freaking out that they're coming to slap the cuffs on her next, and she'll have to turn the kid over to foster care for a while, or something. Her mom's out of town. She left Gavin with a sitter this afternoon so she could go out, but the sitter's only sixteen and has to get home to her own family. She can't stay at Stella's place just in case Stella gets arrested."

I curse again. This is a nightmare.

Chris is far from my favorite cousin—he's kind of an asshole, to be honest, and not the guy I'd choose to date if I were a single mom with a two-year-old—but that's neither here nor there. These are vulnerable people with so much to lose, and I for one don't think Stella should lose her child or Chris his clean criminal record over trespassing on some rich guy's yacht.

Some rich guy...

God. Weaver went from my brave, thoughtful, sexy boyfriend, to "some rich guy" in the blink of an eye.

Maybe I'm not as cool with our class differences as I've convinced myself I am in the past few days.

"There has to be some explanation," I say, tugging at my earlobe as I try to think this through. "Something we're not understanding right now. Weaver wouldn't do this just because people were trespassing. And he wouldn't punish innocent guests and let Mark walk away. That's not the kind of person he is. He honestly isn't a big fan of his nephew."

Steven arches a dubious brow. "Okay, whatever you say."

"I do say," I double down, with only a slight flutter of anxiety in my stomach. I know Weaver, and I know he wouldn't do this...don't I?

"Then text him." Steven crosses his arms.

"What?"

"Text Mark," he says, nodding toward the purse slung over my good shoulder. "Ask him if he's in jail."

I exhale. "I'd rather not. We're not on good terms right now."

Steven frowns. "Why?"

"Reasons," I say vaguely, but he's right. Texting Mark is probably the quickest way to get to the bottom of this. But it will have to wait. Gramps is expecting us, and I don't want to keep him waiting. I start toward the ICU doors again, "Come on, we should see Gramps. We can figure this out after."

Steven catches my elbow gently between his fingers, and I turn back to see an unusually worried expression on my cousin's face. Steven isn't usually much for feelings—positive or negative. He's the chill, steady sort, a voice of reason amongst the chaos of our loud, emotional family.

So, his warning hits differently as he says, "Just be careful, okay? With Weaver? There are things you don't know, Gert, about what went down between him and your mom when we were little. The Olds tried to keep it a secret from all the kids, but you know me. I'm always listening, and Cathy's always talking, and I spent almost every day after school at her house until my dad finally trusted me to stay home on my own. I heard things."

I want to ask him what he heard, but I also want to turn and walk away. I want to head down the elevator, walk out of the hospital, and keep walking until I'm at whatever hotel room Weaver found for tonight. Then, I want to rest my head on his chest, feel his arms wrap around me, and forget everything else but us.

There's no ugly past, no family feuds, no beatings or arrests or criminal charges, there's just the man I love and how perfect I feel in his arms.

Perfectly happy.

Perfectly cared for.

And maybe, perfectly lied to...

I owe it to myself and everyone I love to find out.

But first, I owe it to the man who raised me to tell him how much I treasure him.

I nod, my jaw tight. "Let's grab a coffee after we see Gramps, and you can tell me whatever you've heard."

Steven looks uncertain for a moment, but nods. "Okay. But you're not going to like it."

"That's okay," I say, a humorless smile twisting my lips. "I don't like anything that's happened today.

Might as well add one more topping to the shit sundae."

Steven grunts out a soft laugh. "Yeah. That sounds about right." He rests a hand between my shoulder blades as we walk to the ICU. "Wouldn't be a Sullivan family weekend if there wasn't drama."

He's right, but this is a *lot* of drama, even for our family.

Still, I do my best to put it out of my head as we enter Gramp's room. He looks so small in his bed, despite his ample belly. So small, and so frail. All I want to do is hug him and tell him how glad I am he's alive, but the tubes hooked up to his chest and my sling make that difficult.

I end up resting my forehead on his for a moment and whispering, "Don't leave me, old man. I still need you."

He smiles as I pull away. "Of course, you do." His gaze is tired, but clear as it shifts between Steven and me. "Glad they sent you two. I don't have the patience for the rest of those clowns today. Don't let Cathy in here. If I have to hear her say 'I told you so' about all the butter I put on my lobster roll, I might have another heart attack."

We laugh and promise to keep Cathy away, then move on to discussing the surgery and next steps. Gramps is eager to be home, but they'll be keeping him for five or six days, until they see how he's healing up. Then, he'll need to take it easy for a couple months as he builds his strength.

"We'll need to get help for you on the boat until I'm

back on my feet," Gramps says, scowling as he eyes my sling, seeming to notice it for the first time. "What happened to you?"

"Long story," I say, forcing a smile. "But I'll be out for a while, too. But don't worry, I already have some thoughts on who to hire to fill in for the rest of the season."

"Not the Cooper kid," Gramps says, scowling harder. "He's strong, but he's an idiot, and I don't want an idiot wrecking my boat."

"Not the Cooper kid," I agree, but hold up a hand when he starts running through a list of other people he doesn't trust with his baby. "We'll worry about it later, okay? We have time. Our profits are up over last year. We can afford to take a few days off while I figure this out. And *I* will figure it out," I emphasize. "All you need to worry about it resting up and getting better. I've got this."

And I do.

I can handle staffing the boat and figuring out how we're going to pay a crew and still eek out enough profit to stay ahead of our bills.

What I'm not sure I can handle is the truth.

What if what Steven tells me changes everything? What if it burns what I've built with Weaver to the ground?

Or...what I thought I'd built.

Could be this love is built on shifting sand.

Guess I'm about to find out.

chapter 25

I DON'T HEAR from Sully Saturday night.

I wake up several times, checking my phone for texts I might have missed, but there's nothing.

Sunday morning passes in continued silence, until I begin to worry that something's happened. Maybe her grandfather didn't make it through surgery.

Or maybe...*she's* recovering from surgery and too out of it to use her cell.

Fuck.

I can't believe I didn't think of that.

Yes, she was fine to text me yesterday, but that doesn't mean her injuries didn't take a turn for the worse sometime in the afternoon or early evening. The woman I love could be in a hospital bed right now, and I've been sitting here with my thumb up my ass because I was afraid of pushing her to pick me.

But fuck...I want her to pick me.

She'd be better off picking me. The Sullivans are an anchor, wrapped around her ankle, dragging her down, a fact proven yet again yesterday, when I learned the redheaded asshole from the boat is also a Sullivan.

A Sullivan with an anger management problem, who punched the deputy who showed up to question him about the incident on the yacht and ended up getting himself arrested...

I have to get Sully out of here, away from Sea Breeze and her criminal family.

She's so much better than this. She's an artist with a gifted eye, an incredibly hard worker, and one of the kindest people I've ever known. She deserves the chance to rise in the world, to make her dreams come true without this tangled web of insanity shutting her down at every turn.

With that in mind, I call the hospital to ask if a Gertrude Sullivan has been admitted. The woman says, no, and I sag with relief. When I ask about John Sullivan, she's able to tell me that he's in the ICU and in stable condition.

I thank her and end the call, my stomach in a slow, dread-filled free fall.

I'm relieved that Sully's not lying in a hospital bed and that her grandfather is okay—obviously—but then, why hasn't she called? Why did I sleep in that big king bed alone last night?

"Track her down and find out," I mutter to myself, disgusted by my own lack of action.

This isn't who I am. I don't sit around, waiting for other people to solve my problems. I go straight to the source and address any issues head-on. Sadly, Sully and I haven't reached the point in our relationship where we've enabled location tracking for each other, but there are relatively few places she could be.

And one of them is right across the highway from my hotel.

I pack my things and head for the elevator, checking out on my way through the lobby. At the hospital, I make my way directly to the ICU, where I know her grandfather is recovering, but it's still a little while before visiting hours begin. The nurse on duty at the check-in desk encourages me to get a cup of coffee and come back at nine.

After leaving the ICU, I check the various waiting rooms scattered throughout the floor, but there isn't a Sullivan to be found. I head to the chapel and yoga room next—also Sullivan-free and mostly empty at this early hour—before hitting the cafeteria. I grab that cup of coffee the nurse suggested and wander around the space, finally spotting a few familiar faces in the corner.

I linger beside the coffee station, taking my time adding cream to the burnt-smelling brew as I try to put names with faces. One of the women is definitely Sully's aunt Cathy, from yesterday, but the older woman and the two middle aged men with her are unfamiliar to me.

The most important detail, of course, is that *my* Sullivan is nowhere to be seen.

The knowledge sends another wave of apprehension through my core.

If she didn't stay at the hospital last night, why

didn't she join me at the hotel across the street? Surely, she knows she can call or text me any time of day or night, especially in a crisis.

Second-guessing the wisdom of putting coffee on my irritable, empty stomach, I dump it in a bin and head back to the car. Aiming the Subaru toward Sea Breeze, I consider calling Sully to ask if she's at home, and if I can swing by to talk, but that feels wrong.

She hasn't responded to my last message, why would she reply to another one? She's clearly avoiding me, and the only way to put an end to that is to track her down and insist she tell me what's bothering her.

She's probably angry that you pressed charges against her cousin, right after she begged you not to press charges against her father, the inner voice says, but I'm not buying it.

I pressed charges against *everyone* on that boat, including my own nephew. And Sully isn't the kind to condone destruction of property, especially when that property is a seafaring vessel. She's a lobster woman. Her boat is her livelihood. A yacht isn't the same thing, of course, but that yacht is my home in Sea Breeze. I can't imagine her being okay with fully grown adults boarding my boat without permission and trashing it.

There has to be something else, something I haven't thought of yet.

My stomach growls, as if suggesting perhaps the reason I can't think straight is that I've barely eaten in the past day. I managed to force down some grilled chicken and rice last night for dinner, but the room service was bland and overcooked, and I was too worried about Sully to have much of an appetite.

But this morning, my stomach insists on sustenance, no matter how unsettled I am by my girlfriend's disappearance.

Girlfriend...

I hope she hasn't decided to end things. I know she must be worried about how she's going to help care for her grandfather from New York, but that's one thing about money—it can buy a lot of time, help, and freedom. I can get Gramps a full-time, live-in nurse. And Sully and I can fly back every other weekend to spend time with him.

I'm open to visiting Sea Breeze on a regular basis, but we can't stay here. It isn't good for either of us.

I'm reminded of how "not good" things have been as I pass the boat on my way into town and see a Happy Housekeepers van parked in the lot. Looks like Mark is making good on his promise to have cleaners in to take care of things. Hopefully, he's taken care of hiring temporary staff for the Sullivan boat, as well. The sooner all those ducks are in a row, the sooner we can get out of here.

Fuck being here for the official reading of the will. I'll attend via Zoom from my apartment in New York and deal with the rest of the estate issues remotely or during shorter, weekend trips to Maine.

I should have known better than to think I could make it through three to four weeks in this place. I wouldn't stay three or four more minutes if Sully weren't here.

As if summoned by my thoughts, my focus is suddenly drawn to a wavy blond ponytail bouncing down the street. I tap the brakes, waiting until the ponytail emerges from behind a pickup truck, to affirm that is indeed, Sully.

My heart squeezes tight.

She looks exhausted, with dark circles under her eyes and no makeup on. She also looks...sad.

Or angry?

I can't read her expression before she reaches the door to the Sweet Pussy Café and swings inside.

But that's okay. I know where she is now. I'll find out what she's feeling for myself.

I pull into a parking space farther down the block and start back toward the café, skin buzzing with an unfamiliar sensation I can't place. About ten feet from the entrance, I realize it's anxiety, and exhale a soft huff of laughter.

If only my work colleagues could see me now: Weaver Tripp, the Ice King of Wall Street with sweating palms and a racing pulse. I'm famous for keeping a cool head, even when protestors set fire to the elevator shaft in our building and we had to evacuate down twenty-six flights of stairs.

But then, I've never had this much to lose.

As I push through the door, my heart slamming against my ribs, I'm struck by the realization that work isn't as important to me as I've always thought it was. Neither is status or reputation or all the beautiful things I've accumulated after years of professional success. They're all nothing compared to her, the most beautiful person I've ever known.

Even in a pair of gray sweats and a baggy white sweater, with one arm in a sling and her hair pulled back, she's stunning. I step into the cinnamon and butter scented air and even though the café is hopping this Sunday morning, all I can see is her.

She's seated at the small blue couch in the cat-friendly part of the café, a paper coffee cup clutched in her good hand and a fat gray cat curled up against her with a paw on her thigh, as if to tell her that everything will be okay. She's sad now, but she won't be sad forever.

She won't be sad for another ten minutes if I have anything to say about it, cat, I think as I stride across the room.

Almost instantly, Sully looks up from the carpet, the sadness on her face morphing into a mixture of anger and betrayal that slows my steps.

I lift my hands at my sides, but before I can speak, she sets her coffee down on the table in front of her and jabs a finger at my face. "Don't. Go away. Just...go away. I can't deal with you right now. I have enough on my plate."

I spread my fingers wide. "You don't have to deal with me. I'm perfectly capable of dealing with myself, but we do need to talk."

She shakes her head, rage burning in her eyes even as they begin to shine. "No, we don't. I need caffeine in my system, and then I need to get back to the hospital to see Gramps before morning visitor hours are over. That's all I need to do right now."

"I'll drive you," I offer. "We can talk on the way."

She exhales a sharp breath. "Are you hard of hearing? I said I don't want to talk to you right now. Honestly, I'd be good with never talking to you again."

"Why?" I ask, my own temper smoldering to life. "What on earth have I done except do my best to support you? You could have at least texted to let me know you were okay and wouldn't be joining me at the hotel."

"Sorry, I was too busy learning you put my cousin in jail for trespassing on your boat, even though Mark was the one who invited him on board."

My brows shoot up and hope whispers through my blood, cooling my anger. "Is that what he told you? That isn't what happened, Sully. I arrived to find your cousin and several other people pouring beer over everything, carving up the deck, and ripping open the furniture. I didn't go below, but the sheriff's deputy who came to the scene last night, documented extensive damage to the furniture down there, as well. They did tens of thousands of dollars' worth of damage."

She blinks, her gaze darting over my shoulder to where I'm sure the rest of the café is eavesdropping on our conversation, before she whispers, "I didn't know that."

"Well, that's what happened."

A frown claws into her forehead again. "But that still doesn't excuse having Chris arrested and no one else. That's not fair."

"I didn't have Chris arrested. A deputy went to question him and he assaulted an officer of the law. That's why he ended up in jail."

"It's true," a voice calls out from the other side of the café. "My brother's the one he punched. Dumb move. Kid should've known better."

"Oh," Sully mutters. "That's...not what I heard."

"And I'm pressing charges against everyone who was on board," I continue, grateful that at least a few people in town seem to be willing to back me up when it comes to speaking the truth. "And that includes my nephew. I'm not in the business of sparing idiots' consequences, even if I happen to be related to them."

She nibbles at her bottom lip, looking conflicted, but the righteous indignation is gone.

In hopes of further easing her mind, I ask, "Can we go somewhere private to finish this, please? I haven't looked behind me yet, but we're obviously causing a scene."

"Huge scene," Sully's friend, Elaina, says from behind the counter, her voice cheery. "But please feel free to stay We haven't had a show this good in a long time. The cats are cute, but the gossip isn't nearly as juicy."

Sully sighs as she pushes to her feet. "Can we go upstairs to your place?"

"Sure," Elaina chirps. "Just be sure to yell loud enough that we can hear everything, please. I'll turn down the music so we don't miss any of the good stuff."

Sully rolls her eyes before starting toward a stairwell marked with a "Do Not Enter" sign. She steps easily over the low rope blocking the door and starts up the stairs, not pausing to see if I'm behind her.

But, of course, I am.

I'm going to chase after her as long as it takes to prove that I'm never going to hurt her or betray her. I'm loyal to the fucking marrow, unlike the liars in her family.

It makes me hope Chris spends as much time as possible in jail. He must have been the one to tell her the false story of what happened yesterday.

God knows what else he said, but hopefully I can set that record straight as easily as I did the first one.

And hopefully Sully and I will be leaving here together.

Truly together, in a way that no bullshit story will ever be able to tear apart.

chapter 26

THERE'S no good way to start a conversation like this.

That's why I'd planned on *never having* this conversation.

But Steven was wrong about what went down with Chris.

Maybe he's wrong about this, too, though I have no idea how I'll ever find out for certain. Closed adoptions are private things, and I can't imagine my mother would have done anything but a closed adoption. She wouldn't have wanted anyone to know that she was dumping yet another unwanted kid on her way to her shiny new life.

And Weaver could always just lie, the way he did the first time.

I spin to face him across Elaina's large open living room, but he's already closing the distance between us and dragging me into his arms.

His mouth covers mine, crushing my lips with a

kiss that steals my breath. And even as I tell myself to push him away, I find my good arm twining around his neck, clinging to him as he grips my ass tight and our tongues stroke and spar.

The chemistry between us is just too intense, and I've been craving his touch since the last time he laid his hands on me.

And a part of me knows this might be the last time. Once we talk, we might never be able to touch again. There are things not even *I* can forgive, breeches of trust that there are no coming back from.

But the weak thing that I am, I need him. At least one more time.

His fingers drive into my hair, sending my ponytail holder flying as he makes a fist there. Then his lips are at my neck, his teeth dragging over the sensitive skin as he whispers, "You're mine. This is where you belong. With me. Always."

I shiver, knowing it's true, but knowing it might also be impossible.

But that doesn't stop me from dropping my sling to the floor and helping him ease off my sweater and the camisole beneath. And then he's guiding me to the floor, and his mouth is on my nipples, and I'm begging him never to stop touching, never to leave me.

"Never," he promises, ripping my sweatpants down my legs with one hand as he continues to torture my electrified skin with his mouth.

"That's my girl," he says, groaning as he slides his hand down the front of my panties. "So wet for me. I love feeling you soaked and ready for me to fuck you, baby. I love it so fucking much."

I whimper, lifting my hips to welcome the invasion of his thick fingers driving inside me. He hasn't even touched my clit yet, but I'm already so close it feels like I'm being swept up in a tornado, carried higher and higher into a churning funnel cloud of desire.

And just like with an actual tornado, there's a serious chance I won't survive giving myself to this man again.

He's a danger to my family and possibly the most gifted liar I've ever met.

"I love you, Sully," he says, shoving his own pants and boxer briefs down far enough to bare his erection. I feel his cock feverish against my thigh and fresh heat rushes between my legs. "I'm always going to love you."

Except that.

That isn't a lie.

That's the truth. I can hear it in his voice, feel it in the way his hand trembles as it smooths down the back of my thigh.

Before I can respond, he shoves my knee up toward my ribs and then he's inside me, hot and bare, making me gasp as he fills me. I moan at the hint of pain that swiftly transforms to pleasure as he rides me hard, staking his claim in a way he never has before.

This man has spanked me and restrained me and whispered filthy, forbidden things into my ear, but he's never taken me like this.

Like he can't get close enough...

331

Like he's terrified that this will be the last time, too.

"Mine, you're mine," he rasps as he captures my uninjured wrist, pinning it to the hard floor above my head. "You're mine, and I'm yours. Can't you feel it? This is right, *this* is what we should be fighting for."

I arch my back, straining against his hold as much as my injured shoulder will allow, knowing he won't let me escape. He'll bruise me first, because he knows this is how I like it. Using every bit of my strength to fight him as he fucks me turns me on like nothing I had the guts to even imagine before Weaver.

He's changed me, ruined me, liberated me.

He's an anchor dragging me down to the bottom of the sea and the port in the storm I've been aching for my entire life.

He's my devil and my savior and when he releases my wrist long enough to slap the side of my ass hard enough to send a shock wave through my nervous system, I come like the shameless creature I am.

I come screaming his name and crying out for mercy, but I should know better.

Mercy is in short supply these days.

And Weaver isn't a man known for sparing anyone —his enemies, his friends, or anything in between.

He proves that by burying himself deep before he comes, pumping me full of that baby-making mate-rial he was so damned determined to keep to himself just a few days ago. He pins my hips to the ground, even when I try to wiggle away, forcing me to take every bit of his release, muttering, "Mine, you're fucking mine," as his cock continues to jerk deep inside me.

And once again, I'm flooded with shame.

Because I like it, *love* it. I want him to pin me down and make me take everything he has to give over and over again because he's that deep under my skin.

So deep I'm doubting everything I've ever known and lying in a sobbing heap beneath the man who ruined so many lives.

"Don't," he says, brushing my tears tenderly from my face. "Don't cry, baby. Did I hurt you? I didn't mean—"

"Is this what you did to my mother?" I ask, the words out before I can stop them.

His brows shoot up. "What?"

Tears coming faster, I force out, "Did you get her pregnant on purpose? Or was it an accident?"

His face pales as he pulls out and rolls onto his side next to me on the hard floor. "What are you talking about?"

I drag the back of my arm across my face, wincing as I feel his come slipping from between my legs. "Steven heard Aunt Cathy talking to my mom when we were kids. Not long after Mom left town. She was pregnant, and asked Cathy if she knew anyone who might want to adopt a baby. Someone out of town, obviously, since she didn't want any of the other Sullivans to know. She said she couldn't leave the baby with Dad because...it wasn't his. It was yours."

He scowls and shakes his head. "Jesus. She's fucking insane."

I move my arm, peering up at him. His shock looks genuine, but how can I know for sure? My mother was pregnant by someone, and she and my father hadn't shared a bedroom in a long time at that point. Dad started sleeping on the couch when I was in first grade.

"So, you're saying she was stepping out on my father with someone other than you?"

"I have no idea," he says, indignation creeping in to banish the shock on his features. "I barely knew your mother, and I certainly didn't get her pregnant, Sully. I told you the truth. We kissed a few times, that's it. It was nothing, especially compared to this." He curls his hand around my thigh, his fingers digging into my skin. "Like I said, we shouldn't be fighting each other, we should be fighting *for* each other."

I swallow past the knot in my throat. "How can I believe you?" I sit up, looking for my camisole, then decide to forget it and go straight to pulling on my sweater before reaching for my panties and sweatpants.

He huffs as he stands, hitching up his own pants. "How can you not? I've never lied to you. Your family are the ones who lie. Your mother and your cousin, Chris, and God knows who else."

"Chris and I aren't close, and I know he's not the best person," I say as I stand beside him, feeling the need to make that clear. "But Steven, the person who told me all this, is a good guy. And the baby isn't the only secret he overheard when he was eavesdropping as a kid."

Weaver crosses his arms, his Ice Prince glare in full

effect as he says, "Please, tell me what's next. I can't wait to defend myself from more insane gossip spread by a bored old woman and a child."

"He said..." I pause, not wanting to say the next part aloud. If it's true, he's not the person I thought he was. "He said there was a rumor going around town that not long after you beat up my dad, you almost killed a man in New York. With your bare hands. For no reason."

"There was a reason," he says, making my stomach twist with dread. "He put his hand up my friend's skirt."

I blink, that's bad, but not self-defense. Or a reason to do what I heard he did. "Okay, but...they said he ended up in the hospital afterward, Weaver. That you beat him so badly that he almost died and your dad had to pay off a bunch of people to keep you from going to prison. They said the guy almost lost an eye and had to drop out of college afterward because he couldn't play sports anymore."

As soon as the words are out, I know it's true.

It's written right there, in the shame on Weaver's face.

"Oh my God," I whisper, my hand coming to grip my throat as I shake my head back and forth. "Oh my God, Weaver."

"I told you there was an incident when I went back to the city."

"Not an incident where you almost *killed* someone," I say, shoving my feet back into my boots. "And not where your father had to bribe people to keep you out of prison. What about all your big talk about consequences? Are those just for other people? But when you destroy someone's life, it's okay?"

"I told you. He assaulted my friend. It's no excuse for what I did, but—"

"You're right, it's not." I move toward my sling, but Weaver is already there, snatching it off the floor.

"Please," he says, his eyes pleading with mine. "Let me explain, Sully."

"Give me my sling."

"Please, I—"

"There's nothing to explain. There's nothing you can say to make this better. Nothing."

His throat works. "Then, this is it? It's over?"

"My sling," I say, fighting to keep from falling apart. "Please."

I hold out my hand and he presses the fabric slowly, gently into my palm, practically wrenching my heart from my chest as he says, "All right, but please... get out of this town. For your own sake. And if you ever need anything—money, a reference, an introduction to my gallery owner friend in the city—just ask. I'll do whatever I can to help. No strings attached."

Eyes filling with tears, I rasp, "Please, just go."

"I'm going," he says, tears in his eyes, too. "I love you, Gertrude Sullivan. And I always will."

And then he's gone and I'm dropping back to the floor to sob my heart out.

I cry and cry, open-mouthed, nearly silent sobs that sap what little strength I have left in my body after a restless, painful night of sleep. Then I pull myself together as best I can and clean up the mess Weaver and I made on my friend's floor. But once I'm done, I can't seem to move.

I'm still sitting on the hardwood, a pile of used paper towels and a spray cleaner bottle beside me when Elaina appears half an hour later.

I peer up at her, my puffy, aching eyes narrowing in my face. "What are you doing here? Who's watching the café?"

"No one," she says. "After Weaver left with tears in his eyes, I kicked everyone out and closed up for the day."

My jaw drops. "But Sunday is one of your biggest days."

"I don't care."

"There are still a few tourists out. I saw them on my way in."

"Still, don't care," she says, settling beside me and wrapping her arm around my back. "You need some TLC, bestie. So, I'm going to run you a bath, get you some pajamas to borrow, and then we'll snuggle in my bed and watch Anne of Green Gables and eat chocolate until the pain gets better."

Tears spring to my eyes again. "I can't. I have to get back to the hospital to visit Gramps."

"You'll call Gramps and tell him you that feel like shit and need to rest, he'll understand," she says. "If he could see you right now, he'd insist I take care of you, just like he did when we were kids. We can order pizza too, like at our old sleepovers."

"I loved sleepovers," I sob, tears flowing down my

face again. "Things were so much easier then. Still hard, but so much easier."

"I know, honey," Elaina says, hugging me tighter. "But we'll make them easy again, just for tonight. Just you and me. I've got your back, girl. Forever and ever. Boys will come and go, but I'm yours for life."

She means it, I know she does. And she's so precious to me. I'd die for Elaina in a heartbeat, but is our friendship and the love I have for Maya and Sydney and my family enough to *live* for anymore? Or have I been ruined by the complicated, damaged, dangerous man who just walked out of my life with the sweetest final words any man ever gave a woman?

"I can't understand it, Elaina," I say. "How can he make me feel so safe and wonderful and have nearly taken someone's life with his bare hands, too? I don't get it. Make it make sense."

She sighs. "Oh man. Sounds like we need to talk. But first, your bath. I'll start it now and grab you a coconut water from the fridge. You need to hydrate. You look like you've cried out half your soul."

"Probably more than half," I mumble, rubbing at my scratchy eyes.

"Come on," she says, helping me to my feet. "Come on, my battered little squirrel. A soak will help. Then we'll get you fed and hydrated and when you're ready, we'll talk about sexy sad Weaver."

"He was really sad," I agree, fighting another wave of tears. "I think he really loved me."

"No doubt," Elaina says. "He's a very smart man and you're very, very loveable. But shush. No more boy

338

talk until after you get cleaned up and rest a little. A nap would also be good. I love a mid-morning nap. We can turn on my sound machine and snuggle with stuffed animals like when we were kids. I still have a huge stuffy stash in my closet."

And so, we do. I soak in the bath until my stomach starts to settle, drinking the coconut water while Elaina bustles around outside, getting the room ready for our healing day. Afterward, I put on a pair of her pajamas that fit just fine aside from being way too short, and we nap and eat and watch television and stay in bed until she pops downstairs to feed the kitties their afternoon snack and clean up the litter boxes.

Then, we go right back to sloth mode and she's right, it is healing.

But at this rate, I'll need approximately ten thousand days in bed to mend the gaping misery hole inside me.

"More pizza?" Elaina asks as we finish the last episode of Anne of Green Gables. "Or should I be a good girl and make us a veggie stir fry for supper?"

"Pizza," I say, and she grins.

"I like it when you facilitate my naughtiness. And really, it's best if we eat the leftovers now. They won't be as good tomorrow."

So, we do, but hours later, when the lights are off and my best friend is snoring softly beside me, I can't sleep. I tell myself it's all the cheese, but I know it's not that.

It's Weaver's last words ringing in my ears, and the horrible feeling that I'm never going to find a man like him again, that he was my one in a million and now he's gone and I will be alone and untouched forever.

I don't want anyone to touch me but him.

And memories won't be enough to keep me warm or even sane, not even close. Cursing stupid past me for thinking they would be, I roll over and squeeze my eyes shut, willing my body not to shake as I cry.

chapter 27

WEAVER

THE ONLY THING more devastating than losing the woman you love?

Losing her and realizing you don't have a soul in the world to turn to for comfort, because you've cut every soft thing from your life in your quest never to feel again.

I did an excellent job with that for many years, but now the ice around my heart has melted and I'm drowning in a flood of emotion. I've been knocked off my feet by regret and I'm choking on my own misery, but no one's interested in administering CPR.

And who can blame them?

I'm the first to reach for the check after a business dinner or to offer my home in The Hamptons to a friend for free, but my generosity doesn't extend to anything beyond material things. When it comes to vulnerability and intimacy, I've been a miser, a Scrooge who's only realized how desperately he wants to love and be loved now that it's too late.

It is too late. I don't want to be with anyone else. Sully is the only one for me. Imagining loving someone else the way I love her makes me physically ill. And I only had a little over a week with her. Eight fucking days. It's not nearly enough. I want a hundred more, a thousand. I want the rest of my life. I want to start watching what I eat and exercising even more than I do already so I can stay alive as long as possible and never leave my girl alone.

I suck in a breath, fighting the tears still burning the edges of my eyes.

I won't cry. I don't deserve to, not when this is all my fault. I should have been honest with Sully from the beginning. I should have confessed my sins so she couldn't find them out from anyone else. Though, maybe it wouldn't have mattered. Half the gossip she'd heard wasn't even true, but she was still ready to believe it, because it came from a family member.

No matter how hard I loved her, or how long we were together, that might have always been the case. Even if we'd been together for years, she still would have known *them* years longer. They might have always had their claws in her, able to come between us with a few words.

Or not.

I suppose now, I'll never know.

Willing myself to keep it together, I call my boss, Anthony, back in New York. I wouldn't normally call a colleague on a Sunday, but Anthony and I are friends as well. And he'll want to know that I'm going to be back in the office on Tuesday, sooner than later. We have a big meeting I was planning to attend via Zoom, but being there in person will spare the tech team the trouble of setting up a monitor.

He answers on the second ring, a smile in his voice as he asks, "Small-town life driven you to drink yet?"

"No, it's driven me away," I say, my tone flat, but even. "I'm flying back tomorrow afternoon. I'll be in the office for the meeting on Tuesday."

"Excellent," he says. "Glad to hear it. But if you need to go back afterward, I get it. I know estates as large as your brother's can be complicated to manage."

"I'll manage it from the city. I can't come back here."

He makes a considering sound. "Why not? What happened? Your family melting down from the stress?"

"Something like that."

He grunts. "You know you can share personal details of your life with me, Weaver. I may be your boss, but I consider us friends. And losing a relative is big deal. If you need someone to talk to, I'm here."

And even though I've brushed off similar offers from Anthony half a dozen times, I suddenly find myself spilling everything. From the fight with my family over the will, to the tragedy of my brother's wasted life, to the drama with the illegal seafood empire, to the amazing woman I met and how I fucked it all up before I even met her, by being an angry young man who didn't know how to manage the rage inside him.

When I'm done, I'm not crying, but my voice is

wobbling enough that I have to pause and take a breath as I fight to regain control.

I'm a little worried about what Anthony's going to say, to *think* about his most stoic employee having an emotional outburst over the phone.

But I should have known better. Anthony is a former child math prodigy—one of the reason's he's leading a giant financial firm at the tender age of thirty-nine—but he's also amazing at reading people.

He probably guessed I had this in me all along, a hunch that proves correct when he says, "Well, I figured you had family issues or you wouldn't be buttoned up so tight. But fuck... That's rough, Weaver. And the woman, she sounds great, but maybe she's just too young. An older woman might understand that we all make mistakes in our youth, but people really do grow and change in amazing ways. You're not that person anymore. I can attest to that. I've never seen you lose your cool, not even with Cranston, and he'd try the patience of a saint."

"Thank you." I sigh. "But what I did was more serious than most young adult mistakes."

"It was," he agrees. "But you realized you had a problem and took the necessary steps to fix it and become a better man. I, for one, find that admirable. Maybe she will, too, if you give her some time."

"I doubt it. Her family will encourage her to think the worst of me. And once I sell off the Tripp fleet and throw the entire town into chaos, I'll be even less popular around here than I am now."

"Corporate intrigue in small-town New England,"

Anthony says, his tone eager. "Damn, that sounds like fun. And who cares about being popular? You have to make the decisions that are best for you and your family, even if they don't understand they're for the best, at first. Your instincts are always spot-on, Weaver. You have to trust them."

"I agree. I just wish the rest of the Tripp clan trusted me half as much as you do."

He hums beneath his breath. "Yeah, that's not going to happen. You're too close to this, and they've cast you as the bad guy for the sin of being the one your brother chose to steer the ship. But maybe if you had a high-powered private equity firm interested in the sale of the company... And they advised your family how much they stand to lose if they don't restructure before they're faced with legal conse-quences..."

I snort, and a smile twitches at my lips for the first time since I left Sully. "Except you don't work for a private equity firm anymore."

"No, but I have a very good friend who does. And he's champing at the bit to get out of the city to avoid some relationship drama of his own. I bet he'd love to spend a week in a charming New England town, scaring your family onto the straight and narrow."

"In exchange for what?" I ask. "He won't actually want to acquire Tripp Seafood. As we've discussed, the business structure is inherently flawed. And even if he were comfortable with taking that risk, I'm not. I want to leave my family better off than they were before I took over. Even if that just means protecting them from prosecution and an ugly legal battle down the road."

"Of course," Anthony says. "Honestly, I'm pretty sure he'll do it just for the fun of it and a change of scenery. But I'll ask him. See if he needs anything to sweeten the deal. I'm sure a place to stay would be appreciated."

"He can have the yacht," I say. "It's docked in town." I'll find somewhere else to stay. That would be better anyway. There are too many memories of Sully on that boat. She haunts every inch of it for me now.

"Perfect. He'll love that."

"But if he's up for it, I'll have to stay a little longer," I caution, "to facilitate his understanding of the situation and introduction to my family. I'll have to Zoom into the meeting on Tuesday, after all."

"How about I shift the meeting to later in the month and you take off next week?" he asks. "You have twenty-five vacation days to use before the end of the year, Weaver. I checked. And it sounds like you have enough on your plate up there without working remotely right now."

I grunt. "You're probably right."

"I almost always am," Anthony says. "It's a blessing and a curse. Anyway, let me call Hunter and get back to you."

We say our goodbyes, end the call, and I start looking for a rental for the next week. No one says "no" to Anthony. Hunter's compliance is all but assured.

As expected, in just a few minutes, I get a text from Anthony confirming that Hunter Mendelssohn will be flying in this evening on his private plane. He sends another text, introducing the two of us, and Hunter and I exchange pleasantries for a while before getting down to business.

Turns out we both have homes in The Hamptons, but have somehow managed to miss each other the past three summers since he moved to the city from San Francisco. We make plans for me to pick him up at the small airport outside of town at six and grab dinner to discuss the situation before getting him settled on the yacht.

When we're done texting, I set about tidying the few things I've disturbed on the yacht. Since the cleaners were here this morning, there are already fresh sheets on both the beds, so he can have his choice of rooms. I suppose I could stay here in the guest room, but I want him to have his own space.

And I'm not going to be good company.

I'm grateful to have something to do to keep the heartbreak at bay, but it's still there, roiling beneath the surface, ready to emerge as soon as I run out of distractions. With that in mind, I book an isolated cottage on the bluff for the next week, where I can be a pathetic, grieving human being without any hotel or bed and breakfast guests overhearing.

Then I pack my things, move them to my new place, and head out to the airfield, doing my best not to look at the café on my way through town.

She's still there. Somehow, I just know it.

I can feel her, like a phantom limb my mind refuses to accept is gone for good.

Maybe she's not. Maybe you can try to explain yourself again. Maybe if she knew why you were such a broken kid back then in the first place...

The thought makes my skin go cold and acid rise in my throat.

I can't do that; I can't share that part of my past.

There has to be another way.

But as I collect Hunter from the airport, talk business over dinner at a local bistro, and thankfully discover he's the perfect mixture of clever and charming to win over my family, I can't think of anything else that might help Sully understand.

That's what I want most—for her to understand. Yes, forgiveness and a second chance would be a miracle I'd never take for granted, but if I can just make her understand, maybe she won't hate me.

Or hate herself for falling for a bad man.

That's what tore me apart the most, seeing the depth of her disappointment and knowing at least part of it was for herself. I was her first love, and in her eyes, I was a monster. It's the kind of experience that makes it hard to trust yourself and even harder to fall in love again.

And I don't want that for her. If she won't let me love her, I want her to find happiness with someone else...as long as I never have to see them together.

Just thinking about it makes me want to jab out my own eyes.

Instead, once I've settled Hunter on the yacht, I return to my tiny cottage on the bluff and sit outside in the bitter wind, writing a letter I hope I'll have the courage to send.

chapter 28

GERTIE

IT'S BEEN one hell of a week in Sea Breeze.

The drama is off-the-charts, even by our angsty, conflict-prone standards.

Weaver starts Monday off with a bang by attempting to sell Tripp Seafood to some corporate raider from New York, only for the deal to quickly go south once the dirty secrets behind their success come to light. At least, I'm guessing that's what happened.

Weaver and I still aren't talking, but it's the most logical explanation for a quickly-executed reallocation of assets that effectively ends the Tripps' fifty-year reign of terror overnight.

The Tripps who wanted to stay in the lobster business were able to buy their boats and go fully indie, but at least half the family chose to take the money and run.

Some of them, literally.

Mark disappeared overnight, along with several of his cousins. They're allegedly going south to start a brewery in Massachusetts, but he didn't share his plans with me. Mark clearly doesn't care for me much anymore. Even when he showed up at Elaina's Monday morning to give me the information on the crew he'd hired to work my boat until the end of December, he was curt and distant.

But then, I knew who was really responsible for hiring the workers and arranging to pay them from an account he'd set up in town.

It was Weaver, taking care of me even though we're not even friends anymore.

When we pass each other in town, he doesn't look at me, and I do my best not to look at him. But I fail. A lot.

He's just so damned beautiful, and so...mine.

I tell myself he'll stop feeling like mine with time, and that losing what we had will be easier once he leaves town, but I suspect I'm lying to myself. This will never be easy, but hopefully someday it will become bearable.

As it stands now, I'm barely surviving.

I sleep all the time, only emerging from my bed to visit Gramps and clean the house for his homecoming on Friday.

An in-home care nurse shows up at the door Thursday night to help with that, along with a hospital bed we set up on the ground floor by the fire for Gramps. I don't even bother asking who sent her or who is paying her salary for the next month. I already know, and I'm grateful.

I'm also angry.

This has to end. How am I supposed to start getting over him when he won't stop trying to take care of me?

In all the bustle of collecting Gramps from the hospital and getting him settled, Friday passes a bit more swiftly than the days before. We share a healthy meal of grilled chicken and roasted sweet potatoes with Mia, the nurse, and Gramps spends the entire meal flirting like his heart didn't almost explode less than a week ago.

But Mia, an older woman with sparkling green eyes and a laugh that makes our drafty house feel warmer, doesn't seem put off by it. If anything, she seems as taken with Gramps as he is with her, and I head back to my apartment suspecting I'm soon going to feel like a third wheel around here.

I wonder if that was part of Weaver's plan, too. Did he select Mia with an eye to helping set me free? And if so, is that sweet or...controlling as fuck?

I can't decide.

And I can't muster up the energy to do anything about it.

I stay in bed until nearly noon on Saturday, only emerging when Gramps texts me to come over and watch Deadliest Catch. I do, but talking shit about other fishermen isn't as much fun as usual, and no matter how hard I try to act normal, Gramps notices.

"So, who is it?" he asks, pausing between episodes.

I shake myself from my fog and ask, "What?"

He narrows his eyes at me from his hospital bed, where he's propped up and covered with a thick, cozy blanket from our winter stash. It's getting colder with every passing day now, suddenly starting to feel like winter after the mild autumn. "Who is it? The idiot who broke your heart?"

I blink and shake my head. "What? No one. I don't know what you're talking about."

"You're love moping."

"I am not."

"I know a love mope when I see it. Come on, out with it. Who do I need to kick overboard?" I answer him with a roll of my eyes and he adds, "Was it Mark Tripp? And he left without saying goodbye? Is that it?"

I choke on my next breath and sputter, "What? No!"

"Well, you were sneaking around with him for a while." He shrugs. "I thought it might have become something more."

"You knew?" I ask, my stomach tight.

"I knew," he says with a sniff. "But I liked that you were trying to hide it from me. It felt respectful."

"I do respect you, Gramps," I say. "It's just that there aren't many single people my age in town. And a lot of them are Tripps."

"I know. And I don't blame you. I blame myself. I may have gone overboard a little myself with the Tripp stuff." Before I can pick my jaw up off the ground, he adds swiftly, "I still don't like them, not even close. But they're our neighbors. And now that they're playing by the rules like the rest of us..."

"Wow." I sit back in my armchair. "This is...a big deal."

"It is."

"The end of an era."

"It is. So, date a Tripp if you want. As long as you pick a good one. Luke isn't bad. He's a hard worker, and I heard he just bought his dad's boat and plans to stay in town, not cut and run like the rest of his cousins. He's a good kid, the kind who sticks."

The kind who sticks...

The implication is clear. Luke is the kind who sticks so therefore, he'd be a good match for me, someone who also sticks. But I don't know if that's who I am anymore. Gramps and my family will always be so important to me, but when I think about going back to my old life, I want to crawl in bed and stay there —forever.

But I can't tell him about Weaver. Tripps may be okay to date now, but not Weaver. He's still forbidden. There's no doubt in my mind about that. And it doesn't matter anyway. Weaver and I are over. There's no sense in hurting Gramps by confessing to a sin I'm never going to commit again.

Still, I can't let a chance to be honest with Gramps pass me by. We don't talk like this often. If I let this moment go, I might not get another opening for a long time.

"I'm not going to date Luke, Gramps," I say, my pulse picking up as I weigh the chances that he's going to freak out. They're decent, I decide, but not high enough to make me worry about damaging his heart. "I was actually thinking about going back to school."

His bushy brows lift, but he doesn't look unpleas-antly surprised. In fact, he looks...proud. "Aw, that's great, Gert. I always hoped you'd finish your degree. You starting the online stuff again in the spring?"

"Um, no, I was..." I pick at the loose yarn on the afghan covering my legs. "I was actually thinking of applying to another school. Maybe in Boston or New York, and going for my bachelor's instead of an associate's degree. I'd be able to teach if I have a bachelor's, and I still have some money saved up after I paid for Dad's rehab. It's not enough to pay for everything, but I could apply for scholarships and get a part-time job. I think I could make it work."

I finally look up, surprised to see tears in Gramp's eyes. "Or I can stay," I hurry to add, willing to do whatever it takes to banish the pain from his face. I've only seen Gramps cry a couple times in my life and both were when someone had died. He doesn't get upset easily, and I can't bear to be the thing upsetting him. "I'll stay, Gramps. Forget I said anything. I'm just crazy right now. It's been a rough week."

It has been a rough week, even after deciding that Weaver was telling the truth about not sleeping with my mom and accepting Elaina's assurances that I don't have any obligation to track down the sibling I may or may not have, I'm still reeling.

"You'll do no such thing," Gramps says, his voice gruff with emotion. "You'll go, and I'll pay for it. You've sacrificed enough for this family."

I shake my head. "No, I haven't. I'm happy here with you. I—"

"Your dad left the facility last night," he says, the words landing like another punch to the gut. "He didn't even last a full week. Gary saw him at the pub last night."

I curse, suddenly fighting tears myself.

"I know," Gramps says. "I'm sorry, kid."

"I already paid the co-pay! His bed was eight hundred dollars a day. The insurance only kicked in after I paid for the first three thousand in charges. I can't get it back. It's gone." I curse, swiping at my leaking eyes. "For nothing."

"Not for nothing," he says gently. "Now you know. Nothing you do is going to change things with your dad." He sighs. "Nothing I do, either. I'd be honored to spend the money I've been using to pay your dad's mortgage to help put you through school. I'll be back to work before you know it and—"

"No, Gramps, you won't," I say, my jaw clenching tight. "It's going to be months until you're strong enough, and even when you're cleared for work, I don't think you should. The house is paid for and your retirement fund is in decent shape. If you get an easier part-time job somewhere in town and quit throwing your money away on Dad, you'll be able to cover your bills. It's time for you to quit worrying about the rest of us and take care of yourself."

He huffs. "If you think that's going to happen, you're even crazier than Cathy thinks you are."

My brows snap together. "What? What did she say? Because I swear to God, Gramps, if she's gossiping about me behind me back, I'm going to lose it for real. She's been on my last nerve since the hospital."

"She told Jennifer who told Henna who told her

mom who told Aunt Sue who told the priest who told me that you're... Well, they said you're mixed up with Weaver Tripp."

I gulp and my heart free falls through my chest to crash into my churning intestines. "What?"

"Sea Breeze gossip," he says, still sounding calm, though I know the explosion is coming any minute. He hates Weaver, and for decent reasons. "You know how it is. No one's safe, no matter how hard they try to fly under the radar."

I shake my head but don't say a word. I don't know what to say. I don't want to lie, but I don't want to give Gramps another heart attack, either.

"But she's mistaken, isn't she?" Gramps presses. "You know better."

I sigh and curl deeper into the chair, pulling the afghan up to cover everything but my eyes.

Gramps curses, and I cringe a little lower.

"Honey, what the hell were you thinking?" he says, his tone strained. "He's a psycho. Your dad picked that fight, but you should have seen what was left of him after Weaver was done."

"I did see," I say from under the cover. "I was there in the hospital room with you, Gramps."

"No, you weren't," he says. "I wouldn't have let you see something like that. I made you wait outside."

I pull the afghan down, knowing this isn't the time to hide. "No, you didn't. I was right there, Gramps. I sat in the corner while you held Dad's hand and cried. I'll never forget it. It's one of the sharpest memories in my entire life."

His brow furrows. "Really? I would have sworn..."

"Really," I say. "And that wasn't all Weaver's doing. Dad was in a horrible car crash. I'm not excusing what Weaver did, but...he's not like that anymore. He was really good to me. Really, really good."

Gramps snorts and rolls his eyes hard enough to get his head involved. "Right. Can't wait to hear this."

"He's paying for Mia," I say, deciding to cut right to the chase. "Even though I broke up with him."

Gramps' eyes widen. "What?"

"He's paying for Mia. He's also paying for the crew taking our boat out every day."

He glowers, his brows twitching like angry caterpillars above his narrowed eyes. "Well, he can stop. Right now. We don't need his charity. As soon as Mia gets back from her lunch break, I'll tell her she's fired."

"No, you won't," I say. "You need her, and we can't afford her without help. Not and have any chance of making it through the year without going into debt. Same with the crew. And there aren't any strings attached here. Weaver knows it's over. He barely looks at me when I see him in town. He's doing his best to be respectful and give me space."

Gramps curses, but it's pain in his voice, not anger when he says, "Honey, why? He's an old man compared to you. And cold as a witch's tit. Even as a kid, he wasn't right, Gert. He'd skulk around in the shadows, watching everyone with those X-ray eyes of his, like a creepy little spy."

"Oh, come on, Gramps."

"No," he says, doubling down. "He was a weirdo.

361

And way too quiet. Never trust a kid that quiet, there's something wrong with them."

I frown.

Quiet...

I have enough experience with kids to know that quiet isn't normal. Even shy kids communicate in their own way and open up in situations where they feel comfortable. The only kid I know who was quiet all the time was Maya's nephew, Reese, the one who we later learned was being abused by his dad.

Maya's sister, Mallory, had to get a restraining order against her bastard ex during the divorce. Now, years later, and with plenty of therapy, Reese isn't quiet anymore. When he comes to visit, he's a happy, giggly boy who runs wild through the sprinklers with my second cousins, just like all the other kids.

And suddenly, like that, it all falls into place.

I rise from my chair, letting the afghan slide to the floor. "I have to go, Gramps."

"What? Where are you going?"

"To talk to Weaver. I think I made a mistake." I start toward the front door only to remember that I'm still in the grubby sweats and long-sleeved tee I slept in and reverse course.

"The only mistake you made with that man was getting mixed up with him in the first place."

I pause with my hand on the back door. "No, Gramps. I forgot something important, something you taught me, actually."

He blinks, his cheeks puffing out. "And what's that?"

"You always made it clear that I wasn't defined by the bad things that happened to me when I was little. I wasn't the girl whose mom abandoned her or the kid with a drunk for a dad. I was me, and I got to decide how I defined *myself*. I got to choose to be the girl who was the apple of her grandfather's eye and the best player on the rugby team and a person my friends could always count on."

He sighs, nodding slowly. "And you did a great job of that, kid."

"I know, thanks to you. And the rest of the family, even annoying Aunt Cathy," I say, earning a grunt of amusement from Gramps. "I had a lot of people who loved me and helped me believe in myself. But...what if I hadn't had that? Who would I have become then? I might have been a weird little kid lurking in the shadows with my X-ray eyes, trying to figure out if there were any grown-ups out there that I could trust. That's what happens when kids are let down by the people who are supposed to love them and make them feel safe."

Understanding dawns and his expression softens. "Damn..."

I nod. "Yeah."

"His father *was* a bastard," Gramps says. "Even worse than Rodger. Don't know much about his mother, she didn't leave the house much, but..."

"But it's a safe bet his home wasn't a great place for a sensitive kid to grow up," I say. "And he is sensitive, Gramps. The icy exterior is just a mask. Underneath, he's kind and compassionate and..." I exhale in a rush, "and bossy and frustrating and controlling, but also sweet and generous and he loves me. He really loves me. Even when I told him it was over, he just wanted me to know that he still cared and that he always would."

Gramps eyes begin to shine again. "If that's who he really is. And if you love him back..."

I swallow past the lump in my throat. "I think it is, Gramps. And I know I do."

"Then go to him and talk it through," he says. "But you'd better hurry. He's leaving this afternoon, taking his friend's private plane back to the city. But you can probably still catch him at the airport if you don't dawdle."

I shake my head, knowing better than to ask how he knows that. Gramps knows everything that happens in this town. And he knows me, a fact he proves when he adds, "Skip the shower and just throw some clothes in a suitcase and go, Gert. If he loves you, he won't mind that you're in your pajamas. And if you really love him, you're going to want to get on that plane."

On impulse, I hurry across the room, hugging Gramps with my good arm, getting choked up again as he cradles me close, whispering, "As long as you're happy, baby girl. That's all I ever want. Make sure he treats you like the treasure you are."

"He does, Gramps," I whisper. "He does. I love you. I'll text you soon. Don't fire Mia."

And then I'm gone, sprinting up to my apartment and calling the one cab in town as I throw clothes in my bag. In ten minutes, I'm hustling back down the stairs with my small suitcase, still in my pajamas, but with a ballcap on over my wild hair and my teeth freshly brushed.

Crossing my fingers that I'll be kissing Weaver again before the day is over, I meet Pete at the curb, and tell him to push the speed limit on the way to the airport.

chapter 29

I'M NOT a fan of airports at the best of times, even when I'm safely ensconced in a Platinum Card lounge or a restaurant with private booths suitable for retreating from the turmoil of air travel.

But today, as I sit in the tiny waiting room of Sea Breeze's microscopic regional airport, sipping a heinous martini as a gaggle of women on their way to Las Vegas screech at the other end of the bar/sandwich shop, and a stressed-out toddler wails on the ground near the bathroom, I vow never to step foot in an airport again.

Even if I'm flying private and only have to wait half an hour for the plane to be prepared for takeoff...

Logically, I know it's the fact that I'm leaving without saying goodbye to Sully or mailing that letter I burned in the cottage fire last night that has me feeling so low, but I refuse to think about that now. I'll think about that once I'm back in the city, on my therapist's couch. I have an appointment tomorrow morning, an emergency Sunday slot she opened for me after receiving my message earlier in the week.

We haven't had regular appointments for over eight years now, and Dr. Everett knows I'm not the kind to reach out for help unless I truly need it. No, I'm the kind to wait until I'm on the verge of losing my damned mind to make an appointment, and she scheduled our session accordingly.

I *am* losing my mind.

I can feel it in the prickling in my head, in the buzzing in my ears as I watch myself sip my drink as if from a distance. I look as cool and under control as ever, but inside, I'm spiraling. The pain of losing Sully hasn't gotten easier in the past week. It's only gotten worse. It feels like someone infected me with flesh-eating bacteria that's been gnawing away at my internal organs, hollowing me out. Soon, there won't be anything left inside. I'll be an empty shell that will scatter like ash in the next strong wind.

And that will probably be for the best.

I can't live like this, and I don't want to learn to live without her. I've fallen in love the way I've done every-thing else in my life, with an intensity that's almost frightening. Now, I'm paying the price for that with my sanity.

Sully was right to be afraid of me.

That's what I decided last night, as I sat on the porch in the cold wind for the sixth night in a row, thinking about how easy it would be to climb over the railing and take a long walk off the cliff a short distance away. She was right. I'm broken and unworthy of her. I'm not the violent person I was as a young man, but I'm not "normal" either, and I likely never will be. This is what my particular combination of DNA and childhood environment produced. I've done the best I could with the material I have to work with, but the end result is far from ideal.

Far from being what's best for a beautiful young woman with a giant heart and her entire life ahead of her...

She's better off without any further interference from me. That's why I burned the letter and why I refuse to text or call her before I board the plane, even if I have to drink myself into a mild stupor to dull the longing gnawing away in my chest.

"I'll have another," I say to the bartender, a tired-looking man with a hunched spine and hair sprouting from his ears. "Less olive juice this time, please."

"And I'll have a root beer because it's too early to start drinking," comes a voice from behind me.

A voice I instantly assume I must be hallucinating...

There's no reason for Sully to be at the airport, and no reason she'd join me at the bar if she did have one.

But when I glance over my shoulder, there she is, looking like a supermodel trying to fly incognito in a pair of gray sweatpants, an oversized navy puffer jacket, and a ballcap over her wavy hair. She isn't wearing makeup, either, just something glossy on her lips, but she's still the most stunning woman in the room.

To me, she will always be the most stunning woman in any room.

But for some reason, I can't find the words to tell her that. I can't speak at all. I can only watch, mute, as she sets her suitcase beside mine and slides onto the stool beside me.

She meets my gaze, hers softening as she says, "How are you?"

"Terrible," I rasp out.

She nods. "Me, too. I slept until noon today. These are my pajamas."

"You're still beautiful."

"You, too," she says, her brows shifting closer together. "I told Gramps about you."

My eyes widen.

"Yeah," she says, her breath rushing out. "I didn't mean to, really. It just kind of happened and he was more okay with it than I thought. He also said some things. About you. About when you were a kid, in particular, that made me think I might have been too quick to judge the other day. What you did is still awful and scary, but—"

"Agreed," I say, my tongue finally getting the message that it's time to speak up. If she's here to give us another chance, I can't afford to sit here like a mute and let it pass me by. "But I would never do anything like that again. I swear. I'd cut off my own hands first."

"I know," she says. "On the way over here, I kept thinking about the hospital. How you stood there letting Dad hurt you and barely even fought back, even though you had every right to defend yourself. And well, like I told Gramps, if I hadn't had him in my life to help me heal from all the hard parts of my childhood, I

with a married woman, I want to go back in time and shake some sense into myself."

"But if that hadn't happened," she says, "*we* might not have happened. And I'm really glad we happened."

"Me, too," I say, relief making my entire body feel lighter than it has in days. "I'll cancel the flight and maybe I can take you to dinner? Since we don't have to hide anymore?"

Her lips hook up on one side. "Or I could come with you." She nods toward our bags. "That's why I brought a suitcase. In case you decided you wanted company."

Heart soaring, I nod. "Yeah, I'd like some company. I'd love it, actually."

And I do.

I love her all the way to New York and during the cab ride to my apartment in the East Village. I love her through our takeout meal on my terrace and the tour of my place, and then I love her in my bed, showing her with every kiss, every touch, how much she means to me.

She's the most precious thing I've ever had entrusted into my care and for the next several weeks, I bust my ass to prove it.

By the time we return so Sea Breeze to celebrate Christmas with her family, we're so close, I can read her mind without her having to say a word.

"Don't worry," I say as I park the rental car behind

her spot in the garage. "If things get tense, I'll fake a headache and wait for you in your apartment."

She shakes her head. "No. No way. If things get tense, we'll both leave. They don't get to scare you away. If they want me around, they have to be nice to my boyfriend."

Her boyfriend...

I plan on being more than her boyfriend before this week is through. The ring is burning a hole in my coat pocket, but it isn't time for that yet, not until we clear this final hurdle. If we can make it through a holiday celebration with her family—half of whom still think I'm the Antichrist—then we'll have proven we can make it through anything.

"All right," she says, pressing a quick kiss to my lips. "Let's go, Mr. Fancy."

We're barely out of the car before the door flies open and her grandfather appears, silhouetted against the glowing lights inside. "Get in here, you two! Before you freeze your asses off. It's bitter out there."

"And we have hot toddies," a cheerful voice bubbles from behind him in the kitchen.

As we step inside, I see that it's Mia, his former nurse, dressed in a red sweater with a reindeer on the front and a matching pair of jingle bell antlers on her head. I arch a brow Sully's way and she gives a little shake of her head as she smiles. Apparently, she had no idea Gramps and Mia were family-Christmas-party level friends, either.

"Hey there, Weaver, welcome," Gramps says, giving my hand a firm shake as he closes the door behind us.

"Let me take your coats and you two grab a drink. We're about to start the trivia."

"I'm going to win," Cathy calls from the living room, where half a dozen Sullivans are gathered around the fire. "I always win, so don't feel bad, Weaver. I've got a brain for facts."

"You've got a brain for nonsense," an older man I'm guessing is her husband says from beside her, laughing when she smacks him on the leg.

"Bring me a beer before you start and say hi, will ya, Gert?" calls a feminine voice from upstairs. "I'm still wrapping the kids' presents. I've got to keep going or there's no way I'll be done before Blake drops them off for dinner. We're doing our presents tonight and Santa at my mom's tomorrow."

Sully casts a glance my way, ensuring I'm okay to go it alone while she delivers the drink. When I nod, she calls back. "Okay, what do you want Henna? A lager or a pale ale?"

"Pale ale," Henna shouts. "And a peppermint cookie please."

Sully pulls a face, whispering, "Beer and peppermint? Gross," before snatching the beer from the ice bucket on the kitchen island and pressing a kiss to her grandfather's cheek. "Be good, Gramps. This is the man I love."

"I know, I know," he says, chuckling as she goes. When she disappears up the stairs he turns back to me, adding in a softer voice, "She doesn't need to worry. You've done good since you two left, kid. She's happy and so excited about that show you helped her land at the gallery. We're all taking the train down in February to see it."

"She landed it all on her own," I say. "I just made the introduction. She's the one with the talent."

Gramps beams. "She does have talent. I think she got it from me. I wasn't a bad artist when I was young. I always drew the girls my air force buddies had tattooed on their biceps while we were deployed."

"You're a family with a lot of gifts," Mia says, pressing a kiss to his other cheek, the one Sully missed. To me, she says, "Thank you for hiring me for this job, Weaver. I'm pretty into this guy right here."

"And I'm pretty into you, sweet cheeks," he says, making her blush as he grabs her ass.

Fighting a laugh, I nod. "My pleasure."

"What's your pleasure?" Sully asks, appearing again at my side, slightly breathless, making me think she must have run down the stairs to avoid leaving me alone for too long.

"Nothing," I say, with a smile as I draw her close. "Just feeling the love in the room, is all. Mia and your grandpa are dating."

She glances their way, taking in the canoodling with a dropped jaw. "No way! Why didn't you tell me, Gramps? I thought you were keeping me up on all the gossip."

"Some things are too special to share on Zoom," Gramps says, cuddling Mia closer. "Things like... engagement rings."

Mia holds out her hand, revealing a small, but lovely diamond, and Sully cries out in excitement. She hugs Mia, then Gramps, then Mia again, before turning to me and exclaiming, "Oh my God! You did this. You're a matchmaker extraordinaire. Your first try, and they're engaged in less than two months."

"I'll send the firm my resignation tomorrow," I say in my best deadpan voice. "And hang out my match-making shingle as soon as we get back to the city."

They all laugh and Sully squeezes my arm with an affection I can feel through the heavy sweater she bought me for an early present. It's cream colored and old-fashioned looking and she told me it makes me look like the brooding hero of a gothic romance novel.

I may never take it off.

I like being her hero—brooding or otherwise.

Drinks in hand, we adjourn to the living room to play trivia while the turkey finishes roasting. Cathy does, in fact, win, and Sully's cousin, Steven, comes in second place. I'm down at the bottom, thanks to knowing very little about holiday traditions and being distracted by Sully sitting on my lap.

Even with only part of the family here, there aren't enough chairs to go around.

The rest of the clan apparently elected to spend their Christmas Eve playing bingo somewhere else. Not all the Sullivans are as accepting of our relationship, but that's okay. All the relatives who mean the most to Sully are here and she seems happy. For me, that's all that matters.

She and her father haven't spoken since he left rehab, but apparently, he's at the other gathering, fully aware that Sully has no interest in a relationship with him until he gets sober. Considering he found another relative willing to pay his rent when Gramps withdrew his support, I don't see that happening any time soon, but who knows.

People surprise you sometimes.

I surprise myself every day. I never thought I'd be good at loving someone, never thought I could make a woman want to stay. But every day with my girl is better than the last, and she shows no sign of leaving. We're actually packing up the rest of her things while we're here to send them back to New York.

She's making the move permanent and starting her job as a second shooter to a well-known wedding photographer in January. She may go back to school, eventually, too, but for now, she's excited about moving straight into a career in photography. Within just months of arriving in the city, she'll have her first show and be on track to earn far more than she ever made lobstering.

Not that we need the money, but I know it makes her feel good, to be succeeding when she's doubted her talent for so long.

She shouldn't doubt it.

As far as I can tell, she's amazing at everything she does, a fact she proves by carving the turkey like a professional chef. We settle down to eat at the long table in the dining room and it's by far the best holiday meal I've ever had, filled with laughter and toasts and a generosity of spirit that proves the Sullivans are more than agents of chaos.

They're also people who love and care about each

other and want what's best for the people who matter most.

"She's shining," Cathy whispers to me over dessert, while Sully's in the bathroom. "Whatever you're doing, keep doing it. She's never looked more beautiful."

"She's happy, that's what it is," Steven says, shooting me a tight grin from the other side of the table. "Looks like you are, too."

"Very," I assure him.

He nods and points his fork my way. "Good. Don't take it for granted. Show up every day. That's what makes a marriage work."

"That's right," Henna says from the opposite end of the table, where she's busy wiping whipped cream off one of her kids. "Show up and choose each other every single day."

I can't help noticing that her husband decided not to come in for dinner. Sully warned that he might not be part of the celebration. He and Henna are apparently having problems.

I feel for them. I've only been separated from Sully for a week during the course of our relationship, but that was enough misery to make me positive I never want a repeat of the experience.

With that in mind, I wait until New Year's Eve, when we're dancing with her friends at a party at the cat café, to drop down on one knee.

"Gertrude Sullivan, you are—"

Before I can get to any of the romantic things I'd planned to say, Sully tackles me to the carpet, screaming, "Yes! Oh my God, yes!" over the music as we roll across the floor. Laughing, she kisses me and I kiss her back, until Elaina drops a cat on top of us and demands to see the rock.

We ring in the New Year with congratulations from Sully's friends and birthday cake made for Gideon and Sydney's combined birthdays.

As I lick icing off Sully's nipples later, in the privacy of her apartment, she agrees that getting an extra slice of cake to go was a brilliant idea.

"I'm a brilliant man," I say, sliding her sequined skirt up her thighs to reveal stockings and a garter belt that make my already hard cock sit up and take extra notice. "A brilliant man who would like to fuck you with these stockings on, you sexy little minx."

"Wait until you see the best part." She grins as she rolls over on the bed, showing me the back of the ensemble, a thong that leaves her gorgeous ass bare.

I try to take it slow, I really do, but in just a few minutes, that thong is jerked to one side and I'm buried in my fiancée, making her moan and claw at the bedsheets and call my name as she comes.

As I join her a few strokes later, I send out a silent thank you to all the stars that had to align to make her mine.

"Mine," I murmur into her hair as she's resting on my chest afterwards.

She wiggles a finger into my ribs. "Mine."

"No, mine," I insist, grinning at the ceiling.

"No, mine." She pokes me harder.

"Should we wrestle to see who stakes claim on who?"

She exhales a happy sigh. "Yes, please. Hold me down hard, but let me win at the end."

"Always," I say, all too happy to oblige her.

When she wins, I win, and vice versa. As far as I can tell, that's what love's all about.

And orgasms.

And magic.

And getting to spend every day with your favorite person, the sweet, sexy, precious one who feels like home.

It's about all those things, too.

THE END

Need more dark, addictive billionaire romance?

While you're waiting for Maya's forbidden romance, check out the Bought by the Billionaire series, by my dark romance pen name, Everly Stone. **The first book, Dark Domination, is free on all retailers!**

about the author

Author of over forty novels, *USA Today* Bestseller **Lili Valente** writes everything from steamy suspense to laugh-out-loud romantic comedies. A die-hard romantic, she can't resist a story where love wins big. Because love should always win. She lives in the world with her two big-hearted boy children and a dog named Pippa Jane.

Find Lili at...
www.lilivalente.com

also by lili valente

The McGuire Brothers

Boss Without Benefits

Not Today Bossman

Boss Me Around

When It Pours (novella)

Kind of a Sexy Jerk

When it Shines (novella)

Kind of a Hot Mess

Kind of a Dirty Talker

Kind of a Bad Idea

The Virgin Playbook

Scored

Screwed

Seduced

Sparked

Scooped

Hot Royal Romance

The Playboy Prince

The Grumpy Prince

The Bossy Prince

Laugh-out-Loud Rocker Rom Coms

The Bangover

Bang Theory

Banging The Enemy

The Rock Star's Baby Bargain

The Bliss River Small Town Series

Falling for the Fling

Falling for the Ex

Falling for the Bad Boy

The Hunter Brothers

The Baby Maker

The Troublemaker

The Heartbreaker

The Panty Melter

Bad Motherpuckers Series

Hot as Puck

Sexy Motherpucker

Puck-Aholic

Puck me Baby

Pucked Up Love

Puck Buddies

Big O Dating Specialists

Romantic Comedies

Hot Revenge for Hire

Hot Knight for Hire

Hot Mess for Hire

Hot Ghosthunter for Hire

The Lonesome Point Series

(Sexy Cowboys)

Leather and Lace

Saddles and Sin

Diamonds and Dust

12 Dates of Christmas

Glitter and Grit

Sunny with a Chance of True Love

Chaps and Chance

Ropes and Revenge

8 Second Angel

The Good Love Series

(co-written with Lauren Blakely)

The V Card

Good with His Hands

Good to be Bad

Made in United States
Orlando, FL
13 November 2024